# Books by Thom Collins

*Single Titles*

Closer by Morning

I0658857

Closer by Morning

ISBN # 978-1-78686-012-5

©Copyright Thom Collins 2016

Cover Art by Posh Gosh ©Copyright 2016

Interior text design by Claire Siemaszkiewicz

Pride Publishing

Published in 2016 by Pride Publishing, Newland House, The Point, Weaver Road, Lincoln, LN6 3QN, United Kingdom.

Pride Publishing is a subsidiary of Totally Entwined Group Limited.

# CLOSER BY MORNING

THOM COLLINS

# Dedication

To Liam.

# Chapter One

Matt Blyth was not a morning man. When his alarm went off at five a.m. it shocked him awake. *What the hell?* Dragged rudely out of dreamland, where he'd been sailing across the Atlantic on a luxury cruise ship, to the darkness of his bedroom on Monday morning. Then he remembered the reason for the alarm. Boot camp. Today would be his first session. What had made him think that was a good idea?

He forced himself out of bed. *No time to think about this. Just do it.*

He stumbled to the bathroom and threw water in his face and raked wet fingers through his dark, wavy hair. Ten minutes later, dressed in joggers and running shoes, he was out of the house. He felt nauseated with the lack of sleep but pushed through it. Minor discomfort would not deter him, not when he was set on doing something he wanted. He was twenty-eight years old. In a little over a year he would turn thirty, that first great milestone of age. He was determined to be in his best shape ever when the dreaded day came. Even if it meant getting up well before dawn to slog it out and sweat for an hour before work.

The morning, which felt like the dead of night, was damp and cold. The sky was still ink black as he steered his car off the estate and onto the road that would take him out of town. It wasn't far to the assembly point, a little over two miles. Soon, when he got used to these God-awful early rises, he wouldn't need the car, he would jog to the meeting place. But not yet. Not today.

Matt turned on the radio. Music usually got him going but the radio was tuned to a local station, just in time for the news. He let it play. He liked to know what was happening in the area, as well as getting the sports results and weather.

The lead item blasted away the final cobwebs of sleep.

*"Durham Police have cordoned off an area of the river bank in the city following the discovery of a body late last night. Police refuse to speculate whether the death is connected to that of student Conner Welsh, whose body was discovered just two weeks ago downriver of the latest finding. Mr. Welsh was severely beaten before being strangled. Durham FM News will bring you further information on the latest death as we receive it."*

Two bodies dragged from the river within a fortnight. That was unheard of in a small city like Durham. Murder of any kind was rare. He hoped the latest death was nothing more than an accident — a tragic coincidence — in no way connected to the murdered student. Drunk students had always been drawn to the riverbank. Too much alcohol and a loss of balance could have fatal consequences. From what he'd heard, Conner Welsh, the previous victim, suffered a nightmare ordeal before going in the water. He prayed it hadn't happened again.

The story continued to trouble him as he followed the winding country road, though he tuned out the rest of the bulletin and missed the sports update. The image of the murdered student had been a regular feature in the local press these last two weeks. A smiling, happy boy. Young and good-looking, a university student, Conner had everything to smile about. But some sick bastard had thought otherwise. Matt hoped they quickly found who was responsible, for the sake of Conner's family and the wider community.

Thin fingers of light began to crawl across the sky when he pulled into the car park at Binchester Woods. A handful of vehicles were already parked and a group of people in sports clothes were limbering up and stretching against the picnic table.

So there were others just as crazy as he was, coming out to exercise at this early hour.

There was no sign of Annabel's Fiat among the parked cars. Typical. This crazy venture was her idea. "C'mon, Matt," she had enthused in the office kitchen. "We'll motivate each other. And think how great it will be to get it over with so early in the day. No more having to drag our tired butts to the gym after work. Our evenings will be our own."

He had texted her the night before to make sure she was still up for the challenge.

*Definitely* she had replied and had added a smiley face.

Matt locked the car and headed toward the group of people. There were four men and three women, all of them swaddled in layers from head to foot.

"Is this the meeting point for boot camp?" he asked, certain it must be. Why would they be here otherwise?

A large man stepped forward. He carried a hardback notebook and a pencil. "It is. I'm Clint. I'm instructing the group today."

"Hi." They shook hands. "You spoke to my work colleague on the phone. Annabel Faith. She made the booking for both of us."

Clint consulted his little notebook. "Matt, is it?" He ticked him off his list. "Is your friend with you?"

"No. But she only has to come from town. She shouldn't be long." She had better not be.

Clint was huge. Exactly how Matt imagined a boot camp instructor would look—an enormous, ex-military, brick shithouse. With his steely crew cut and dark, hooded eyes, he looked like a hard case who would take no prisoners. He was sexy too, in a strange, scary way. Not really Matt's type, but he could see the appeal.

Clint enquired about his current level of fitness.

"Decent, I'd say. I train at the gym three or four times a week and like to run at weekends. I eat plenty of protein and take it easy with carbs. I'm just looking to improve my overall levels of fitness." All true, if slightly exaggerated.

Clint looked him over closely before making notes in his

book. "Good. Any health concerns I should know about before you start?"

"None."

"Sure? This is an intense course."

"That's what I'm looking for. Something I can't get at the gym."

Clint nodded, satisfied, and closed his book. "You've come to the right group. Whipping bodies into shape, that's what I'm known for. No messing, no time wasting, no excuses—just exceptional results. A guy in my group last year made the front cover of *Men's Health* magazine. Those are the kind of results I aim for."

Matt stretched while they waited for the rest of the group to arrive. Clint told him they would leave at five-forty-five sharp. "Get here later than that and we'll be gone."

There was still no sign of Annabel. Punctuality wasn't one of her strong points. If she intended to turn up at all. Knowing her, she would still be curled beneath her duvet. He was mad for listening to her in the first place. She never came through, always full of enthusiastic ideas but with little success in achieving them.

More vehicles began to pile into the car park and soon there was a group of around twenty assembling for the class. They were mainly men, aged twenty through to mid-forties. Intense, serious-looking men who didn't mess about over fitness. Real go-hard-or-go-home types. Maybe it was a factor of the unsociable hour, but there wasn't much conversation going on. That suited Matt. Nobody wanted small talk at this time of day.

He cast an appraising eye over the group. They were fit, masculine, real men's men, but, a little bit like Clint, he found them rather asexual. Not his type at all. Not that he was looking anyway, but hey, a little eye candy could provide great motivation.

Just before the appointed start time another vehicle pulled into the car park and a man in blue running pants and a gray hoodie jumped out and jogged toward Clint.

They spoke briefly and the instructor made a few hurried notes in his book.

Matt's interest was piqued by the new arrival. This was more like it. Even from a distance, he could see this guy was something very special. With short, dark blond hair and a light beard, he was as manly as the rest of the group but seemed to lack the focused intensity that made them so fearsome.

He even smiled as he left Clint to join the group. A lovely, winning smile that wrinkled the corners of his sparkly eyes and illuminated a broad, handsome face.

"Hi, guys," he addressed the group as a whole in a warm American accent.

"Hi," Matt replied while the others responded with a non-committal grunt or nod.

Unselfconsciously, the newcomer began to stretch.

Matt found it hard not to stare. Wow. This guy looked good from a distance but was even better close up. He had the broad build of a man in his thirties and, though he was swaddled in layers like the rest of them, Matt could discern the strong lines of his shoulders and butt through that clothing.

But it was his face, with its twinkly eyes and golden skin, that was so exceptionally handsome.

Matt, with his wavy brown hair, brown eyes and angular face, was good-looking. He wasn't vain or conceited about it, he knew he was attractive, but couldn't help feeling inadequate beside the glorious American. With a face like that, he could do anything he wanted and the world would accept it—model, actor, politician, king.

*Take it easy.* Matt turned away. It was the only way to keep from staring.

He had the beginnings of an erection.

He'd wanted eye candy and now he had it. He'd have to be careful that the American didn't become a distraction rather than a motivation.

Clint Dexter's boot camp was advertised as the toughest,

most effective workout in the county. *Hard work and effort get results!* proclaimed the poster in the window of his town center fitness studio. *Nobody trains you harder.*

It was no lie.

Without equipment, weights or gimmicks, Clint pushed his group on the most intense and physically grueling workout Matt had ever known. Clint was old school in his methods. Like an army sergeant breaking in the new recruits, he drove them uphill and into the woods. There was no let-up. He shouted and blew whistles, breaking up the run with demands for press-ups, squats, lunges, then straight back onto the track, going higher up the steep hill. There were no breaks. No moment to catch a breath.

Matt believed he was in good shape. Epic mistake. Every muscle in his body seemed to ache. His lungs were ablaze as he drew one arduous breath after another. *Shit.* He'd never known anything like this. And it didn't stop. For the whole hour Clint worked them hard—no slacking, no respite.

Matt was glad to see he wasn't the only one struggling with the course. He might be the newbie but even the seasoned old-timers were taking it badly. Everyone was red-faced and grimacing with pain.

Finally Clint guided them back down to the car park. It was over.

"Make sure you all stretch down thoroughly," he shouted as he walked among the group. Most people were bent double, clutching their knees and gasping. "You'll pay for it later if you don't take the time now."

"Some group, eh?"

Matt realized that he was standing beside the handsome American. The course was so exhausting that he'd stopped paying attention to the blond hunk after the first five minutes. His hair was soaked, plastered to his head, and his face burned red, yet he exuded a sexiness that would have caught Matt's breath if he wasn't already wrecked.

Matt struggled to speak. "My first time," he gasped.

"Yeah? Me too. I thought I was fit until this morning. This

guy has destroyed me."

"I doubt anyone is fit enough for this."

The American laughed. "You could be right. I've had personal trainers in the past. Let me tell you, none of them worked me half as hard as this dude. Not ever."

"Think you'll do it again?"

"Absolutely. A month of this and we could compete as Iron Men."

"You might be right. If we survive a month. My heart might not be able to take it."

"I'm Dale," he said. "Hi."

"Hello. I'm Matt."

"Nice to meet you, Matt," Dale said cheerily.

Matt was struck again by just *how* good-looking Dale was. God, his eyes — they were as blue as a cloudless August sky.

As he stretched his tired muscles, Matt tried not to be affected by the proximity of Dale, but it wasn't easy. It wasn't just the way he looked, it was his manner and the confidence he exuded. Even the smell of him, the sweat from all that hard work, was an aphrodisiac. It was a long time, if ever, since a man had had such a devastating effect on him. When Dale bent over to touch his toes and gave Matt the full benefit of his glorious rump, he had to turn away. Tenting the front of his pants with a hard-on was *not* the kind of first-day impression he wanted to make.

The sun finally put in an appearance, breaking weakly through the clouds above the jagged tree line.

"I've got to beat it," Dale said, straightening up and thrusting a hand at Matt. "Will you be here for the next session?"

Matt took his hand and was transfixed by those eyes. This must be how a rabbit feels as he's about to become road kill. "Wednesday? Yes, I'll be here." Truthfully, he hadn't been sure he had more than one early start a week in him, but that was before he met Dale. If he needed a reason to drag his tired butt out of bed, this was as good as he'd find.

"Great. I'm glad to see I'm not the only new guy. We're in

this together now. Got to give those regular guys a run for their money, don't you think? So I'll see you Wednesday. Bye for now, Matt."

Dale jogged toward his car, giving Matt one final glimpse of his beautiful bouncing butt.

What was that? Matt felt as though he'd been picked up, spun around and dropped back down again. Had Dale been flirting? Or was that just American friendliness? Probably, Matt reasoned. He was so used to British reserve and surliness that he'd misread the signs. Dale was being friendly, that was all.

He shouldn't hope for more.

\* \* \* \*

Two hours later, showered, dressed and breakfasted, Matt walked through the doors of Benedict and Taylor, the long-established law firm where he'd worked since finishing college, ready to face the day. He *really* was ready. Despite the early start and punishing routine in the woods, he felt amazing. More energized for a Monday morning than anyone had a right to be. Maybe it was worth it and those people who worked out before the rest of the world had had their first cup of coffee weren't as crazy as he'd always thought. Exercise did have its benefits, besides meeting sexy strangers, and this early feeling of energy was a previously undiscovered one.

One look at Monica, sitting bleary-eyed on the reception desk, chugging from a bucket-sized carton of takeaway coffee, convinced him he was right.

"Rough night? Rough weekend? Year?" he asked.

"Very funny," she sneered, booting up the computer. "It's Monday, unless you've forgotten. Only freaks come in to work on Monday with a smile on their face."

"I'm smiling, aren't I?"

"Like I said—freaks!"

She sipped her coffee, looking him up and down. In his

12

dark blue suit, pale shirt and narrow tie, clean shaven with his unruly hair combed into a neat style, he bore little resemblance to the wild creature who had stumbled out of bed all those hours before. Wearing a suit each day was part of the job and Matt Blyth wore it well. Six-foot-two with broad shoulders and a slender waist, he had the classic male physique that suits were designed for. The cheapest, off-the-rack two-piece still looked great on him.

"You *do* look unusually happy," Monica said, narrowing her eyes. "Why? Did you have a lottery win over the weekend? Or did you strike it lucky in other ways? A tumble in the sack?"

"It's the joy of life, Monica. You should try it sometime."

"Huh? You should try sitting here eight hours a day, five days a week and listen to people bitch because they can't get an appointment. See how joyful you feel then."

Matt's office was on the first floor of an imposing Victorian mid-link terrace in the heart of the old city. He bounded up the stairs, two at a time, to retrieve the planner from his desk. *This is ridiculous.* Surely he couldn't feel this good because of a little extra exercise. If so, he should have done it years ago.

Every morning from nine till nine-twenty Edward Benedict, senior partner in the firm and Matt's direct boss, held a brief team meeting in the ground floor conference room. The aim was to assess any outstanding work, go through what had come in overnight and fix what everyone had to do that day.

Edward was at the head of the table when Matt entered. He was a well-built man in his mid-fifties, with thick gray hair and a broad, often red face. He regarded Matt with serious eyes over the top of his wire-framed glasses. With the table only two-thirds full, Matt was glad he wasn't the last to arrive.

"Morning," he greeted the room and took a seat beside Trish Coleman, the firm's bookkeeper. She had been with the practice almost as long as Edward.

"Have you heard?" Trish asked as he poured a glass of water from the jug on the table. "There's been another murder in town."

"I heard they had found a body. Have they confirmed it's murder?"

"Not officially. Not yet. But I've heard it from various sources already this morning. It looks *exactly* like the boy they found the other week. Same circumstances and everything."

"Shit. Poor kids. Have they ID'd the body?"

"Not that I know of." Trish Coleman, with contacts in most other law firms and within the police force itself, was the first person to find out everything. Whatever she said would be easy to dismiss as gossip but Trish had been right about so many things, so many times before, it was stupid not to listen. Gossip was her life. If she decided to change careers she would make an excellent journalist. Her contacts were outstanding. "There's something else," she said, relishing the power of her knowledge. "The first victim, Conner Welsh — what hasn't been released so far is that he was severely assaulted — sexually. Before and after death."

"My God."

"I know. Isn't it awful?" Her eyes were indecently excited. "There's potentially a serial killer. A *sexual* serial killer. On the loose, right here in Durham."

"That's all idle speculation," Edward said firmly. He'd never approved of Trish's gossiping. Gossip worked both ways and he was suspicious of any information about the firm she might share with a rival in return for tittle-tattle.

For Matt, the shine was taken from his previous good mood. The discovery of another corpse was bad enough without the prospect of a sexual predator stalking the city. Unlike his boss, he was inclined to believe what Trish said. She was rarely wrong. The police needed to move quickly on the case before anyone else was killed.

Annabel Faith was the next to arrive. Edward glanced

frostily at his watch as she came in, but it was not yet nine o'clock. Annabel had joined Benedict and Taylor six months after Matt and had been his best friend in the practice since her first day. There was less than a year between their ages and Annabel was like the young sister he had never had.

In a black trouser suit and silk blouse, Annabel had clearly spent some considerable time getting ready that morning. Her makeup was immaculate and her soft blonde hair had been straightened into a sharp style. Matt looked her up and down.

"So what's your excuse? Hair dryer emergency?"

"Sorry, sweetie, but I just couldn't face it. Not this morning."

"Neither could I but I still made the effort. It's what we agreed after all. You could at least have sent a text and told me you weren't coming."

"I didn't think you'd have your phone on you." She helped herself to a breakfast muffin from the pile on the table and sat beside him. "I said I was sorry, sweetie."

"I told them you would definitely be there," he lied. "The instructor was really pissed. The entire group waited for you."

Her mouth widened, as she was about to take a bite. "Oh my God. Really? Were they mad? What did they say about me?"

Edward called the meeting to order. Not everyone was there yet, but a bit like Clint Dexter, he was a sucker for punctuality and starting on time. Matt decided to keep quiet for a while. It would do Annabel good to stew a little.

As usual, Edward went around the table, getting his staff to read out one by one what they had listed in their diaries for the day. It was the standard list of mundane matters, the kind of work that kept modest firms like this one ticking over.

"I've got two clients at court this morning," Matt said when it came his turn. "Magistrate's stuff over at Newton Aycliffe. One breach of the peace and one driving offense.

Both are pleading guilty so it shouldn't take more than an hour. I was going to spend the rest of the morning preparing a trial I have tomorrow."

"Which trial?" Edward observed him over the rim of his glasses.

"Newby versus Lewis. A family matter. Dad is going for access rights to his son."

"Difficult?"

"Mother is being difficult but I think we can win. Her main argument against our client getting access is that he has a new girlfriend. Nothing to do with his suitability to have the boy. If I can get that across to the judge, I think I can get our client what he wants."

"Good. And this afternoon?"

"Appointments every half hour until six. Two new cases. It's a full schedule. And I'm on call tonight. This morning is the only time I have to prep the trial," he added hastily. Edward had a habit of spotting what he perceived to be gaps in his workers' schedules and filling them, with little consideration for the amount of work required before and after even the most mundane case.

"That's fine. Annabel?"

Less prepared, Annabel blustered through a sparse calendar and tried to make herself sound busy. In reality she had little going on that morning, other than a few follow-up phone calls, and only appointments booked for the afternoon. Edward saw straight through the ruse.

"Take the files from Matt for the magistrate's cases. You can handle the sentencing. Matt, take the morning to prepare your trial for tomorrow. I think you'll need it."

"Thank you, sir. It's appreciated."

"You bloody crawler," Annabel said afterward, coming to Matt's office to collect the files she needed for court.

He laughed. "I didn't ask for this. The boss saw right through that crap you gave him. You've got bugger all to do today."

"I like to keep things light on Monday, you know that."

"So does Edward, *that's* your problem."

She pulled up a chair and sat, leafing through the files without taking much notice of what was inside. It was routine stuff. Nothing she couldn't deal with on the fly at court. "So how did it go this morning? Were they really pissed I wasn't there?"

"You'd love that, wouldn't you? But no, they weren't pissed. Nobody noticed to be honest, except me. This guy Clint, he doesn't wait around for people. If you're not there on time, too bad."

She flicked her hair across her shoulder. "What's he like? The instructor? A hottie or nottie?"

Annabel was a serial fiancée who had recently broke off her latest engagement. She was back on the market and finding a new man was her number one priority.

"He's okay. He's very fit but probably not your type."

"Hmmm. How old?"

"Fortyish. Thereabouts. It's sometimes hard to tell with those really muscular men. Too much muscle can be ageing. He might not be as old as all that."

"I need to find out for myself."

"Then you need to get your butt out of bed on Wednesday and be there at five-forty-five."

"You're going back?"

"I am. Unlike you, when I commit to something I see it through."

He decided not to tell her about Dale. Not yet. Selfishly, he hoped Annabel wouldn't show on Wednesday. He wanted the American to himself. At least until he had time to figure him out. The more he thought about him, the more convinced he became that Dale had been showing definite signs of interest this morning. Crazy, for sure, but Dale was so goddamn beautiful, he couldn't pass up the opportunity of seeing him again.

Even if it was just a sweaty yomp around the woods. When a man looked as good as he did, a moment of his time was better than nothing.

# Chapter Two

The boy, not yet twenty, slept peacefully in his bed. The white sheets were thrown back to the waist as he lay, one arm flung carelessly above his head, the other open wide. His body was lean and smooth, the muscles of youth flourishing as they transitioned from adolescence to manhood. His bare chest rose and fell with the regular rhythm of sleep. Peaceful and content, he was oblivious to the danger standing less than three feet away.

If the boy opened his eyes he might not see the man across the room. His black clothes and hooded face merged almost seamlessly into the shadows. Barely breathing, not making a sound, the man was quite undetectable. Until he stepped out of the darkness and approached the bed.

He stood over the boy, silently watching.

The boy moaned softly in his sleep and raised a hand to scratch an itch above his right nipple. It was an unconscious action and his eyes remained shut.

Unlike the eyes that watched him from the slits of a balaclava. They glistened in the darkness, almost burning in their intensity—full of evil. The man was as still as a statue, until suddenly he made his move.

The boy stirred, aware that something was off. By the time he opened his eyes it was too late. The man was on top of him, crushing him with superior strength and weight. A black cord wound around the boy's neck. Before he knew what was happening, the man's hands drew tight. Desperately the boy scrabbled at his throat. Teeth bared, mouth open, he struggled to breathe. Tighter, tighter, the man drew the cord.

The boys eyes bulged and his tongue protruded obscenely from his mouth.

The man was merciless.

Finally, it was all over.

The killer released his hold, sitting back to admire his efforts.

Stillness and quiet returned to the small bedroom.

"Excellent. Cut!" yelled a voice from the darkness.

The room was flooded with light and the dead boy opened his eyes, looking somewhat bewildered and vacant.

Dale Zachary eased his weight off the body beneath him and pulled off the killer's hood.

"Are you okay?" he asked, rolling off the bed so the boy could sit and catch his breath. It may only be acting but the brutality of such a scene could have a disconcerting effect on the performers.

The boy, a young actor called Rory, pushed up onto his elbows.

"I didn't hurt you, did I?" Dale asked.

Rory shook his head. "Not at all."

Playing the unfortunate first victim in a new TV series, *Blood Falls on Stone*, was a big deal for the young actor. His biggest role to date. Dale knew there was nothing he or anyone on the crew could do to dampen this guy's enthusiasm. He'd been that inexperienced newbie back in the day. That's why it was important for him to look after the kid, even when he was wringing his neck.

Elton Weaver, the director, strolled over. He was short, overweight and chewing gum. His minty breath failed to cover the stink of gin. It seemed to leak from every pore. "Good one, guys. Let's do another take of that. This time, let's see you really go for it. Dale, I want you to let him have it. Don't hold back. Rory, I want you to put up a bigger fight. Struggle, twist and kick. Fight the fucker with all you've got. Let's see how badly you want to live."

"Okay," Rory said, happily flopping back on the bed and pulling the covers into place.

"Are you sure?" Dale asked the director. "This is TV after all. Can we really get away with this? Seems like we've gone pretty far already."

"Trust me. We can get away with all sorts of things these days. I want the violence to mean something. For the audience to feel the pain of your victims. It'll contrast well with the slower-paced dialogue scenes. If Aunty Beeb gets cold feet, we can always substitute the earlier stuff."

The scene was pretty violent as it was but, despite his reservations, Dale gave the director what he wanted. The second take was far more disturbing and mean-spirited than the first. Rory fought back. Coughing, spluttering, fighting for his life. The more he struggled, the harder Dale played it, pressing down with all of his strength and weight.

When the director called "Cut" again he was shaken. He pulled off the mask and gasped for breath. *Shit, that was intense.*

Elton rushed forward, delighted. "Perfect," he roared. "Just perfect. *That* is going to be the watercooler moment for this show. Twitter will go into fucking meltdown and everyone will talk about it. Fuck *Broadchurch* and *The Fall*. We'll give people nightmares for weeks. They'll sleep with the lights on the night this goes out. Ha."

Dale wasn't so sure. He had a suspicion they had crossed a line and the TV company would insist on using the other version, but kept his opinion to himself. Elton was the director. His job was to give the director what he wanted. Besides, Elton's track record was impeccable. His last show had won a slew of BAFTAs and Emmy awards. He had the respect of the entire industry. He hadn't achieved that by playing things safe.

Rory didn't look quite as bright-eyed as he had before. He face, neck and chest were flushed and blotchy. He was out of breath.

"Still hanging in there?" Dale asked.

The boy raised his thumb and smiled.

"You did good," Dale said, patting his shoulder as he got

off the bed.

They spent the rest of the afternoon shooting close-up and insert shots. Dale's hands around the cord as he throttled the boy. Rory's legs thrashing about the bed. Dale's eyes, narrowed with hatred, through the balaclava slits. Hard work, but not as grueling as playing the scene in its entirety.

Around five Dale was released for the day. His scenes were over. Rory was not so fortunate. Filming would continue until late, covering the aftermath of the murder. The discovery of his body by his girlfriend and the ensuing crime scene investigation. Standard cop show stuff. But, as the killer, Dale was no longer needed.

He walked gratefully back to his trailer. A rare early finish. It was just what he needed after a tough day. Early morning boot camp probably wasn't the wisest way to kick things off when he had so many tough scenes to film, but he was glad he'd made the effort. Keeping fit was a mandatory part of the job for an actor like him and he hated every minute he spent at the gym. Boot camp was the perfect solution – get in early, train hard and get it over with. Job done.

Meeting hot men, like that guy Matt, was a bonus.

He was already looking forward to the next session and another encounter with the dreamy Matt. He was some looker all right. Tall, dark and handsome – the perfect English gentleman. The kind who only seemed to exist in movies – until now. Dale smiled. He was no romantic. Odd that Matt should arouse those kinds of feelings. With his strong, angular face, straight nose and wide mouth, he was better looking than any Hollywood pretty boy.

Wednesday, Dale resolved, he would make the effort to get to know him better. Find out who he was, what he did, whether he was straight, gay or bi.

Preferably one of the last two.

Not that any of it mattered. Dale had no time in his life right now for the complication of romance.

They were two weeks into a three-month shoot for *Blood Falls on Stone*. Serial killer Daryl Stone was the role of a lifetime, but playing him wasn't easy. Dale had worked too hard to win the part to lose focus now. The casting process had dragged on for months as the British producers searched for a recognizable American face to star in their thriller. Of all the names rumored to be under consideration, his was the least known. Several TV stars and movie actors were in the running. There was also competition from talented British actors with an American profile. While Dale had a sizeable list of IMDb credits that could match any of those guys, most of what he'd done was shit. Lousy rom-coms, cheap horror movies and a string of uncommissioned pilots.

Being based here in the UK while the producers were casting was a big plus. He was also generating excellent reviews for a play in London when the director came to see him. Elton Weaver was impressed enough by his stage performance to arrange a screen test with *Blood Falls on Stone's* leading lady, Roxanne Maxwell, a glamorous powerhouse of talent. Roxanne had made her name in her late twenties as a film actress. Now in her mid-forties, she had spent the last decade carving out a career on TV and stage. Pairing Roxanne with an award-winning director like Elton ensured *Blood Falls on Stone* would be a TV event.

Dale was determined to be part of that.

He smashed it in the screen test, giving everything he had.

The producers wanted a bigger name but Elton said they didn't need it. They already had Roxanne Maxwell. Of all the actors he'd tested there was no one as good as Dale Zachary. He was the man they needed to play the sexy, charismatic and terrifying killer Daryl Stone.

He was cheaper than all the others too. A fact, Dale had no doubt, that went in his favor.

Dale entered his trailer. He might be cheap but at least they'd provided that.

He took off his costume and hung it up for the wardrobe assistant to collect later. Daryl Stone was a tough nut to play and took him to some disturbing places, especially on days like this when they were shooting a murder scene, but he was no method actor. The character came off with the costume. Daryl Stone did not go home with him.

As Dale stepped into his own jeans, there was a knock at the door. "It's open," he called, pulling on a black T-shirt.

Aaron Oxford was a production assistant on the series. He was thirty-two but looked younger. His brown hair was thick and lustrous, falling heavily across his brow, above friendly brown eyes. He wore a full beard, chocolate brown without a hint of gray.

Dale, known through his career for his fresh-faced, clean-cut good looks, had grown a beard at the request of Elton for the role. He was still getting used to being a man with a beard. His was shorter, more trimmed than Aaron's, but the most shocking thing about it was just how much gray it contained. He was only thirty-four, less than two years older than Aaron, and yet his beard was so much more aging. As soon as the shoot was over, this thing was history.

"You were great today," Aaron said, stepping into the trailer. He was tall, rangy and heavily tattooed. He smelled good too, wearing a fresh, citrus scent. It suited him. "You going straight home?"

"Yeah. It's not often I get to leave early. Got to take advantage. I'm going to take a long hot soak, learn my pages for tomorrow, then an early night."

Aaron closed the trailer door. "Lucky you. I'm stuck here till the end." He took a purposeful step toward Dale.

They had known each other a couple of weeks. There was nothing in it, besides physical attraction. Two lonely people working together far from home.

"I thought you might like me to take care of something before you leave." Aaron smiled, rubbing a hand across the front of Dale's jeans.

"I'm pretty beat," he protested weakly.

"Don't worry. I don't have much time."

Deftly, Aaron undid Dale's belt and fly and shoved his jeans and underpants to mid-thigh. His cock thrust forward, ascending rapidly to full hardness. Despite good intentions, a man's dick will always betray him. Aaron dropped to his knees and took Dale's cock into his mouth.

* * * *

Dale Zachary, the middle of three brothers, had been born in Pennsylvania, popular with girls from a young age. All of the Zachary boys had been, inheriting their blond, blue-eyed good looks from their Danish mother. As his body had developed through puberty, muscles growing and balls dropping, the girls had really started to notice him. The Zachary brothers, each a year apart, had been a handsome bunch, but Dale, who had the least interest in girls, always had seemed to be the favorite.

He had been more interested in sport than chasing girls. Happier on the track than hanging around the arcades and cinema. Running, jumping and wrestling, he'd excelled at them all. It hadn't been just natural talent that'd brought him success, but hard work—lots of it. From an early age, he hadn't been a slacker.

Dale's first crush had been Danny Segal, captain of the school wrestling team, but it was Danny's cousin Susie who'dd claimed his virginity. With her soft blonde hair and overly developed boobs, fifteen-year-old Dale had known what he should fancy, rather than the hot jock in the wrestling singlet.

"Don't worry," Susie had said. "I know what I'm doing."

They had been in the spare bedroom of Danny's house during a party for his sister's eighteenth birthday. Susie had been two years older than Dale and he had no reason to doubt her claim. She'd said she knew what she was doing and he'd believed her. It had been exciting—and frightening—as she had led him away from the party and wedged a chair against the unlocked bedroom door. Susie's tits had been the talk of the locker room. The guys on the team would have all settled for a glimpse of those unfettered breasts, but she had been there on top of him,

24

pushing those massive boobs right in his face. Dale had wanted to laugh but doubted Susie would see the funny side. With steely determination, he had followed her lead.

Susie's polished fingers had guided his hard manhood between her legs and Dale had been enveloped by her warm, sticky pussy. It hadn't felt too bad. Hell, it actually had felt pretty good. Normal even.

He had read that crushes on members of the same sex were a common part of growing up. It was something most guys went through. Susie's welcoming, voluptuous body had convinced him that his feelings for her cousin had been nothing more than that—a phase. He'd grow out of it soon enough and, when he did, he'd be as normal as any other guy.

He'd had a lot of girlfriends after Susie. Through high school, as he had excelled on the wrestling team and in the drama group, he had become one of the more popular boys. His easygoing nature and wholesome good looks had put him at the top of many girls' fantasy lists.

It had been another girlfriend, Sherilyn, who had persuaded him to enter a modeling competition while he'd been at college in New York.

"You're crazy." He'd laughed. "I'm no model. Who wants to stand around looking dumb all the time? All I know about fashion are jeans and T-shirts. I'd suck."

Undeterred, Sherilyn submitted his photo to the competition. She had known he had the look. Dale had won first place and a contract with a New York agency. What started as a laugh and a way to earn extra cash had quickly led to high-profile campaigns for jeans, underwear and aftershave. He had the face and the body to go far and he quickly had, traveling all over the world to promote the brands he had been attached to.

Despite the fame, the money and the traveling, he had soon realized that his early opinion of modeling was correct. It wasn't for him.

Through it all, he had been dismayed to find that the

phase he had gone through of fancying other guys had been slow to pass. It hadn't gone anywhere. Though he had still slept with women, he hadn't been able to stop looking at other men. Traveling had afforded him the opportunity to experiment. Discreetly, away from home, where nobody had known who he was. It seemed reasonable, that if he scratched that itch, maybe it would go away.

Sex with women had come to be something he had enjoyed, even if he'd often found himself thinking of other men during the act, but sex with a man had been something else—something out of this world. *Oh God*, it was wrong. So, so wrong. Why had it felt so good—so right to him?

But it couldn't be. He wasn't *that* kind of man. Dale had suppressed that aspect of his sexuality. If he kept it under wraps and satiated it rarely, away from home, with strangers who didn't know him and who he'd never see again, he could lead a normal life. Be a normal man. Have a family someday.

His high-profile modeling had led to him being cast as the love interest in a teen TV show. Like modeling, the role hadn't required him to do much except stand around and look decorative, but it had been a foot in the door to the career he really wanted. He'd always been a passionate performer in the school drama group and had kept up acting classes during his poster boy years with a view to someday moving on.

From the TV series, he had progressed to his first film role—Chuck, the all-American football hero boyfriend of the second lead in a schmaltzy teen romance. The movie had been awful but a decent success at the summer box office. It had been his next role that really changed things.

*An Axe in the Dark* had been a bandwagon-chasing addition to the torture porn genre, which was currently in vogue. Dale had a sizeable role, the obligatory hunky boyfriend of the leading lady, but it was the elaborately staged murder of his character that had become the film's major talking point. In just a pair of tattered shorts, he had been hanged ingloriously on a meat hook while the ax-wielding killer had hacked him in half. The unsettling, but timeless juxtaposition of beauty and violence, combined with some of the most realistic gore effects ever seen in a movie, meant the film and *that scene* had been a huge hit—two weeks at number one in the American box office.

Dale had gone from support player to top billing in his next run of movies. The films themselves had been interchangeable, a roster of romantic comedies and gory horror films, but the parts improved. In the years that had followed, he had become a familiar face in TV shows and direct to video movies. Sadly, his biggest film, an earthquake movie with an enormous budget and an all-star cast, had been a huge flop. He had been far from the worst thing in it, but the movie's failure had put an early end to his hopes of being an A-list leading man.

But he was still working steadily. That's all any decent actor could hope for.

"Got another horror picture for you," his agent had announced.

"Another one?" *An Axe in the Dark* might have given him a career but it had sure as hell typecast him too.

"It's a good one this time. Two months in Europe. Expenses. Top billing. Decent money. They want you. They're not looking at anyone else."

With no jobs pending, Dale had boarded a plane for Prague with little idea how this low budget indie film was about to change his life forever. *It's in the House* was identical to any of the other found footage ghost stories cluttering up the multiplexes. He hadn't even looked at the script until he was on the plane.

He had been glad to get out of town. He'd been secretly involved with a married businessman for almost a year when the guy's wife had found out. She never had discovered the identity of her husband's lover but came pretty damn close. He'd hoped to land the lead in an NBC pilot later that year. A whiff of scandal now would ruin that opportunity for good.

The hokey thrills of *It's in the House* came at just the right time.

Laura Kinnear had been originally from London. Working as a makeup artist in New York and Los Angeles, she eventually had found herself on the set of a low-budget horror film in Europe with Dale Zachary. She had been just a year younger, with a tomboyish attitude and filthy sense of humor. Dale had never met a woman quite like her. Always cheerful, and even in the makeup chair at seven in the morning, she could make him laugh harder than any comedian he'd seen.

Most mornings he hadn't been able to wait to get on the set to see her. Finally, a woman he really clicked with. A woman who had been able to banish all those foolish notions he'd had about other guys. By the end of the second week they had started sleeping together and when the movie had wrapped, Laura had returned to Los Angeles with Dale.

He had scored the lead in the NBC pilot but the network failed to take the show to series. It didn't matter. By autumn, Laura had become pregnant.

"I'm gonna take care of you, babe," he'd said, delighted with the news. He was going to be a dad.

They'd married before their son was born. At last he had become a real man with a wife, a child and a half decent career. Life couldn't get much better. When not working, Dale had spent all the time he could with his new family. He was a hands-on dad, just like his old man had been with him. It was important for a kid to have a father figure. To lead by example.

Those old forbidden feelings refused to die but by keeping busy with work and family he had kept them at bay. For a while at least. His sex life with Laura had ended almost as soon as their son Jack had been born. It had been a relief not to have to go through the motions and he'd believed Laura when she'd told him that she was too tired to do it after a long day with the baby.

* * * *

For several years, Laura had even convinced herself that was true. Dale had been discreet most of the time, deleting his Internet history, but she'd found out accidentally, while searching their computer for an old contact, the kind of porn he got off to. The shock hadn't lasted long. She'd suspected for a while that he had more than a passing interest in other men. She'd heard the rumors about him from before they had been married. She had chosen to dismiss them back then. All sexy young actors were tarred with the gay brush at some point in their career.

Only with Dale, she had known those rumors were more than jealousy or bitchy gossip. Her husband was gay. Laura Zachary had come to terms with that fact before he did.

At the start of 2011 and after eight years of marriage, Laura had filed for divorce and moved back to the UK, taking Jack with her.

* * * *

Dale hadn't been bitter about the divorce. He'd been deceiving his wife. She deserved a man who could love her in the ways he couldn't. But he couldn't live without his son. If Laura wanted to bring the boy up in England that was fine, but he hadn't wanted to let her do it without him.

Most of his work had been shown on TV or DVD in England. Finding an English agent to represent him hadn't been difficult. He had done another run of Euro horror films and landed a couple of high-profile theater roles, but basically he had been starting his career all over again. Building a reputation, putting his name out there.

When he had finally tested for *Blood Falls on Stone*, Dale Zachary had been ready for that breakthrough.

Dale was renting a house for the duration of the shoot rather than living out of a hotel. Most of his adult life had been spent in hotels, apart from the eight years he'd been married. Even then, he'd spent a lot of time working away.

He was sick of suitcases. Besides, Jack was living with his mother in Kent and he wanted somewhere nice for the boy to stay when he came to visit.

The house was one of only five properties developed on the site of an old farm. The original farmhouse, barns and outbuildings had been converted into luxury country accommodation. Dale was renting the smallest of the new dwellings. Formerly a single-story cattle shed, the original stone building had been gutted and redeveloped into a modern, two-story, high-spec cottage. Situated on a steep bank with outstanding views of the countryside and Durham City in the distance, the house and the location were perfect.

In February the nights cut in early and it was dark by the time he pulled into the small courtyard of the property. There were lights in one his neighbors' houses but none of the others were home from work. He had met a couple of the neighbors when he'd moved in but they kept to themselves and didn't bother him, which was just perfect. He spent all day being looked at. Away from the studio, he valued his privacy.

Coming home to an empty house sometimes bothered him. It was crazy. He'd spent more years on his own than he ever had married, but he still yearned for the wonderful evenings he'd spent with Jack when they were a family unit.

Someday, he would get around to buying a place of his own—a proper place, not a temporary rental. He was determined not to live alone. He'd get a cat if he had no other option.

The cottage smelled delicious as he entered. Mrs. Butterman, the local woman he hired to look over the place, came in three mornings a week. Today was one of those days and he discovered the source of the smell in the kitchen. A wonderful beef casserole bubbling away in the slow cooker. *Wow.* It must have been slowly stewing all day and the smell was quite incredible.

Just as well he went to boot camp with this treat in the pot for dinner.

He emptied his gym bag into the laundry basket and wandered through the cottage, turning on lights and closing curtains. He switched on the kitchen TV to give a little background noise. He couldn't stand the silence when he was alone.

He poured a neat whiskey, opened his mobile phone and dialed the most frequent number.

Jack answered on the fifth ring. "Hi, Dad. What's up?"

"Nothing up. I finished work early today and wanted to ring you before dinner."

"How come?" There was a lot of background noise. There always was when he spoke to Jack. Laura had remarried, had another kid and the house was full with the chaos of a young family. The noise was a painful reminder of what he'd lost.

"Just wrapped my scenes for the day. Fortunately it happens. You've done your homework?"

"Nearly. I've done the stuff for tomorrow."

"What about the rest of it?"

"It doesn't have to be in until Thursday. I'll do it tomorrow."

"Is your mom okay with that?"

"She's fine."

"Sure?"

"*Dad!*"

"Okay."

He never tired of hearing Jack's voice. The boy had lost all remaining traces of the American accent he'd had when Laura had relocated back to the UK. Growing up with a British mother, he'd always sounded more English than American. Now the transformation was complete. Still, he took after Dale in other ways.

"Got soccer practice this week?"

"Dad, it's called football here. *Football.* Yes, Wednesday night, straight after school."

"I've never understood that crazy game. You'll have to teach me sometime. I can't wait to see you play."

"I hope I'll get picked for the school team."

"Why don't I get us a ball? When you come up this weekend, you can practice your ball skills and show me some of what you've achieved."

"Have you got a yard to play in?"

"The biggest yard you've ever seen. There are fields in all directions. Miles and miles of them. I promise you, Jack, you're gonna love it."

After another ten minutes Dale reluctantly ended the call. He could talk all night but the boy was almost twelve. He had better things to do than listen to his old man.

He hated not being there with Jack. But at least they were only separated by a few hundred miles. The UK was just an island. Not the whole fucking Atlantic.

# Chapter Three

A rotund custody officer led Matt along the narrow corridor of Bishopgate Police Station, a barren and colorless place with solid cell doors on either side. Despite regular visits, the custody cells still made him nervous. It was the confinement. He could only imagine the panic and claustrophobia that would set in if he were locked behind one of those doors.

It was coming up on eight o'clock on Monday night and Matt hadn't been home yet. The call from the police station had come through as he was finishing up his final appointment of the afternoon. One of their clients was in custody. The sergeant said they would be ready to interview him within the hour. It wasn't worth going home to come straight back out. On his way to the station, he stopped at a supermarket and bought a bunch of bananas to tide him over.

The client had been accused of rape. There was little chance of getting home before midnight if the charge was as serious as that.

Gary Draper was a regular customer of Benedict and Taylor, though Matt didn't know him personally. One of the more senior lawyers usually handled his business, but as Matt was on call, it fell to him to deal with any after-hours business. It was the luck of the draw. Some nights on duty resulted in no calls at all, while others were so busy he was lucky to snatch an hour or two of sleep before getting up to face another day.

The custody officer unlocked one of the doors and swung it wide open. "Your lawyer is here," he barked, allowing

Matt into the cell.

The room was sparse and gloomy with just a padded bench to sleep on and a stainless steel toilet without a seat. Gary Draper sat on the bench in shirtsleeves. The jacket of his suit, together with his belt and tie, had been confiscated

"Hi, Gary." Matt walked forward and shook his hand. His grip was weak and clammy. Matt introduced himself and explained his role as duty officer.

"When will I get out of here? I've been in this room since ten o'clock. They lifted me before I even got to work."

Matt sat beside him. "We're going to the interview room in a few minutes. Depending on how that goes, they'll either release you or hold you for further questioning. They can hold you here for up to twenty-four hours and within that period they have to allow you eight hours' sleep. When that time runs out the police will have to release you, charge you, or apply for an extension on your detention. That'll give them an additional twelve hours before they either charge or release you."

"Shit. This is stupid. I haven't done anything."

"Have you had any experience of police custody?"

"God, no. I've never had so much as a speeding ticket." A note of panic crept in with the anger in his voice.

Gary Draper was not typical of the clients he usually represented at the station. Most of their criminal cases were seasoned regulars. By eighteen years old they knew the procedure inside and out. The prospect of custody held no fear for them. Not like Gary, a corporate client, used to conveyance and property deals. For Gary, looking at the inside of a police cell for the first time at thirty-seven was a big deal. A very big deal.

"You've been accused of rape," Matt said.

"I didn't do it. Rape. God, no, never."

"During interview the officers are going to put the allegations to you and any evidence they've gathered. Do you have any idea what these allegations are about or who has made them? It relates to an incident on December nineteenth last year."

Gary nodded. "I know what it's about. But there *was* no rape."

"Tell me your side."

"Victoria Smith. She's the one who's saying all this about me. I've known her for years. I'm always seeing her out and about. She likes to flirt when she's had a drink but she's not my type. She's married for a start. Though I don't think that's ever held her back, not when she's on one of her girls' nights out."

"What happened on the nineteenth?"

Gary rubbed his palms against his thighs. "I went out after work. Christmas drinks and all that. A few of us stayed later than planned. We went to Love Shack. That's where we ran into Victoria and her mates. They were merry, flirting and all the usual antics. I think she got her eye on me that night and decided I was the one."

"You had sex?"

He nodded sheepishly. "I should have said no, but it was Christmas. I was drunk. So was she. We all were. I took her to the Travelodge in town and we stayed the night."

"And the sex?" Matt asked. "Was it consensual?

"Yes. As consensual as sex between two drunk people can be. We were smashed. Falling all over each other. It couldn't have lasted more than a few minutes."

"Did she ever ask you to stop? Say no? Did she seem uncomfortable with what you were doing?"

"No. To be honest she made all the moves once we were on the bed. I sort of lay back and let it happen." He looked Matt straight in the eyes. "I didn't rape her."

"What happened afterward?"

"Nothing. We fell asleep. We were there all night. She even woke me up to have sex again but I just wasn't up to it."

Matt made rapid notes throughout Gary's version. "Why do you think Victoria is making this allegation now?"

"To cover herself. The police—they've taken my phone.

But if you look on Facebook—there are photos. I only saw them myself last week, but someone's put photos up of that night in the club. Victoria and me in a booth, kissing. There's one of her on my knee with her hands down my pants. It's not pretty. But I think she's saying all this because of those pictures. To cover her ass, 'cause her old man has seen them."

Matt asked Gary to retell the story a second, then a third time, looking for inconsistencies, for something he might be holding back. Matt had developed a skill for spotting liars and smelling their bullshit. It was an essential part of the job. This didn't smell like shit. Gary was telling the truth. He would bet on it.

"When we go through to the interview, you have the right to say nothing. You don't have to answer any of the questions. But my advice to you is to tell the officers exactly what you've told me. Keep calm. Don't lose your temper. Just tell your side of the story."

Gary nodded. His face was several shades whiter than when Matt arrived. "I can't believe this is happening. All because of a drunken mistake. I wish I'd never gone out that night."

"Sadly, it's more common than you think."

"I could go to the prison because of a drunken shag."

"Let's worry about the interview first. One thing at a time."

The custody officer came back and escorted them to an interview room. It was a standard box room with a desk, four chairs and a clunky voice recorder. Matt and Gary took their places on the far side of the table. Matt laid out his notebook and pen while waiting for the interviewing officer to arrive. Gary exhaled anxiously and glanced around the narrow room. The criminal justice system is a frightening beast to those unfamiliar with it.

"Just relax," Matt said. "Tell your story exactly as you told it to me."

"It's not a story," Gary snapped. "It's what happened, for

36

fuck's sake."

"Calm down," he said firmly. "If the police see you're rattled, they'll use it against you. Tie you in knots. Keep your head and stick to the facts, just the facts. You'll be fine."

He nodded. "Okay. Sorry. I didn't mean to bite your head off. It's been a stressful day." The door opened again and two plain-clothes police officers entered, taking their seats across the table. Matt's heart sank when he saw who the second officer was... Jamie Dench.

*Shit!* Why did it have to be Jamie?

Detective Constable Jamie Dench.

Matt's ex-boyfriend. Barely an ex at that. They had been together for two years and had been separated for less than three months. This was only the second time he'd seen Jamie since their split.

Jamie gave him the barest flicker of a smile as he pulled in his chair.

Thirty-three years old, with short dark hair and even darker eyes, Jamie had always had a serious look about him. This wasn't his game face. It was how he always looked.

The other officer, Detective Sergeant Sophie Talalay, was a by-the-book police officer. A career woman who got results with hard work and effort. Matt had a lot of respect for her. She was a tough nut at times — a pain in the ass when you were on opposite sides — but she was one hundred percent fair.

Without any preamble, Jamie activated the voice recorder and DS Talalay gave the formal introductions for the tape. She took the lead on the interview, questioning Gary about December the nineteenth and his night with Victoria Smith. He gave a strong account. Hearing it for the fourth time, Matt couldn't detect a single inconsistency in the story. No outlandish embellishments or minute attentions to detail that gave away the lies.

When it came to what happened in the hotel bedroom, Gary was resolute in his account — Victoria Smith had participated willingly.

"The hotel was her idea," he insisted. "We could've gone back to my place, but she said we were less likely to be recognized somewhere neutral. Get on to the hotel. They must have CCTV in the lobby and the corridors. They'll show how it was."

"Did you buy Victoria any drinks that night?"

"Yes. But it was Christmas. I bought everyone a drink. It's what you do."

"Did you slip anything extra into her glass?"

"No."

"Not even an extra shot or two?"

"No."

The detectives were clutching at straws. It was obvious. They had nothing to go on except Victoria Smith's version of events, which was riddled with inconsistencies. At one point, after a particularly desperate question, he made eye contact with Jamie, who looked away embarrassed. This interview was nothing but a fishing expedition.

They had nothing.

An hour later, they'd got no more from Gary than what he'd told Matt when he'd first arrived. Gary was taken back to the cell while the officers consulted on the interview.

"Is it worthwhile hanging around?" Matt asked. Their clock was ticking. They would have to talk to Gary again very soon, otherwise he was entitled to eight hours' sleep. If they weren't going to speak to him until the morning, he might as well go home.

"Hang on ten minutes," Jamie said. "Then we'll let you know either way."

Matt wrote up his notes as he waited. In a strange way he was glad to see Jamie again in circumstances such as this. Where they could maintain a degree of professionalism, detached from their messy history.

They had met for the first time in a similar situation to this. Matt had been a fresh faced, recently qualified solicitor when he'd got a call to represent a woman accused of stealing vodka from an out-of-town supermarket. Jamie had still been a uniformed PC, and the arresting officer. Some men look good in uniform. Jamie wasn't one of them. Pale and lanky, the standard kit had seemed to swallow him. He had reminded Matt of a little boy playing at being a cop. It had been quite endearing, with his pretty, but miserable face, swamped in the clothes of authority. It had been obvious that Jamie took his role very seriously because of the way he looked.

He later explained that he had to take himself seriously if anyone else was going to.

They had seen each other a lot like that in the beginning. As a rookie solicitor, Matt regularly had been sent to the police station to deal with the minor criminal jobs. His more experienced colleagues didn't want the hassle of dealing with shoplifters, drunks, vandals or anti-social behavior. Jamie always seemed to be around when he'd attended. As they had got to know each other, Matt had realized that Jamie's po-faced, often dour demeanor concealed a dry, very funny sense of humor.

The rapport they had shared led to the offer of a drink and their first proper date.

They couldn't have been more different. Matt came from a middle-class family with happily married parents. He had been privately educated and excelled both in the classroom and on the playing field. He'd always known he wanted to be a lawyer, just like his father, and had studied hard to make that dream come true.

Jamie came from a broken home. His warring parents had separated for good when he was thirteen. His teenage years had been a nightmare. He'd hated school, his parents and his mother's new boyfriend. He'd alienated the few friends he had, preferring the company of a video game to real people. He had drifted aimlessly after school, one job after another — laboring, bar work, shelf stacking, cleaning — until he had eventually joined the police force in his mid-twenties.

Police work had been the breakthrough he'd needed. All of the hatred and anger he'd battled since childhood could be focused on to single outlet—catching criminals.

Getting his own place, gaining independence, building a career, Jamie had been happy for the first time in his life. Almost. Building relationships was a skill he hadn't mastered. One-night stands never had been his scene. Right from the start, from the first date, Jamie had been looking for a boyfriend, not a casual lover. He'd come on strong. Too strong for most guys to handle. His relationships had tended to fizzle out after a few weeks. Six months had been the record before he'd met Matt.

Jamie had come along at just the right time for Matt. Throughout college, he'd been out there having fun. He'd played the field with one-night stands and casual lovers. He never had been a complete slut—not like some of the guys he'd run into. Hell, some of those guys had put themselves out two or three times every day—never satisfied. But Matt had enjoyed it. Why not? He had been a young guy, curious and hungry to experience new things. All part of growing up, right?

With Jamie, he'd finally been ready to experience something more serious. Nothing heavy, but he had been looking for a boyfriend. Jamie was cute and funny and very different from the scene-orientated, app-savvy boys he had been used to at college. Most of the time they had got along well. Jamie had been moody and difficult, especially when their work had brought them into competition. He hadn't thought it was right for Matt to defend the shit-bags he worked so hard to lock up.

Matt had been too easygoing ever to let work come between them, but Jamie had been so sure he was right that he hadn't been able to let it go.

When he'd asked Matt to move in with him, Matt had known that it could never work.

It had been the beginning of the end.

"We're done for tonight," Jamie said, returning to the

interview room. "We've decided to bail Draper till next week."

Matt gathered his notes. "You can't charge him. Not on that evidence. You have nothing and his account is tight."

"There'll be further investigations and we'll take prosecution advice."

It was standard practice in almost all sexual assault cases. It was such a political hot potato that the police had no option but to take it further.

"Same time next week. We'll have a decision to charge then."

Matt made a note of the date. It wasn't his case but being Monday night he'd have to deal with the after-hours interview again. That suited him fine. He liked seeing a job through to completion.

Jamie stood awkwardly in the doorway. Uncomfortable, as if they had never been close or intimate. "How, er…have you been?"

"Good. Busy. You too? I haven't seen you around much." Matt's voice sounded false and overly cheerful. He was almost as bad at this as Jamie was.

"I've been around," he said sheepishly, stuffing his hands in his pockets.

Why was this so awkward? Maybe because they were unused to it. After all those college flings, Jamie had been Matt's first proper boyfriend, the first one to mean anything. He'd never had to deal with a break-up or the emotional baggage that came with it. Before Jamie, he had been used to both partners moving on when the novelty wore off.

"Are you seeing anyone new?"

Jamie shrugged. "Not really. There was a man in Durham. We went out a couple of times but it didn't come to anything. How about you?"

For no reason the image of Dale, the guy from boot camp, flashed into his mind, together with the realization that he liked him. *Really liked him.* Enough to ask him out? *What? No way. This is insane.* He was probably straight anyway.

But it was a nice, if unexpected thought.

To Jamie, he said, "No. I'm not looking for anyone right now."

"So why did you break up with me?" The words rushed out of Jamie's mouth. He looked as shocked to be saying it as Matt was to hear it. "Oh God. I didn't mean to say that."

"But it's what you were thinking?" Matt said carefully.

"I guess it was. It wouldn't have come out otherwise. An unconscious gesture."

"Jamie, we've been through it all, God knows how many times. You know the reasons."

Jamie's dark eyes glistened with unspilled tears. They had moved on, but Matt could see the pain in his eyes. Their break-up was still too raw. The issues of the last six months of their relationship were as unresolved as they'd ever been. Going over it now, in the damn police station, wouldn't help.

Matt stood. "I'd better be going," he said, injecting some of that false cheerfulness into his voice. "It's been a long day. I'm starving."

"Of course," Jamie said, forcing a smile that was too broad, too desperate. "No need for you to hang around. Like I said, we're going to bail Draper to next Monday. I just need to process the paperwork. You don't have to stay for that. He'll be out of here in half an hour."

"I'll get going then," Matt said, rushing for the door. He hated himself—handling Jamie *so* badly—but he'd been granted an exit. He had to take it.

"I miss you," Jamie said as Matt headed out of the door, just quietly enough for Matt to pretend he hadn't heard.

# Chapter Four

Turning up for boot camp on Wednesday was so much easier with a motivating factor—Matt. Dale Zachary had thought about Matt a lot since the first session, which was strange in itself. Dale was too old to be harboring boyish crushes on a stranger. He was thirty-four, for Christ's sake. Even so, Matt had not been far from his thoughts for the last two days and he was looking forward to seeing him again. Leaving the cottage at five-twenty, he was kind of nervous. An excited feeling in his stomach. It was similar to the nerves he experienced before going on stage.

It was a morning like all the others that week—cold, dark and damp—but none if it affected him. He was too busy thinking about Matt, his anticipation building. Afraid to consider the possibility that Matt might not return for the second session.

Matt—the last thing he thought about when he'd turned out the light for bed and the first thing on his mind when the alarm sounded at four-thirty. He had it bad.

In a strange way, it was nice feeling like this—naive and excited. Kind of stupid, but cool just the same.

Some of the shine was knocked off that excitement when he arrived at the assembly point.

Matt was there all right, looking rugged with an unshaven face and unruly bed hair, but he wasn't alone. There was a woman with him. A very pretty, if overly done woman.

*Shit.* Those gay vibes he'd felt were a false alarm. What a pity. He'd been so sure Matt was into him.

"Hi," he said, jogging gently toward Matt and the blonde woman. "You made it back. I'm glad to see that."

Matt's face split into a grin so wide and charismatic it brightened even this miserably damp morning. "Hey, Dale, glad to see you too. This is my colleague Annabel. A no-show on Monday but she finally made it."

Dale detected an emphasis on the word *colleague*. Not girlfriend. Maybe it wasn't so bad after all. His spirits lifted. "Hi, Annabel," he said cheerfully.

"Hello," she replied politely.

Annabel had put a considerable amount of effort into her appearance this morning. All of the other girls in attendance were practically dressed and fresh-faced. Not this lady. She must have been up since three constructing her look. She was fully made up — powered with glossy red lips, smoky eyes and false lashes. He'd played on stage against actresses wearing less makeup than this. Her hair was blown and fluffed and swept into a soft ponytail that was supposed to look casual, however was anything but. She wore skintight purple leggings, silver running shoes and a pink hoodie covered in some kind of glitzy message. If this was how she looked to work out, he could only imagine the time it took her to dress for a big event.

"No ill effects from Monday?" he asked, turning his attention back to Matt.

"None. I thought I'd be stiff as a post afterward but I felt amazing. It must be doing me some good already."

"*Oh please*," Annabel drawled, looking at Matt but angling her body toward Dale. "Stop trying to sound so macho. No one feels that good after just one session. Tell the truth — you were crippled."

"Not so." Matt took her comment in good humor but Dale disliked her tone of voice — sarcastic and bitchy. The kind of girl who put her friends down to make herself feel better. "I felt great afterward. Honestly."

"I did too. This Clint guy, he pushes us all hard but he knows what he's doing, don't you think?"

"Absolutely."

"Huh." Annabel sighed, sticking out her chest. "You

boys, what are you like? All talk. I want to see some action before I believe either of you."

*Lady,* Dale thought, *I don't know what tree you're barking up here, but mine is sure as shit the wrong one.*

Clint Dexter approached with his ever-present notebook. "Welcome back, gentlemen," he said, ticking them off his list before turning to Annabel. "What happened on Monday? Did you sleep in?"

Matt laughed out loud until she shot him a look. She turned to face Clint directly, all fluttering eyes and jutting tits. "I'm here now," she preened. "But go easy on me. You don't want to break me on my first day."

*Isn't it a bit early for all this flirting?*

She was wasting her time. The instructor was immune. "I don't go easy on anyone. Not ever." He looked her coldly up and down before walking away.

"Wow." Matt smiled. "You're working your charm this morning. Looks like you scared him already."

Annabel tossed her ponytail, unperturbed. "Just need to get these guys warmed up, that's all. They'll come round eventually."

Dale admired her confidence. However misplaced it was.

Having completed the course once before didn't make it any easier. Clint was a tough taskmaster and put enough variety into the session and the course that it was impossible to predict or be prepared for what he threw at them next. Dale was impressed. This dude was good and he knew his stuff. Some of those stars back in Hollywood would kill for a trainer like this.

For most of the course, Dale kept pace with Matt. There was no chance to talk, Clint worked them too hard for that, but he was happy enough to run beside him, to share his quiet company. A couple of times Dale deliberately hung back so he could take a peek at Matt's bodacious butt as he ran uphill. Sneaky, but he didn't feel bad about it, not when he could look at an ass like that.

At one point, Matt glanced behind and caught him

staring. There was a moment of uncertainty and Dale was convinced he'd got it *so* wrong. Then Matt cracked a broad smile and, with a conspiratorial look, kept running. The smile was infectious.

*God, he is beautiful. Sexy too.*

There could be no doubt now. Not after a look like that. Annabel *was* just a colleague after all. Matt was definitely interested in him.

Wasn't he?

Self-doubt lingered. Dale just didn't have it in him to make the first move. Not under circumstances like this.

Exhausted and elated, they made it to the end of the course. Dale's heart pounded inside his chest. That had been some workout.

Annabel looked far less composed than when she'd started. Her blonde hair had gone to hell, clinging to her face and neck in sweaty strands. Her makeup was a lot more resistant—lips, eyes, powder were all still perfect.

As much as Dale wanted to hang around and talk to Matt, there just wasn't time. He was pushing it even coming here this morning. They needed him on set and in costume by eight.

"Are you going for the triple session?" he asked, as they headed back to their cars. "See you Friday?"

Matt's brown eyes sparkled in the gray light. "We're on a roll. Wouldn't miss it."

Annabel watched them both with a huge shit-eating grin on her face. Whatever she thought she knew or suspected, he didn't have the time or the interest to find out.

"Got to go," he said reluctantly. Annabel was spoiling his plans just by being here. Today he'd intended to find out more about Matt, with a little probing, disguised as small talk. No chance of that with her looming over their shoulders, alert to every word.

Dale headed to his car, feeling less euphoric than he had after his first session. *Never mind, there's always Friday.* Maybe Annabel would fail to drag her ass out of bed again.

As he started the engine there was a tap at the window. It was Matt.

Delighted, Dale opened the window. Matt smiled uncertainly and handed him a business card. *Matt Blyth – Solicitor* it read.

"I wanted to give you this. My contact details are all on there. Office, mobile, email. I thought you might like to stay in touch. I don't know... We could do a training session together. You know, away from the group."

Dale looked from the card to Matt's lovely face. "A training session?"

"It doesn't have to be." Suddenly Matt was blushing. "We could go for a run or a drink. If you want to keep in touch that is."

"Oh, I do." Dale beamed. "I really do. How about I call you later?"

"Great. I'll look forward to it."

\* \* \* \*

Annabel came into Matt's office in a flurry of excitement as he prepared his files for court. She looked remarkable, given that less than two hours before she had been gasping her way up and down the hills. She wore a pale gray trouser suit with a cream silk blouse. Her hair had been washed and straightened and her makeup was fresh and businesslike. She was a remarkable woman, never seen looking anything less than her best.

Dramatically, she threw a copy of the local newspaper *The Echo* onto his desk and pulled out a chair. The entire front page was dedicated to the murder of Olly Raymond, the young man pulled from the river on Monday. The story was the main headline on the news again that morning. Police were reluctant to connect the killing to that of Conner Welsh two weeks earlier but social media moved faster than any police conference, and the public had already linked the two.

"I knew there was something familiar about him," Annabel said.

Matt looked at the front-page photo of the dead boy. Another young man, only twenty-five, tragically taken too soon. He looked a lot like the previous victim, with dark hair and a handsome face. It was no surprise that people were speculating. If one killer was responsible for both deaths, they clearly had a type. "It says this boy was a barista at a coffee shop in town. We must have seen him around. Do you know where he worked?"

"Not the victim." Annabel grabbed the paper, turned the page and slammed it down in front of him. "*Dale.*"

There was Dale's photograph, right beneath a title that screamed *Death Imitates Fiction: Murder bears similarities to grisly TV show.* Matt stared at the headline and the photograph. The story related the eerie similarities between the recent murders and a TV show currently filming in and around Durham.

"Dale's an actor?"

"Yep. I knew there was something about him when he walked out this morning. At first, I thought we might have met before but couldn't place him right away. It came back to me as I was driving home. There was a feature on *North East Tonight* a couple of weeks ago when they started filming this show. They interviewed Roxanne Maxwell and Dale. Dale Zachary. That's his name."

Matt looked at the photo again. It showed a smiling Dale, without the sandy beard. *Dale Zachary – American Star*, read the caption.

"I've never heard of him," Matt said. His knowledge of film and TV shows was pretty sparse. He had a good memory for faces and names but when it came to celebrities and actors, he couldn't retain it. There was too much happening in real life to give much thought to the rich and famous.

Annabel, on the other hand, knew everything. An avid reader of *Heat, Closer* and *Hello!*, she knew all the actors in *EastEnders, Coronation Street, Hollyoaks* and *Emmerdale* and when she wasn't caught up watching soaps, she was immersed in celebrity talent shows—dancing, skiing, roughing it in the jungle, she watched them all.

"Dale Zachary," she announced, "is rather famous."

"You didn't recognize him this morning."

"Not at first but I got there eventually. I think the facial hair threw me. He doesn't usually have a beard."

"So what would I have seen him in?"

"*An Axe in the Dark.*"

"The horror film?"

"That's the one. You must have seen it. Everyone has."

Matt nodded. He remembered watching it on TV when he was at university. Late at night, when he was alone in his room, it scared the shit out of him. But he watched so much from behind a pillow, he could hardly remember it. "Dale was in that?"

Annabel made a swinging ax motion. "He got hung up and chopped up. It was awesome."

Matt thought hard. Yeah, there was a really hot guy in that movie who came to a nasty end. He was the main reason he had kept watching. Once the guy was dead, he'd begun to lose interest in the film. *That was Dale?*

"I'll have to look him up," he said.

"Do it now." She pointed eagerly at his computer. "We might find some naked pictures. I'm sure I've seen him nude in a movie before."

Matt laughed. "I'd love to but it will have to wait. I need to get to court."

"I'll do it," Annabel said, taking out her phone. "I'll text you if I find anything juicy."

"Don't you have any work to do?"

"It can wait. Come on, Matt. How often do we meet a gorgeous American celebrity? Don't you want to check out his fine Hollywood arse?"

"His arse, which I'm sure is very lovely, can wait. Unfortunately I can't."

Matt's case was listed at Bishopgate Magistrates for ten a.m. He arrived with fifteen minutes to spare but his client wasn't there yet. Checking his phone, he found that Annabel, true to her word, had texted a photo of Dale's naked butt.

*This is from a film about six years ago,* she wrote, *but, from what I saw this morning, he might have got better with age.*

The picture was a hazy screen grab of Dale stepping into the shower. Only the side of his head could be seen but it was recognizably him, minus his beard. But his ass—oh my God, his ass—was ripe and round. Manly and meaty. A real man's butt. Perfect.

Matt's cock came up hard. A boner was the last thing he wanted to take into court. He pocketed the phone and spoke to one of the clerks.

"I'm going to wait in the solicitor's room. Could you let me know when my client arrives? I'm waiting for Jenna McNab."

The clerk nodded and made a note on his list.

The waiting room was packed. If his client had been on time, they could have jumped to the front of the list. As it was, she would have to take her place when she arrived and might not get dealt with until late morning or even this afternoon. Matt was already prepared on this case. It was a straightforward assault. Jenna McNab was going to plead guilty. It was his job to put forward mitigation and get her the best sentence. The prosecution would ask for custody. He would argue the case for probation and a community sentence.

He'd brought a couple of other files to work on while they waited. There was no such thing as a spare moment in this job. Annabel often tried to wing it, arriving at court unprepared. She'd fallen foul of the magistrates dozens of times, then had to face the wrath of the senior partners when she'd got back to the office. Getting bawled at for losing the case did little to improve her motivation.

Matt hated to lose any case. That was the only incentive

he needed to work hard.

The room set aside for solicitors was basic. Just a few tables and chairs and one phone. No computers, laptops or facilities other than a watercooler. It was the perfect place to read through a case file. He'd often achieved more in an hour here than a full morning in the office where the phones were a constant distraction.

There was another lawyer waiting when he arrived. Danny Frost sat at one of the tables with a case file six inches thick open in front of him.

"Hi, Danny, how are you doing?"

The lawyer looked up and smiled warmly. "Hello, stranger."

Almost forty, Danny had the verve and energy of someone fifteen years younger. He bore the deep tan of a recent holiday. His dark hair was rapidly turning gray. At the rate he was going, he'd be a full-on silver fox in another year or two.

Danny was the only other openly gay solicitor he knew in the area and they had always got along well. He was an outrageous flirt without overstepping the line, but Matt suspected that given just a hint of encouragement Danny would be all over him.

"Have you seen the news this morning?" Danny asked.

"The murder? Sure. Shocking isn't it? To think that it's happening right here in our community. If this was a big city, it would almost be expected, but not in Durham."

"I knew him," Danny said, putting down his pen and looking at Matt with wide green eyes. "Olly Raymond. The latest victim. He worked at the coffee shop on Sable Street. Just down from our office. I even asked him out last year."

"Shit, Danny. That's awful. I'm sorry. Are you okay?"

"Sure. I'm fine. We didn't know each other all that well. Went out a couple of times but it didn't really come to anything. He never said as much, but I got the impression after our first date that Olly thought I was too old for him. I think he only saw me again out of sympathy."

Matt smiled softly. "Too old? You? Hardly. You've got more energy than I have."

"There was about fifteen years between us. I think that was too big a deal for Olly. Still, he was a nice lad. A really nice lad. I can't believe anyone would want to hurt him."

"Any news of an arrest?" Like Trish at the office, Danny was always a good person to ask if you wanted to know what was going on.

"Fuck no. The police round here haven't got a clue."

"According to *The Echo* they're playing down any connection with the other murdered boy."

Danny's eyebrows shot up. "They're connected all right. It's all over Facebook. Haven't you seen it?"

Matt shook his head.

"What connects them," Danny said, "is their sexuality. Olly Raymond and Conner Welsh were both gay. Those stupid plods are playing it all down but come on—both boys are gay, both are from Durham, they look so much alike they could pass for brothers and they're found dead within a fortnight of each other." Danny's usually bright demeanor had taken on a serious expression. "Someone is picking up and murdering young men—gay men—in our city and the police are doing fuck all to warn the community. It stinks. It fucking stinks."

\* \* \* \*

Since the unexpected appearance of Annabel had spoiled his intention to chat up Matt, Dale's day had not gone as planned. But Annabel's unwanted intrusion was nothing compared with the shower of shit that rained down on him when he got to work.

The production was using the empty buildings of an old primary school as their temporary studio and offices. The building had a sad, gloomy feeling that worked perfectly for the show. It was due for demolition later in the year. Something local residents were dead set against. The solid structure was over one hundred and forty years old and loved by the community, many of whom had been educated there. Its current use by a TV company proved that it was not yet ready for the wrecking ball. Dale had even signed a petition by residents campaigning to save the old school buildings and agreed to pose for a photo for the local paper.

Arriving at the studio direct from boot camp, he saw half a dozen people gathered at the gate. They brandished homemade placards, which they waved at passing motorists, many of whom gave a blast of their horn as they passed.

He was all for saving the school but someone would have to ask these guys to turn it down. They couldn't have those car horns blaring while they were trying to shoot a take.

It was only as he pulled into the car park that he noticed their placards had nothing to do with the proposed demolition. *Stop the Bloodbath. Save Our Children. Violence Breeds Violence.*

What the hell was that about?

By the time he had showered and changed into costume, the crowd outside had doubled.

Roxanne Maxwell was in the makeup room. She was already dressed in the black designer power suit of her DCI character and her luxurious auburn hair was being fixed into a businesslike wave around her face. Roxanne stared at a computer tablet while the hairdresser worked.

"What's going on?" Dale asked, taking the chair beside her. "Are those guys outside extras or something? I didn't notice any crowd scenes in today's script. Have they changed the schedule?"

Roxanne raised her cool gaze from the tablet and regarded him in the mirror. "Haven't you heard the news?"

"This morning? No, I listen to music on the way in," he said. "It helps me to focus. All that noise on the radio—DJs and presenters—it's all too distracting when I'm trying to get the lines in."

"You know a couple of local boys have been murdered?"

He nodded. He had seen that story on TV last night.

Roxanne raised two finely arched eyebrows. "Remind you of anything?"

"What? *Us*? The show? How?"

"Good old social media," she said. "Someone was quick to point out a similarity between the deaths and the TV show about a murderer currently being filmed on their doorstep. Rumors and hash tags filled in the blanks."

Another round of horns blasted outside.

"Shit. What did Elton say? Have we put out a statement?"

"Elton is livid. Some of the comments posted online suggest the protestors have seen at least some of the script. They're not one hundred percent off in some of the things they accuse us of. The publicity department is working on a statement right now. Hopefully they can defuse the situation before it gets worse."

"Don't count on it," Dale said. "An old buddy of mine worked on a movie that angered some animal rights protestors. They heard a horse had been killed during the shoot. It was complete bullshit of course. No animals were ever injured. But word got out just the same and it spread like fire. It closed down the production for three weeks."

The crowd of protestors grew over the course of the morning. As well as cars, they had started using whistles and bullhorns to add to the disturbance. Unlike a purpose built studio, working within the old school building was like shooting on location. Sets had been constructed in the gymnasium and assembly hall but none of them were sound proofed.

"Let's just get the fucking scene shot," Elton hollered. "If we get the visuals, we can re-record the fucking sound later."

It was a fair suggestion but not easy to achieve. Nerves and tempers were frayed by the jarring noise outside. Lines were fluffed. Cues were fucked. Lighting, acting, cameras — everyone was off their game.

Between botched takes, Dale grabbed his phone and tried

to get an idea of what was happening online. The profile of the murdered boys was tragic. They were both so young. It made his flesh prickle to look at their photos. It was no stretch of the imagination to see either of them as prey for his character Daryl Stone. They fitted Daryl's victim profile exactly.

But it was nothing more than a deeply sad coincidence. Their show hadn't finished filming, let alone been seen by anyone. The suggestion that it could influence a murderer was impossible — ludicrous. Not that he believed TV or film had an influence on people's desire to inflict violence anyway. It was blood lust. People acted on their desire to hurt others because they wanted to.

By the time they broke for lunch, only a fraction of that morning's work was complete.

"Why don't we go out and talk to them?" Dale suggested. "Roxanne, Elton and me. Maybe we can calm things down. It's got to be worth a try."

"No fucking way," Roxanne said flatly. "They've got TV crews out there now. It's a damn circus. Publicity can deal with this. It's their job. Not ours!"

Dale retired to his trailer to catch the local lunchtime bulletin. The murder investigation was rightfully the lead story with police still refusing to confirm a connection between the deaths of Olly Raymond and Conner Welsh. The bulletin then cut from a live broadcast at police HQ to the protest outside the studio.

There had to be forty people out there now, together with a live news crew. The reporter seemed to revel in the ignorance and scare mongering that had ignited the situation in the first place.

"*Blood Falls on Stone* is a violent thriller starring Roxanne Maxwell and American actor Dale Zachary. The series follows the investigation of a perverted serial killer praying on young students in a college town. The chilling similarities to events right here in Durham cannot be ignored. Protestors today are calling for production on the series to be stopped."

The reporter turned to interview one of those protestors, a middle-aged woman full of indignation and anger.

"It shows an utter lack of respect for the victims, their families and our community," the woman seethed. "It's sick shows like this and their glorification of violence that has led to the deaths of two innocent men."

*Oh fuck.* Dale shut off the TV. This was turning into a nightmare.

* * * *

It was a long-running tradition on Wednesday night for Matt to get together for dinner with his best buddy, Conrad. The guys had been friends since school and the bond remained unbroken. Despite college, employment or any other responsibility, their friendship remained tight.

It was Matt's turn to entertain. Conrad O'Brien was a much better cook than he was but Matt would never be presumptuous enough to expect his friend to do the hard work every week. Once a month they ate out, but tonight was just a regular evening at home.

It had been a good day for Matt. After his workout with Annabel and the gorgeous Dale Zachary, he'd got the result he wanted at court. Jenna McNab had been spared jail and given an order with the probation service to carry out one hundred and twenty hours of unpaid work. He'd spent the afternoon with three new clients and had a couple of hours to prepare his case for tomorrow. It was a pretty successful day.

By the time Conrad arrived for dinner he was ready to unwind with a few drinks and good company. They were in the kitchen of the comfortable two-bedroom semi he rented on the outskirts of Durham.

Conrad sat at the table, thumbing through news pages on his tablet, while Matt was at the cooker assembling the rice, chicken and curry sauce to make up that evening's dinner.

Conrad was twenty-eight with short dark hair and a slender build. He hadn't changed much since their school days. While exercise and genetics had caused Matt to broaden and thicken throughout his twenties, Conrad was as tiny now as he'd been at fourteen. It suited him, though for years he'd hated it. Matt remembered all the guys he'd brushed off when they had hit on him and called him cute.

"I think you might be barking up the wrong tree," Conrad said, putting down the tablet to refill his wineglass. "It says here that Dale was married. He's even got a kid."

Matt stirred the pan of chicken. "Annabel said he was divorced."

"Looks that way." Conrad had the tablet again and was tapping at the screen. "Looking through some of these movie forums, there's nothing here to indicate he's gay or even bi. A few suggestions here and there but nothing you don't read in discussions about any hot actor. It's idle speculation with nothing to back it up. Sorry, sweetie. I think you're out of luck."

"Damn." Matt finished his wine and poured another glass. "I feel like an idiot now. Giving him my card like that."

"Guys must hit on him all the time. I'm sure he's used to it. No big deal."

"I wasn't *hitting* on him. Just gave him my number. I didn't make a move or anything. Thank God."

"He is beautiful," Conrad said. "Wow. Check out some of these galleries. You do have good taste."

"Have you seen any of his movies?"

"Mmm. I've seen that one with the ax. And this pretty bad rom-com. Can't remember what it was called, but he was the only reason I kept watching. He took his shirt off a lot in that movie."

"I need to do some homework. Check out a few of the films he's been in."

"It won't get you anywhere."

"But I'll get to see him with his shirt off."

They both laughed. Matt plated up their food and they ate at the kitchen table. It was nothing special. The sauce was from a jar but it tasted okay and the chicken was moist. Good company mattered more than great cooking.

"Did I tell you I ran into Jamie the other night?"

Conrad's eyes widened. "No. Where was he?"

"At work." Matt told him about their unexpected meeting at the police station.

"How was he?"

"The same." Matt sighed. "Serious. Businesslike. Until the end of the interview when he took me to one side to tell me he misses me."

"For a smart cop, he can be very slow to get the message."

Conrad was the best kind of friend—loyal, supportive, funny. He worked in the sales office of the art house cinema and theater in town. Working tirelessly for low pay in a job he loved. He was currently raising funds for a small theater group that supported actors with disabilities. The group wanted to stage a new, specially written play later in the year, but with the government cutting funds, it was going to be a struggle.

"I hope to have some charity nights at the theater throughout March and April. I also need prizes for the raffle we're having a week on Saturday. Do you think your bosses might make a donation?"

"Free legal advice?" Matt asked. "It's not the most exciting of prizes."

"Maybe not." Conrad chuckled. "What about your Hollywood friend? Do you think the lovely Mr. Zachary might consider donating a prize?"

"I don't know."

"Will you ask him?"

"Shouldn't you approach him through the TV company?"

Conrad pulled a face. "It takes too long. Especially now that they'll have sack loads of hate mail to open."

"Poor Dale. I hadn't thought of that." The protest outside the studio had been all over the news when Matt came home. The shit had really hit the fan. Though the program itself was taking the hit, rather than the actors. For now, at least. Moral outrage had a habit of getting personal fast.

"So, you'll ask him?" Conrad persisted.

Got to love him. When it came to a cause, Conrad didn't quit. "Maybe."

"Not maybe. Do it."

"Okay," Matt relented, laughing. "He's got my number. *If he calls me, I'll ask him.*"

*If he calls me.*

It was hardly likely to happen.

Was it?

# Chapter Five

"The next cunt to blow a fucking horn will regret the day they were torn from their mother's womb." Hung-over and pissed off, Elton Weaver was an explosive ball of anger. His face was puce as he ranted.

"He's going to have a heart attack if he doesn't calm down," whispered Aaron Oxford. He was standing with Dale at the side of the set. Filming always involved a lot of standing around but today they had done little else.

Rather than looking better in the morning, an evening of news coverage and social chatter meant the crowd outside the studio had trebled in size. With the identity of the real killer unknown, the frightened community had come out in force to attack the one target they were able to — the TV company responsible for a fictional murder.

Adding to the tension on set, leading lady Roxanne Maxwell had called in sick. "Migraine," her assistant had informed the director. "Roxanne's migraines usually last at least two days."

"Tell Roxanne to put some fucking painkillers down her scrawny neck and make sure she's back on set tomorrow morning." The assistant blanched under Elton's venom. "We're only two weeks in. It's not too late to replace her and begin reshoots with a new actress on Monday. I hear that my first choice actress for the role has become available and she loves the script. See how Roxanne's migraine feels after that."

Roxanne's absence put extra pressure on Dale. Without her, they had to concentrate on his scenes. With the bleating car horns and whistles reaching new levels of intensity,

Elton wisely decided to focus on non-dialogue scenes that could easily be re-sounded later. Dale spent the morning climbing in and out of windows, skulking in dark alleys doing creepy, stalkerish stuff. Finding the right mood for the scene wasn't easy. Still, with the constant racket outside, it was easier than delivering dialogue.

Nevertheless, it was a long, arduous morning.

"I still think we should put out a statement," he told Elton while they waited for the set to be relit. "A few careful and compassionate words could defuse this whole situation."

The stench of stale gin oozing out of Elton was stronger than ever. The old man must have hammered it last night. "Let the PR team handle it. They put out a statement first thing this morning."

Dale had read that statement. It was a shallow gesture, absolving the production of responsibility while offering scant compassion for the murdered boys. "It was bullshit. Listen to the noise out there. It obviously did no good. *We* need to say something."

"Forget about it," Elton said dismissively. "Your job is here, playing a part. Focus on that."

At last, they broke for lunch. Dale's trailer was on the back of the school building, farthest away from the protestors, but even there he could hear the horns and whistles.

He had a headache. Hardly surprising. He swallowed two painkillers and turned on the TV, hoping to drown out the noise. There was a talk show on. Four people sat around a table, offering noisy, underdeveloped theories on the correlation between real life violence and what was seen on screen.

"It's Roxanne Maxwell who I feel most disappointed by," the lead mouthpiece said. "That such a wonderful, classy actress would demean herself by appearing in an awful show like this *Blood Stone* thing."

"Opinions are like assholes," Dale said, turning off the TV. Everyone might have one but after a morning from hell, he didn't want to listen to these loud-mouthed broads.

There was a knock at the door. Aaron Oxford entered without waiting for an answer. Oh, Aaron—cute, available Aaron. The last thing Dale felt like was sex, which was the only reason Aaron came knocking around lunchtime.

"Hell of a day, eh?" Aaron leaned against the kitchen counter, brushing his fingers down the front of his T-shirt. Caressing the taut muscle beneath.

"Only halfway over." Dale sighed. He opened the fridge and took out a Diet Coke.

"Elton just blew another stack." Aaron chuckled. "He's bawling out the sound guys. Like any of this is *their* fault."

"He needs to calm down. He'll have a stroke if he's not careful. With all the booze and his temper, he's a prime candidate."

"Roxanne hasn't helped. Cheeky bitch. Leaving everyone else to deal with the backlash."

"Listen, Aaron, I could really do with some time alone right now. My head is killing me and I need to get it together for this afternoon."

Aaron's smile wavered temporarily. He puffed up his chest further and narrowed his sexy eyes. "I know a good stress reliever. Let me take care of you."

Dale held up his hands. "Any other time and I would love to. You know I would. But not today."

Aaron licked his lips and grinned. "How about a blow job? Just lie there and relax. You don't have to do anything. I'll take care of you."

Dale shook his head. "Sorry, buddy."

Aaron came closer, undeterred. "I love it when you come in my mouth. The force of it. The taste. Don't deny me that. I haven't eaten since breakfast."

"Dude, really. It's not gonna happen. Take no for an answer, won't you?"

Aaron flinched, no longer smiling. Dale felt like the biggest asshole. Shit. He had nothing to be sorry for and yet Aaron was acting as if he were the one in the wrong.

Aaron shrugged. "Okay, whatever. It's not like you to say

no, that's all."

"Today I am. It's no offense to you. I'm just not in the mood."

"You're *always* in the mood."

"Not today."

Aaron left without an argument. His parting look was enough to leave Dale feeling lousy. This wasn't meant to be a big deal. Just a couple of horny guys away from home, helping each other out. It didn't mean he was available for sex on tap. No emotional attachments. That was the agreement. For God's sake, he made no promises and didn't expect anything in return.

In the past, he was always careful about the liaisons he made on set. He chose his lovers wisely for their discretion and subtlety. Ensuring they set clear boundaries from the start. He must be getting old. He was getting careless. He'd fallen into bed with Aaron far too quickly.

Aaron was a really nice guy. Great-looking and the sex was hot. But Dale wasn't interested in anything more than sex.

Now he didn't even want that.

There was something else — someone else — he wanted.

Someone for whom he felt more than just a sexual attraction.

Matt Blyth.

A guy he'd only just met on Monday and who hadn't been far from his thoughts since. Matt evoked feelings and emotions unlike anything he felt for Aaron. Unlike anything he'd felt for another guy. Ever. Strange feelings. Unusual feelings. Like falling in love. But it couldn't be. That was impossible.

Dale pulled Matt's business card from his wallet and looked at it for the millionth time. It was already creased and worn from handling. Last night, at the cottage, he'd lain on the sofa and turned it over and over in his hands. Summoning the courage to call his mobile. Never quite getting it.

Despite all the hints and not-so-subtle glances, he still wasn't sure that Matt was interested in men at all, let alone him.

He looked up the company website. Benedict and Taylor. There was a great photo of Matt in the staff directory. Handsome in a dark blue suit, softly smiling. He looked so different from the disheveled sweaty boy he was used to seeing at boot camp. Suited and booted, clean-shaven — the contrast in images only made Dale want him more.

He read the brief biography. Where he came from. Where he went to college. The places meant little to him but the information made him feel closer to the handsome man in the photograph.

*What are you waiting for?*

It had been a miserable twenty-four hours. Thinking about Matt was the only brightness he'd had. What did he have to lose?

Dale grabbed his phone and dialed Matt's number. His heart beat faster as he waited for it to connect.

"Hello."

"Matt? Hi, it's Dale. Dale Zachary. From boot camp. How are you doing?"

"I'm great. I doubt you can say the same. Tough couple of days, eh?"

"You saw the news then?" It made him smile. In a small, far from ideal way, Matt had taken an interest in what he was doing. "Not the kind of publicity we would have hoped for."

"It'll blow over. These things always do."

"I hope so. These guys are angrier at us than the guy who's actually out there doing the killing." Dale took a deep breath. "Listen, I'm calling 'cause I'd like to take a break from all of this shit. What are you doing tonight? Feel like getting together?"

Silence. *Oh shit. Totally misjudged this.*

"I'm not doing anything. I would love to," Matt said. "What did you have in mind? Hitting the gym?"

"No. God no. Something more relaxing. I was thinking drinks. Maybe something to eat."

"Sounds good. Just the two of us? Or a group of people?"

"I don't know that many people. It'll just be the two of us. If that's okay with you."

"It's very okay with me." A pause. "Dale, can I just ask so we're clear from the start. Is this a…date?"

Dale's heart raced. "Would you like it to be?"

Boom. Boom. Boom. Heart thundering. Had time stopped running?

"Yes," Matt answered at last.

Dale smiled widely. "Then, yes. It's definitely a date."

* * * *

After the call from Dale there was nothing that could spoil Matt's afternoon. Not even his boss, Edward Benedict, who told him to head over to the police station. An early morning drug raid had rounded up seven of their clients and the police wanted to interview them all. Annabel and Derek Reed were already there but the cops wanted to crack on with the next interview before the others were completed.

"Fine, but I need to be out of there by five-thirty. Annabel will have to cope on her own after that," he asserted. It was her night on call. Let her do some work for a change.

Matt wanted to get home in good time to prepare for his date. A date with Dale Zachary. Ha. That was one in the eye to Conrad and Annabel, who both insisted he was deluded in thinking Dale was interested in him.

Dale had made it very clear on the phone. It was a date. "With all the heat I'm getting over the show we'll have to be careful. I don't want to go anywhere too public where people might hurl abuse all night."

"I would offer to cook but I'm pretty lousy in the kitchen," Matt admitted.

"Don't worry. I'll ask around this afternoon and text you later when I find somewhere discreet. Does dinner sound good? Or would you rather go somewhere livelier? A show, maybe?"

"Dinner would be great. I'll leave it up to you."

Matt was beaming when he hung up.

He'd never had a real date before. Jamie had been his only proper boyfriend and his idea of a romantic night was pizza and a movie. Tonight would be a whole new experience, in all sorts of ways. He could hardly wait.

But there was a job to be done first.

The police station was a scene of chaos when he arrived. There were extra cops on duty to cope with the raids and the cells were all full. He checked in with the desk sergeant.

"I'm here for the drug interviews. Benedict and Taylor client."

The harassed-looking sergeant shook her head. "You'll have to take a seat and wait it out. All of the interview suites are full. As soon as one comes free, you're next."

Typical Annabel. She must have sold the boss a sob story about not being able to keep up with the demand. In reality, she could have handled this on her own. The police couldn't process the suspects any faster than they were.

Matt took a seat and waited. He sent Conrad a text, informing him of his date. The reply came back immediately.

*Fantastic news. Hope it goes well. Don't forget to ask about a charity donation.*

Hell, Conrad just wouldn't quit. Matt put a reminder on his phone to ask Dale later. Maybe he would sign a photograph they could put in the raffle. Knowing Conrad, that wouldn't be enough. He added another note to ask Edward whether the firm would help out too.

A shadow fell unexpectedly across him. "You're getting to be a regular in here."

He looked up. Jamie. In a crumpled blue T-shirt and jacket. His eyes were puffy and dark, as if he hadn't slept in days.

Matt smiled, keeping it friendly. There was no point in being a dick about this. "I've seen more of you this week than all of the last three months. Were you part of this drugs sting?"

He nodded. "Just an extra pair of hands in the round-up. The operation has been ongoing for months. I wasn't involved in that."

That explained the tired eyes. He must have been up since three preparing for the dawn raids.

*Now what?* Jamie stood awkwardly in front of him. Their smiles were forced. The atmosphere was uncomfortable. Matt searched for something to say but even work-related trivia eluded him. He hoped Jamie wasn't working up to another 'let's try again' speech. Judging by the look on his face, he had something on his mind.

He opened his mouth to speak.

Just in time, the custody sergeant shouted over. "Matt, you're on. Interview room four. Your client's already in there."

*Perfect timing.* Matt stood and smiled softly at Jamie. "Catch you later," he said, hurrying for the exit.

* * * *

Time didn't make the pain any better. Seeing Matt again — twice this week already — hadn't just reopened an old wound, it had made it bleed profusely. Watching him walk away caused a tightness in Jamie's chest. A feeling of panic raced through him. He had to pause and take a breath to steady his nerves.

It was a huge mistake, their split, and he blamed himself. He'd been working too hard and had taken their relationship for granted. Matt had been neglected. Jamie got that. It wouldn't happen again.

But Matt had been so certain, so cruel, telling him it was over. How could anything be over when the feelings were so strong? Seeing him again only reinforced that.

They needed to talk. Not here. That much was obvious. Matt clearly felt awkward speaking to him around the police station and wouldn't open up. No surprise really, given it was Jamie's job that had driven them apart. It was understandable that he had negative feelings about this place.

Matt wasn't seeing anyone else. Not when he'd left him and not now. Someone would have told Jamie if he was. That bloody Annabel for a start. She would take great delight in informing him that Matt had a new lover. He still had access to Matt's Facebook profile too. Though it had hurt when he'd first changed his relationship status to single, it was a comfort now to see it remain so. Matt didn't post a lot but he was often tagged in photos posted by others. Jamie looked at those pictures with a mixture of dread and excitement. But there were no signs that he'd found a new man yet.

No. Matt was still very much single. Seeing him this week, after so long apart, maybe that was a sign for them to get their act together.

Jamie was man enough to make the first move.

No time like the present. He would do it tonight. Go around to Matt's place after work. They would have that long-overdue talk. Put right their differences.

He had this weekend off so the timing was perfect. He would take Matt out. They could go up to Newcastle, to the multiplex cinema in town. Grab a pizza. There was a new Channing Tatum movie out this week. A perfect date movie.

Yes, he resolved. Enough messing around. It was time to win Matt back.

He headed to the locker room. He knew he looked like shit. He'd been up half the night. His eyes, which were naturally dark anyway, resembled two coal pits. But he had plenty of time. He'd go home, grab a couple of hours' sleep. Have a long bath and a shave. Smarten up. He would look like a very different man when he knocked at Jamie's door that night.

"Dench," Richie Rogers, a detective constable in Jamie's division, hollered through the open locker room door. "Wilmhurst is looking for you!"

"What for?"

"Fuck knows. But he's got a real mean face on. Better not keep him waiting."

Damn. It had been a long and difficult day. The last thing he needed was the inspector nagging him for a fuck up he wasn't yet aware of.

DCI Wilmhurst was a tall, hook-nosed man in his late fifties. He was always immaculately dressed in three-piece suits and polished brogues. His tough, no nonsense attitude commanded respect from his team. Wilmhurst was a man who demanded efficiency from his staff. Mistakes may be human but Wilmhurst didn't tolerate them.

He was typing as Jamie knocked on his office door. Barely glancing in his direction, he barked, "Come in. Sit."

Jamie did as he was told, sitting patiently while Wilmhurst rattled the keyboard, designer glasses perched on the end of his hawk nose. Finally the inspector stopped and focused his scrutinizing gaze on Jamie.

"Good result with the drug squad today?"

"Yes, sir. Every last suspect was brought in."

"Good. How did you mind working for a different unit?"

Oh no—tough question to answer without pissing someone off. What did Wilmhurst want to hear? It was no secret within the force that Jamie was climbing the career ladder. He'd been accused of brown nosing his bosses, but he saw every job as a chance to impress.

"I appreciate every opportunity I'm given to experience the full range of police work, sir."

Wilmhurst took off his glasses and looked at him more closely for a good thirty seconds. "All right. You've got your wish. I've been asked to spare two of my officers to help out MIT investigating these murders in the city. I'm putting you forward."

Jamie's pulse quickened. "Thank you, sir."

"Don't know how long the secondment will last but I can't let you go permanently. I'll make moves to get you back in a couple of weeks if they don't release you first."

"Thank you, sir. I really do appreciate your faith in me. This is a wonderful opportunity."

"Hmm." He put his glasses back on. "Two young men are dead. I don't know what's *wonderful* about that. Report to DCI Frank Redgrave at the city center station, seven a.m. tomorrow. I'll see you in two weeks."

"Yes, sir. Thank you, sir."

Secondment to the murder squad. Yes, the next step on the career ladder. He would do all he could to make sure he stayed up there.

# Chapter Six

Getting ready for his date with Dale was a more hurried affair than Matt had hoped. He didn't get out of the police station until almost six and was pissed to find Annabel had left at five-fifteen. He rushed home and showered, lathering up his muscles with his favorite Molton Brown shower gel — cracked black peppercorn.

He had shaved for work that morning. There was a dark stubble across his chin but he decided to save five minutes and omit the second swipe of the razor. Dale had a full beard anyway. A little five o'clock shadow wouldn't bother him.

He dressed quickly. Snug cotton briefs, dark blue jeans and a black jersey. Dale had texted to say dinner wouldn't be anything formal. Thank God. Matt spent all day in a suit. The last thing he wanted in the evening was to put on another shirt and tie.

He was finally ready a full fifteen minutes before his taxi was due. Time enough for a drink to steady his nerves. He wasn't nervous exactly, it was more like excitement. A giddy sensation in his chest that spread all through his body.

He fixed a vodka and Coke and carried it into the living room, where he could watch for the arrival of his taxi. He dialed up a playlist of pop music on his iPod and let it play, dancing excitedly from one foot to the other.

Did Dale dance? Probably not. He didn't look like that kind of guy. Nightclubs and gay bars were probably not his scene. Not that it was Matt's idea of a good time either. He preferred the atmosphere of a good pub and live music to the hedonistic beat of a club. He'd learn more about Dale tonight and discover what they had in common.

Car headlights swept across the room. He moved toward the window. If this was the taxi, it was early.

A man walked up the drive.

Matt's heart sank when he saw who it was.

Jamie.

Of all the times.

Matt met him at the front door.

"Hey." Jamie beamed. He looked much fresher than he had at the police station that afternoon. He wore jeans, an open-necked shirt and jacket. He'd had a shave too. Matt smelled his aftershave before he reached the door. Subtle, it wasn't.

"Hi," Matt said carefully. Some sixth sense warned him Jamie was after something. "Is something wrong?"

"No. I just wanted to talk to you. Mind if I come in?"

"It's not a good time, Jamie. I'm on my way out."

"Oh." His smile faltered. "I thought we could talk, that's all. Can I come back later?"

"Not really. I don't know what time I'll be home. It could be late."

Jamie suddenly looked nervous. Matt had an awful hunch he knew what this was about. Something they had resolved months ago. He *knew* something had been going through Jamie's mind this afternoon. He should have predicted this.

"Seeing you again this week has made me realize that it's not really over between us."

"You're wrong, Jamie. It is over."

"How can you say that? We were so good together. Not perfect. I know that. Nothing ever is. But we were a good match, weren't we? I can be moody and difficult, but I was better when I was with you. *You* made me better." His dark eyes implored. "Please, Matt. Don't leave it like this. Give me another chance. C'mon, please."

How could they be playing this bloody scene again?

"Jamie, I've given you other chances. Lots of them. We

didn't break up without trying. We tried damn hard to make things work between us. But they didn't. Don't bring it all up again. You need to move on."

"I can't." His voice was barely a whisper.

"I have," Matt said softly, hating himself for the pain his words caused. The anguish was clear on Jamie's face. "Sorry, but it's true. I'm not saying this to hurt you, but I've moved on. You must too."

"I don't believe you. I felt it this afternoon. There's still something there."

"There isn't." God, how many times had he said this already? Their relationship hadn't come to an abrupt end. It had died a slow death. Jamie had always looked back with a rose-tinted perspective. Even their good times hadn't been that great. "Look, I'm going on a date tonight. I wouldn't have been so cruel as to tell you that but you leave me no choice."

He stared at Matt with wide, wounded eyes. Betrayed eyes. "With who?"

"No one you know. Someone I've only just met."

"Are you fucking him?"

"No. We've just met," he snapped, and was immediately angry at having to defend his behavior. "It's none of your business who I fuck. One man or fifty, I'll sleep with whomever I want. You know why? Because I'm single and I can."

Jamie's face twisted. Matt thought he was going to cry. It was an expression he'd come to know well. Jamie opened his mouth wide and sucked in deep breaths, fighting the urge to let the tears spill. His eyes glistened.

"Fine," he choked. "Do… Do what you want."

He turned and hurried to his car. On other nights, Matt would have gone after him. Maybe tonight, under different circumstances, he'd have followed him again, but he stayed where he was. The emotional cord had been severed. Jamie might be stuck in the past but Matt meant what he had said. He was moving on.

Jamie's unwelcome appearance couldn't spoil the night. Not a chance. Jamie would say he was being heartless but there was nothing he could do. That chapter of his life was over.

It was time to start a new one.

* * * *

Matt was meeting Dale in town, at the bar of the River House Hotel. He'd only been there once before for a private function, but whoever had recommended this place to Dale had chosen well. It was a traditional hotel in keeping with the ancient city. Decorated in a modern, yet classic style. It was quiet and understated. They wouldn't have to worry about the public outrage surrounding Dale's TV show in a place like this.

He headed straight to the bar. As predicted it was small and quiet. A couple of businessmen sat at a table in one corner. A woman in a smart suit was having a glass of wine alone.

"Over here." A familiar American accent caused his heart to skip.

Dale rose from a sofa in another corner of the room. Something inside Matt went crazy at the sight of him.

*Take it easy. Be cool.*

Dale looked amazing in dark blue jeans, which clung perfectly to his solid thighs. He wore a red checked shirt with the top two buttons undone, offering a tantalizing glimpse of his chest. Just a hint of body hair showing. He smelled good too. A fresh, expensive smelling scent that was perfectly suited to him. It struck him, not for the first time, just how good-looking Dale was.

*My God, he's simply beautiful.*

"Come on, take a seat."

Matt's butt had barely touched the sofa when a waitress appeared with a bottle of champagne in an ice bucket.

"Hope you're not hungry yet," Dale said, smiling wide,

showing great white teeth. "I thought we could have a drink before going through to the restaurant."

"No, I'm good." The truth was he had no appetite for anything but Dale. He had never been smitten so quickly by anyone. His eyes roamed, trying to take in all of him. Those dazzlingly blue eyes. That smile. His hands. His chest. His hair. *How did I get so lucky?*

"Are you okay?" Dale asked, still smiling.

Matt pulled himself together. He was acting like a randy teenager. "Absolutely." They raised their glasses. "Cheers."

The champagne was cold and dry. Delicious.

"How are you anyway? Tough couple of days, eh?" He'd caught the local news in the car on the way home. The controversy about *Blood Falls on Stone* had not abated. It was getting worse.

"Hanging in there. This has all come out of the blue. The saddest thing is that the press is more interested in what *we're* doing than they are in the actual victims. Real people are dead. We're just pretending. It's messed up."

"I think it's the combination of the two that makes it so newsworthy. A local tragedy together with the glamor and excitement of a TV show. It must be like Christmas to these reporters."

"I just wish they'd move their attentions to what matters, rather than what we're doing. Know what I'm saying?"

"I do. But murder, that's not a very common event in a small city. Especially crimes of this kind. Most of the murders I've encountered in my career have been domestic in nature. Big budget TV dramas—well, they're even rarer in a place like this."

"Let's not talk about it," Dale said, fixing him with his beautiful eyes. "I came to get away from all that. Tonight I want to find out all about you."

His nerves evaporated quickly. Dale was such an easy man to be around. As they took their time drinking the champagne, Matt told him about his life and his work. He opened up in a way he wouldn't have thought possible with a man he'd only just met.

"So you are single?" Dale asked with a twinkle in his eyes. "I don't want to go stepping on anyone's toes."

"Yes," he said. "I'm very single. I have been for about three months." That was as much as he wanted to say about Jamie. There was a story he didn't feel like sharing, especially after tonight's little drama.

After an hour they went into the restaurant. Like the bar, it was intimate. There were only ten tables and tonight just six other diners. It was decorated with a library theme. Rows of leather-bound volumes covered one wall, while portraits of famous authors adorned the others.

A soft-spoken waiter seated them and presented the wine list.

"More wine?" Matt joked. "On a school night?"

"Ah, let's live a little. I don't know about you but I fully intend to take a rain check on old Clint's boot camp tomorrow morning."

"I don't think there's any chance of me making it."

"Good." Dale looked at the menu. "Any preference?"

"Red," Matt answered. "After the champagne, I feel like something deep and rich."

Dale ordered a bottle of Amarone.

Two bottles of wine on a weeknight. There was no way Matt would rise for boot camp after that. He'd have to be careful driving to work in the morning too. Maybe he should call Annabel and get her to pick him up. She owed him a favor after today's police station stunt.

They took their time over the menu. Matt wasn't in the mood for anything heavy. He chose pan-fried scallops with chorizo and black pudding to start and sea bass with potato croquets and crushed peas for his main course.

"What's black pudding?" Dale asked.

"It's kind of a sausage made from pig's blood and oatmeal. It sounds disgusting when described like that but trust me, it's absolutely delicious."

"Okay," Dale said warily. "I'll take your word for that but

all the same, I'll pass." He ordered the same starter minus the black pudding and a medium steak for his main course. "It's not adventurous, I know, but if steak is an option I can never resist. I hear they're great here too. From a butcher's right across the street."

It was a fantastic meal in wonderful company. As the plates came and went, they gently quizzed each other, opening up about their pasts. Matt had never met a real celebrity before, but there was no ego to Dale. He was as normal and down to earth as any guy he knew.

He talked about growing up in Pennsylvania and the importance of family and his son.

"How long were you married?" Matt asked.

"Eight years." Dale took a sip of wine before saying, "I don't regret it. Not a bit. But I do regret staying married to Laura for so long. I held her back. If we'd got divorced sooner she could have got on with her life. Ours was a marriage in name only most of the time. We have a great relationship now and if we hadn't been together I wouldn't have such a fantastic son."

Matt nodded thoughtfully. "I never had that doubt. You know, about sex. I only ever liked other boys. The notion of getting together with a girl... It was never a possibility."

Dale shrugged. "I always knew I liked guys but it took me a long time to accept it. I was in my late twenties before I realized this wasn't just a phase. That I wasn't going to grow out of it."

"Being in the public eye can't have helped."

"No. Not when your career amounts to playing the boyfriend of the hot chick. Those roles didn't amount to much but they were all I had. If word got out that I liked dick, those one-dimensional parts would be passed to the next pretty boy. In order to keep working, I had to keep quiet about all that."

"Isn't it different now? There are so many openly gay actors. They all get work."

Dale rolled his eyes. "And what work do they get? The

gay kids in *Glee*. The gay men in HBO comedies and dramas. I'm not putting that down, it's just not for me. Besides, it's not only my career I have to think about. I don't want my son to grow up being bullied as the kid with the fag dad on TV. Maybe when he's older it won't be such a big deal. But I can't do that to him. Not yet."

The waiter returned to ask if they wanted dessert. They were both too full but ordered liqueur coffees to finish the meal. Matt couldn't stop looking at Dale the whole time. The color of his eyes looked deeper than the Atlantic in the soft light of the restaurant. Dale looked right back at him, a sexy smile on his lips.

"So… What now?"

Matt's spine prickled. "Well… What do you suggest?"

"We're taking it as a given that we're blowing off boot camp in the morning?"

"Absolutely."

Dale leaned in closer. Matt mirrored him.

"Then I want to fuck you," Dale said slowly, eyes sparkling. "I've wanted it since you walked in. To tell the truth, I've wanted it since I set eyes on you on Monday. Your face, your body, your ass – you've been driving me crazy."

Matt's cock, which had been idling in a state of semi-stiffness, was suddenly very hard.

"I don't care how we do it," Dale continued. "Top. Bottom. I go either way. All I care about is getting close to you. Getting my hands on that body of yours before it drives me insane."

Beneath the table, Matt rubbed his calf up against Dale's. "Let's get out of here."

\* \* \* \*

They managed to contain themselves in the taxi but it was hard. So very hard. Matt wanted him with every fiber of his body. The temptation to grab his crotch as soon as they slid onto the back seat was immense. To take hold of his head and mash their lips together. But he controlled himself, keeping his hands on his knees and staring at the back of the taxi driver's head as they traveled back to town.

There was more than enough controversy surrounding the *Blood Falls on Stone* production without the lead actor making headlines for getting it on with another man in the back of a taxi.

They made the decision to go to Matt's place. It was nearer.

Nothing could hold them back once they were through the front door,. They were all over each other in the hall, their mouths locked in passion. Matt's hands tore at Dale's body. He quickly explored the muscle of Dale's back through his clothes, slipping lower to settle on the hard curve of his butt. *Wow — that ass is stacked.* He gripped it in both hands and pulled Dale's hips tight against his own, feeling the hard urgency of his cock.

Dale's hands were just as persistent, going farther. He slipped down the back of Matt's jeans and planted his hand against bare skin.

"Oh man," Dale sighed between open-mouthed kisses. "What an ass. Where's the bedroom?"

They left a trail of clothes in their wake, from the door and all the way up the stairs. By the time they reached the bedroom, they were down to their underpants. In hurried snatches, Matt tried to take in the detail of Dale's body. His hairy chest and belly. The fine lines of his pecs and shoulder muscles. He was toned — no surplus flesh on his hunky frame. All the things that turned him on in a man. But there was no time to take it all in. Their passion and hunger was too intense for that.

"Matt, Matt, you've got me on fire."

Matt tore down Dale's underpants, releasing his thick, circumcised cock. He wrapped his fist around it, feeling the satisfying weight and girth. Dale groaned as he squeezed and tugged the shaft. He cupped his balls, nicely shaved, between his hairy thighs.

Clearly not wanting to miss out, Dale shoved down Matt's pants and grabbed his dick. He took delight in his foreskin, tugging the folds back and forth across the head.

They fell onto the bed naked and arranged themselves into a sixty-nine position, taking each other's cock in their mouth. Matt slowed, only briefly, to explore Dale's dick with his lips, kissing the head, teasing the sensitive triangle of skin beneath the tiny opening with his tongue, eliciting a drop of pre-cum to the tip. He licked and tasted before taking the shaft, as much as he could manage, into his mouth. It wasn't easy. Dale was big. But the hot wetness of Dale's mouth around his own cock was potent encouragement. Soon he was taking him so deep that his nose pressed against his silky smooth ball sac.

His slid his hand behind to take hold of Dale's meaty ass, slipping his fingers into the hot crack. He explored the hairy crevice and located the small, fiery opening. Dale tried to groan as he tested the ring with just the tip of his finger but his mouth was full. Soon Dale was exploring him the same way, slipping his fingers into Matt's lightly furred butt crack and teasing the opening.

"Oh man," Dale gasped, releasing his cock. "I want you to fuck my ass. You gotta do it." He jerked his hips, pushing his ass against Matt's fingers.

"You want it?" He teased, sliding his finger inside.

"Oh God. Yes. Yes! *Fuck me!*"

"Only if you fuck me too," Matt insisted. He wanted to experience Dale in every possible way.

"Oh, I'll fuck you all right. Fuck you real good. But you first. My ass needs it more."

Matt hurriedly reached for a bottle of lube and a condom from his bedside cabinet. Dale rolled onto his back and raised his legs, presenting his beautiful ass. Matt put on the rubber and lubed his fingers. He spread the slick lube all around Dale's opening before slipping his fingers inside to ease the passage.

"That okay?"

Dale hooked his arms around his knees and hitched his butt higher. He looked directly at Matt, dark and intense. "Just fuck me, Matt. Fuck me. I want your dick."

Matt spread more lube over his condom-covered cock and climbed onto the bed, kneeling between Dale's thighs. He leaned in, guiding his cock to the opening, and felt the resistance give. Dale opened to him. Matt pushed a little more until the head of his cock entered Dale's tight ass, then slowly and smoothly sliding to the hilt.

"Oh yeah." Dale smiled a mile wide, then raised his head from the bed, his mouth seeking Matt's.

It was heaven. On top and inside the most ruggedly handsome man. All of Matt's senses were alert to him. Taste, smell, touch, even the sound of their bodies in motion. Bare skin sliding against skin. But his ass—*oh God his ass*—so smooth and hot, holding him so tight. Matt stayed still, allowing Dale time to get used to the fullness inside.

Dale's hunger was insatiable. He wrapped his legs around Matt's waist. "Don't hold back. I can take it."

They fucked long and hard, all over the bed, in every position. Matt pulled out to take him from behind, then Dale was on top, like a cowboy. Side by side, Matt gave it to him in a spooning position. They eventually came back to the first position and it was Matt's favorite, on top of Dale, kissing him, looking into his eyes.

"Gonna come," he gasped. He held Dale tighter and buried his head in his shoulder, inhaling the smell of his skin and came long and deep. He felt the pull all the way from his toes, through his thighs, his balls, his belly. His cock pulsed with one intense wave of pleasure after another as he blew his load and his soul into Dale's welcoming bottom.

Matt eased back onto his elbows. Sweat dripped down his face, blurring his vision.

"Wait," Dale said urgently. "Don't pull out. Not yet." He slid his hand between their bodies and gripped his dick. "Oh."

He closed his eyes. His face flushed deep pink. He bit his lip. He gripped Matt's cock even tighter as his body was racked with paroxysms of pleasure.

He opened his mouth in a silent scream as he spurted hot wetness against their bellies.

They came apart, gasping for breath and smiling.

"*Jesus*. That was damn fine."

They both burst out laughing. The euphoria after great sex was a buzz like nothing else.

They cleaned up with tissues and Matt padded down to the kitchen to fetch a couple of glasses of water. The sex, together with all that wine, had given him one hell of a thirst. Dale was under the covers when he returned.

Considering they had only just met, the sight of Dale in his bed was a welcome one. He looked totally at home there.

"Hope you don't mind," he drawled. "It was getting kind of cold without you."

"Let's do something about that."

Matt slipped beneath the covers into Dale's warm, comforting embrace. He pressed against his body, savoring every lean inch of him.

"This is a nice place. Have you lived here long?"

"A couple of years. It's just a rental, so not mine at all, but I love living here. It's perfect for work and not far from the city if I want to go out. I can even walk to town in good weather. When I save up enough money to buy a place, I'd like something just like this."

Dale's hand rested on the naked curve of his waist. "Is that your ideal scenario? To own your own place?"

"Yes. But it won't happen this side of my thirtieth. You need to save a fortune for the deposit on a decent mortgage. My parents have offered to help but I want to do it for myself."

"What do your folks do?"

"Dad's a lawyer, like me. My mam's got a little shop. They work hard. I want them to spend their money on themselves, not me. They should get out there and see the world. Take a few cruises. Travel. They deserve it."

"I think you might be the perfect boyfriend," Dale said, squeezing his hip. "You tick all the boxes. Insanely hot. Big dick. Cute ass. Handsome. And nice to his folks. What more could anyone ask for?"

"I can think of one thing," Matt said softly, reaching for Dale's cock. "A man who keeps his promise. You owe me a return fuck."

Dale rolled over, pinning him down with his weight, cock already hardening. "Well now, that must make *me* the perfect boyfriend too, because I always keep my promises."

\* \* \* \*

From outside, a light could be seen in the first-floor bedroom window. Most of the other houses on the estate were in darkness. It was past midnight and tomorrow was another working day.

Anyone taking one last look out of their window before bed would not see anything amiss.

The shadows between the garages of number thirty-nine and forty were completely black. Dark enough to conceal the figure of the man within them, even if he wasn't dressed in black. He had the controlled stillness of a natural predator. He would not be seen unless he wanted to be.

His gaze was just as unmoving. Watching the window of the house across the street. He didn't have to see in to know what was happening inside. He'd seen the haste with which the men had entered.

They were fucking.

They couldn't wait.

They had no self-control.

Unlike him.

As the minutes of the night ticked away, he kept on watching.

# Chapter Seven

Friday morning the protestors were waiting outside the studio when Dale arrived. But not even they, with their hateful banners and angry calls to quit, could dampen his mood. Nothing could bring him down. Not today.

Not after a night like that.

He didn't get much sleep. Didn't need it – or want it. Not when he was with Matt. Oh boy, what a night. It wasn't just the sex, though it had been pretty mind-blowing. It was the interactions between them, deep into the night, talking back and forth. Listening. Learning. Discovering each other.

How was it even possible to feel so strongly for someone you had just met? Dale didn't know, but he did. Matt was someone very special. The more time he spent with him, the more he felt it. Not only handsome and sexy – those things were obvious to anyone with eyes – but warm, funny and intelligent. He was the complete package.

If Dale didn't know better, he would say he had fallen in love. But he couldn't say that. Not yet.

The first person he encountered as he hurried to his trailer was Adrian Nelson, a talented stage actor playing the young detective on the show, sidekick to the imposing Roxanne. He was tall and rangy with an untidy mop of curls and a large nose.

"How's it going?" Dale beamed.

Adrian frowned. "A happy face. How nice. I hope it lasts. Roxanne is back and she's got as much cheer as a Russian winter."

"Ah. She must have got Elton's message about the avaiabilty of his first choice. Not a happy lady, eh?"

"That's putting it very mildly. She's got a face like a smacked arse. And compared to the face on Elton, *that's* a good thing. Hang on to that happiness for as long as you feel it. This is going to be a very long day."

"It's gonna take more than a disgruntled actress to bring me down," Dale said. He meant it too. He had two whole days off after this. His boy, Jack, was coming to stay. Dale had been looking forward to that for too long to let anyone spoil it.

Now, to add to his joy, there was Matt. It was with great reluctance that Dale had left his bed that morning. In an ideal world he'd slip back in there tonight, but that was impossible. As much as he wanted to be with Matt, spending quality time with his son was more important. This weekend would be all about the boy.

Matt understood. They would stay in touch and maybe, just maybe, there was a chance they could get together again on Sunday night when Jack went back to his mother's.

Until then there was work to do.

Dale changed into the costume that was laid out in his trailer. When he wasn't killing people, his character, Daryl Stone, was a teacher at the sixth-form college, lecturing impressionable teens. It was a huge challenge as an actor to portray the conflicting sides of the character—the caring teacher and the psychotic killer. As he dressed in today's wardrobe—chinos, plaid shirt and blazer—he put thoughts of his personal life to one side and concentrated on the twisted mind of Daryl Stone.

He headed to the makeup trailer with that morning's script. He knew the lines already but an actor could never be over-prepared.

Roxanne Maxwell was in the chair when he arrived. While a makeup assistant and hairdresser busied around her, Roxanne glowered at the screen of her mobile phone, furiously thumbing the keys. She didn't look up or acknowledge his arrival.

"Morning," he said cheerfully, sliding into the chair beside her. She might have a face like a horse's ass but it wasn't contagious. "Hope you're feeling better today, Roxanne."

She raised her eyes from the phone and stared at his reflection in the mirror. Her lips were narrow and tense. The poor makeup girl had her work cut out trying to get color on them.

"Not really," she said frostily. "I don't appreciate being dragged from my sick bed by some third-rate director. You know the little bastard threatened to have me replaced? The gin must have addled his tiny mind. They're selling this crap on me, not Elton bloody Weaver. It's my name above the title. I'm the star of the show. No offense."

"Huh. None taken."

"If he had any damn sense he'd close the production down for at least a week. Until this whole mess is sorted out."

*Mess?* This crazy woman thought the murder of two young men was a mess?

"That would be too expensive," he said calmly, refusing to be drawn into her anger. "I doubt we're insured for things like that. Besides, the producers were breathing down Elton's neck, insisting he keep the show on the road."

"Have you heard the fucking racket they are making out there? Next week we're supposed to shoot locations. How are we going to do that if the moral crusaders decide to follow us?"

"It may calm down after the weekend."

"Not likely." She brandished her phone in his direction. "Have you seen what they are saying about me on Twitter? Me, for fuck's sake. What did I ever do to deserve this shit?"

\* \* \* \*

Roxanne's mood did not improve once they got to the set. They were trying to shoot a scene in which the detectives, Roxanne and her sidekick Adrian, asked questions of pupils and teachers at the school of one of Daryl's victims.

Dale and Adrian were word perfect on every take while Roxanne blew every line.

"For fuck's sake," Elton screeched, blazing onto the set. "It's not fucking Chekhov. What can possibly be so difficult?"

*Oh crap.* This was exactly what she'd been building to, provoking the director to the point of explosion.

"What is so difficult is trying to work on the utter anarchy of *your* set. I can't even think straight with all that noise out there. *You* need to do something about it."

"You don't have to *think,* duckie." Elton's voice was as sharp as a blade. "It's all written down for you. All you have to do is learn the words and repeat them. Like a parrot. It's called *acting.* Give it a try it sometime."

The resulting clash went off louder than New Year's fireworks, so deafening that the sound of the protestors outside was finally reduced to background noise. Adrian Nelson rolled his eyes as he and Dale stepped to the side of the set.

"This could take a while," Adrian said wearily.

"Maybe it'll be better afterward. Once they've cleared the air." Dale sounded hopeful.

"TV fucking Choice Awards," Elton screeched. "I didn't know they gave awards to blocks of wood. What did they carve you out of? Oak or elm?"

"You gin-soaked old fairy!"

"I'm going for a smoke," Adrian said. "Send someone out to get me when this is all over."

Things only got worse over the course of the morning with Elton and Roxanne at each other's throats. The protest outside seemed to be getting louder too, as though they sensed they were being upstaged by the drama inside. This couldn't go on for much longer. The entire shoot was descending into chaos.

During the downtime, of which there was plenty, Dale checked his phone for messages. Everything was set for his weekend with Jack. Laura would put him on a train when he got out of school, first-class carriage, with instructions to speak to no one, and Dale would meet him at Durham station at eight that evening. It wasn't ideal. The alternative was for Dale to drive down early on Saturday morning, meeting Laura at a collection point midway on the A1.

"Boring," Jack had protested loudly. "There's nothing to do in a car. I want to take the train. C'mon, I'm not a kid. I'm not going to talk to pedophiles in the carriage."

Laura had been appalled but Dale had been quietly glad the boy was worldly wise and smart to such dangers. "You can call him every half hour of the journey," Dale had assured her. "What harm can he come to in a first-class train carriage?"

Reluctantly Laura had agreed to the exchange.

No message yet from her to call the visit off. He'd been half expecting it, given the hullabaloo around the shoot. Maybe it was just a big story for the local news and not gaining as much attention nationally.

Mid-morning, he was pleased to receive a text from Matt.

*Thanks for last night. One of the best. Can't wait to do it again.*

Neither could he. His night with Matt had sure put a spring in his step today. Work was impossible, regardless of the on-set drama, when all he could think about was Matt and his amazing body. And the sex. *My God – the sex.* That had never been so good. Not with anyone. Fucking, getting fucked, kissing, sucking, rimming. All night long, they couldn't get enough of each other. Coupling and uncoupling in every way imaginable.

With other guys, Dale couldn't wait to get away once it was over. There was an awkwardness after sex that always made him uncomfortable. But not with Matt. He had wanted to hold him and kiss him until they had been ready to go again. Pretty soon they both had been.

Elton eventually called an early lunch. His fights with Roxanne were getting them nowhere. The director, actress and producers retired to a production room where they could thrash out their considerable differences in private.

Dale was suddenly starving. He hadn't eaten at all since leaving the restaurant with Matt last night. God knew he'd burned off some energy since then.

Instead of retiring to his trailer, he headed to the catering truck with the rest of the crew. No healthy lunch today. He needed protein and carbs. He loaded his plate with a beef burger and thick-cut chips and took a seat at a table with the lighting guys.

There was only one topic of conversation—the bust-up between director and leading lady.

"I've never worked on any set when I saw attitudes as unprofessional as those two," said a bearded, tattooed engineer named Phil.

There were murmurs of agreement around the table. Dale refused to comment either way. There were a lot of weeks ahead of them. He wouldn't be drawn into taking sides. Roxanne and Elton might be speaking to each other by this afternoon but would hold a grudge against anyone who spoke against them in the meantime.

He'd worked on enough sets to know there was nothing more fragile or toxic than ego.

After lunch, he went back to his trailer to catch up on the news. There were no new developments in the murder case though it was still the lead item on the local bulletin, with the protest outside the studio getting near equal coverage.

As Dale began preparing for that afternoon's scenes, there was a knock on his trailer door—Aaron.

He hovered in the doorway, not coming in without an invitation. "Hi," he said, cute smile in place, puppy-dog eyes effectively wide. "Are you in a better mood today?"

Dale smiled, not too encouragingly. "I'm always in a good mood. But I am kind of busy."

"Too busy for a blow job?" Aaron winked, licking his lips.

"Afraid so." Why didn't he just tell the truth? *I've met someone. As nice as the lunchtime blow jobs were, they're over.*

*No more.*

"Your loss." Aaron shrugged, closing the door behind him.

* * * *

Matt had been in a terrific mood all day. Nothing they could throw at him in the office could spoil it. Annabel had obviously known there was something up the second she had collected him that morning.

"Whoa. I know it's Friday and all that but you are way too cheerful for this time of the morning. What's up?"

He'd decided, before she'd arrived, that he couldn't trust her with his good news. There had been too much at stake for Dale, especially right now, to let her in on the secret. For a lawyer, she'd been hopelessly indiscreet. He could have sworn her to secrecy, but within hours, the news of his date with Dale Zachary would have been around the office, Twitter and on Facebook.

"I had a few too many drinks with Conrad last night, that's all. Didn't feel safe to drive this morning."

"Very wise. I had eight drivers at court last week who were caught out by the cops with their early morning spot checks. They all thought they were safe to drive the next day." Annabel had floored the accelerator as an amber light changed to red. Her driving was far from perfect, even when sober. "I thought you were going out with Conrad tonight."

"We are, this was just…an unexpected piss-up. How was boot camp?" he asked, changing the subject.

"Didn't make it," she had said, ignoring the angry car horns of other drivers. "Didn't even set my alarm. I knew last night there was no way I could get up for that this morning, as much I would like to see the tasty Dale again. And Clint for that matter. I got a definite whiff of interest there."

It was a busy day at work and the time flew. Court

appearances, police station interviews and scheduled appointments. He didn't even stop for ten minutes to grab a sandwich for lunch. None of it bothered him. He went through the day on a euphoric high. Just the thought of Dale got him buzzing and looking back to last night.

He'd never been screwed so well. Not by anyone. And he'd never wanted anyone more. Usually one orgasm was enough — roll over and go to sleep. But with Dale, he hadn't wanted to stop. Ten minutes after coming he had been hard again, ready for more. And how great it had been to go to bed with a man who was as versatile as he. Most guys he'd been with were bound up in roles, top or bottom, with no negotiation. Matt had always enjoyed it both ways and Dale did too. They were in and out of each other's bodies all night long.

The memory made him smile. And got him hard again.

There was a possibility of them getting together on Sunday evening, depending on how the weekend with Dale's son went. Matt could hardly wait and prayed nothing would come up to prevent it.

After work, he went home to change. The bed that he'd hastily straightened that morning still smelled of Dale. He held a pillow to his face and inhaled deeply. He wouldn't change the sheets until Sunday. If he couldn't spend the weekend with Dale, he could at least sleep with his scent.

He showered quickly and put on fresh underpants — white briefs — and socks. He dressed in jeans, a blue shirt and a navy pullover. It was a cold night with frost in the forecast, so he chose a pair of brogues and his dark blue tweed blazer. He was meeting his friend for a drink in town and wanted to look good, but not as if he were cruising. He was off the market, at least till he saw how things played out with Dale.

The champagne bar in Durham overlooked the River Wear. On Fridays and Saturdays it was standing room only but Matt arrived just in time to secure a booth and order a bottle of Veuve Clicquot.

Conrad came in as the waiter brought the bottle and an ice bucket to the table.

"Have we got something to celebrate?" Conrad asked, sliding into the booth beside Matt. He had also managed to change after work and wore a white shirt and checked jacket.

"A treat, that's all," Matt said, as the glasses were filled. "I think we deserved it. Cheers."

"Cheers."

They clinked glasses. The champagne was perfectly cold and tasted delicious. Though they often met here—it was one of the most popular bars in town—they rarely splashed out on the fizzy stuff. House wine or happy hour cocktails were more within their budget. But tonight, without Dale, Matt wanted to indulge.

"You look like you've already had a treat or two," Conrad grinned. "I can tell by your face that last night went well."

Matt returned the smile. "You could say that. You could also say that it went absolutely incredibly."

"Come on then. Don't be coy. Tell me everything. What's it like to fuck a movie star?"

Unlike Annabel, Matt knew that whatever he told Conrad would stay between the two of them. They'd been friends for too long and shared too much to let each other down. Lowering his voice to avoid unwanted evesdroppers, he told Conrad about his date, leaving nothing out.

"Wow," his friend said at the end of the story. "That's some night, you randy bastard. Did you expect to go so far with him?"

"Depends what you mean by far. Sleeping with him— absolutely. My God, Conrad, if you had seen him you would understand why. I've never met anyone before who I found so physically attractive. He's ten out of ten gorgeous. There's just no way that I'd turn down the opportunity of going to bed with him. If it were only a one-night stand, I'd still do it. It was the other stuff I didn't expect. The talking, the intimacy, feeling so comfortable with someone I knew next to nothing about."

Conrad looked at him closely. "It sounds to me like you've fallen in love."

"It does, doesn't it? But I can't have. That's insane. You can't love someone after a few days, can you? After only one date?"

Conrad suddenly sang the chorus of *Love at First Sight*. They both laughed.

"Thank you, Kylie, but I don't think that's the case just yet."

Conrad refilled their glasses. "Until it hits you, how could you know? But I can tell you this, I've never seen you beam quite as much as you are tonight. Whatever Dale has done for you, you look good for it."

"Thank you."

"I don't suppose you asked him about helping out with a charity donation?"

"No, sorry. Had other things on my mind."

"Hmm. I don't doubt that. You'll ask him next time, though, won't you?"

"I'll do my best."

By the time they had finished the bottle, the bar was heaving. The sound of talk and laughter all around was at a deafening volume. Time to move on. Matt hated it when a place got too crowded. He used to love the crowds and the action. Not anymore. He was getting old, almost thirty, but so what?

They went to another bar on the same road. It was just as busy but, because the venue was more than double the size, it didn't feel so crowded or restrictive. Matt found a place to wait in a quieter corner of the room, while Conrad fought his way to the bar to get them each vodka and Cokes.

It was past nine-thirty. Dale would be with his son by now. He wondered what the boy was like, whether he knew about his father's love life. This would take some getting used to if things developed between them. Matt hadn't been involved with a man who had the complication of a family. Dale had given the impression that things were good between him and his ex-wife, no reason it should be a problem for Matt.

Give it a rest, he warned himself. One night of lust and he was already thinking about the future and relationships. Time to slow down and enjoy things for what they were, one day at a time.

Danny Frost came into the bar after ten. The lawyer was in the company of a couple of other guys. They were about the same age as Danny but lacked his trim physique and outgoing attitude—they looked like middle-aged men, where Danny looked timeless. He wore a tight-fitting black shirt, which not only looked great against his holiday suntan and graying hair, but showed off what great shape he was in.

"Matt," he greeted, "twice in one week. This is an honor."

Matt noted Conrad's eyes widen at the sight of the older man and he changed position to get closer. Oh yes, he liked what he saw. Why not? Danny looked incredible. A total DILF. Matt made the introductions and didn't miss the way Danny looked Conrad up and down as they shook hands.

Well, well, he would never have thought of putting these two together. But why not? They seemed to hit it off. Danny's friends were less friendly and made little effort to engage with Matt while Danny and Conrad got acquainted. Eventually he excused himself and went to the bathroom.

He checked his phone. Still no messages from Dale. He had to stop doing that. They weren't teenagers. Dale was a busy man. There was no reason for him to text all the time.

The bar was really heaving now. It was a struggle to get through to the bathrooms. He couldn't be bothered with all of these people. It was a cattle market. He appeared to be the only man in here who wasn't on the make. It would be time to move again soon. Always better to stay ahead of the crowd.

Matt was finishing off at the urinal when a voice behind him said, "Why did you stand me up this morning?"

He turned to find Clint Dexter standing there. Even now, dressed casually in shirt and jeans, off duty, the boot camp instructor was a huge and imposing figure. His brow was furrowed and the set of his mouth could almost be interpreted as a smile.

"Oh, Clint. Hi. I didn't recognize you for a second." A lie. There was no mistaking him.

"Not up to it today?"

"Sorry, no. I didn't have time. Early start at work." Why was he lying? He was under no obligation to attend every session.

"Your American friend didn't make it either." Clint's pale eyes looked directly into Matt's.

"He has a lot going on," Matt said brightly. "I expect he was busy too."

"Hmm," Clint said, folding his tattooed arms. "I saw the news. All that shit about his show. You could be right about him. And your…girlfriend? No sign of her today either."

"Yeah, Annabel's not really a morning person. I don't think you'll see a whole lot of her. But I'll be there Monday. Bright and early, with bells on."

"I hope you are. To get any kind of results you have to put the work in. It takes commitment."

"Like I said, I'll be there." Clint made him uncomfortable. His tough attitude was great for motivating tired people on the course, but not here when he was trying to unwind. "Better get back to my friends. See you next week."

"You will," Clint said as he walked away. "You showed great stamina. You have potential. You could get amazing results if you do the work."

Conrad was alone when he returned. "Where's Danny?"

"His friends dragged him away. I don't think they liked us."

"Miserable fucks," Matt said.

They both laughed.

"He was nice though. I really liked him."

"I could tell. I think he liked you too."

"What's his story? He is single?"

"He's single. He hasn't been in a relationship the whole time I've known him. But he's a nice guy. Funny too."

Conrad raised his mobile. "He left me his number. Said to call him tomorrow."

"Excellent," Matt said. "Meet for a coffee. See how you get on."

Conrad smiled. "I think I will. God, I haven't been on a date in ages. Seems old-fashioned in this age of apps and instant sex."

"It's not that old-fashioned. I went on a date with Dale."

"And look how *that* turned out. You've really started something."

It was true. He had started something. And it was something he couldn't wait to continue.

# Chapter Eight

In the two weeks since Dale had last seen his son, Jack already looked different. He was twelve years old and growing fast. *Too fast*, Dale thought. He was missing out on so much. Even when he and Laura had been together he was never around as much as he'd wanted to be. Location shoots and long working days had made him miss out on much of Jack's childhood.

And pretty soon he would be a man. There was already a hint of shadow on his top lip. Not yet a teenager and he'd be shaving soon enough.

It struck Dale afresh every time he saw the boy after a period apart — that sense of loss for everything he was missing.

Saturday morning Dale took Jack shopping in Newcastle. He'd have liked to have shown him around Durham. There was so much to see in the old city. They even had a castle. But there was too much heat in Durham. Too many angry residents with an ax to grind against the TV show. No way was he going to expose his boy to any of that.

Only half an hour up the motorway, Newcastle was far enough for him to feel safe with his son.

Still, he was taking no chances. Ordinarily his face wasn't famous enough in the UK to prevent him going about like a regular Joe, but that was all before this week. He'd been in every local paper since Wednesday. He couldn't to run the risk of being recognized. Not with Jack.

He downplayed it in jeans and a thick winter sweater, his hair and brow concealed beneath the low peak of a baseball cap. Just like any other dad taking his son out for the day.

Except not many regular dads wore caps around here, not like in the States anyway, but it was the most incognito disguise he could think of.

Jack said he needed a new pair of boots for playing football. Laura had warned him about spoiling the boy, but hey, when he only saw him for a couple of days a month, he had the right to spoil him.

"Dad, can I have an iPhone?" Jack asked as they walked through the mall. The soccer shoes were already in the bag, together with a new England sports kit and a stopwatch.

"Don't push your luck," Dale said. "You've got a phone already."

"But it's crap."

"What's the matter with it?"

"It's not an iPhone. Not even a smart phone. It's a crappy pay-as-you-go handset."

"You can make calls, can't you? Send texts?"

"Uh-huh."

"Then it's good enough. Your mother will go ape over all this soccer stuff without me sending you home with a new phone."

"Can we go to Starbucks then?"

Jack reminded him so much of himself at that age, though he couldn't remember being quite this confident or outgoing. It was like looking back in time. Jack was the double of him. He had the same blue eyes, same jawline, same nose. His hair was a much paler shade of blond but Dale had been the same as a kid, darkening in his mid-teens to the color it was now.

"What do you want?" he asked, as they entered the coffee shop.

Jack ordered an oversized iced coffee, topped with a mountainous serving of whipped cream and chocolate sauce. Dale rolled his eyes. Just as well the boy had inherited his love of sport. He'd be the size of a house if he didn't work that shit off.

"Does your mother let you have drinks like this?"

"As if. She won't even come to Starbucks," Jack said. "I'll find us a seat while you wait."

*He's got me wrapped around his little finger*, Dale thought affectionately. Things would be different if he was a full-time dad, but he wasn't, so here they were buying three hundred bucks' worth of sports gear and eight-hundred calorie drinks.

"Why are you in the newspapers?" Jack asked when Dale joined him.

"What?"

"Over there." He pointed to a guy across the café, reading a folded newspaper. On the flip side of the page there was Dale. They'd used a picture from one of his old rom-coms. There was also a photo of Roxanne on stage.

"It's nothing," Dale said, sitting down. "Just something to do with the show. Drink your coffee."

"So are you properly famous now?" Jack asked wide-eyed. "Hardly anyone at school knows who you are."

"Sssh. That's the way I like it, so keep your voice down." He hoped he could shield Jack from the worst of the *Blood Falls on Stone* controversy. That was one of the perks of him *not* having a smart phone. He couldn't follow that shit on social media.

"Wouldn't it be cool, being recognized?"

"Not today. Or any day. Being famous isn't important, Jack. It's doing a good job that matters."

"Chris Coleman says he's seen one of your films. He says you got chopped up with an ax."

Dale started, staring at his son. "You haven't watched that movie, have you?"

"Got nothing to watch it on, have I? I'm not even allowed a computer in my bedroom."

"Good. You don't need to watch movies like that. They're too frightening."

"*Frightening*?" Jack laughed. "I'm not scared of cheesy horror films."

"Cheesy, eh?"

"According to Chris Coleman. He said that film was *soooo* bad it was funny."

"Spend a lot of time with Chris Coleman, do you?"

"Not really. We're in some of the same classes but he's a bit of douche. He's the only boy in school who's heard of you, that's all."

Dale's eyes widened. Nothing like the honesty of kids to keep you grounded.

* * * *

Matt spent a quiet morning at home. Last night's drinking had left him with a heavy head. He stayed in bed until nine-thirty. After a week of very early mornings it was a luxury to sleep late. He woke from a sweet dream about Dale and rolled over to inhale his scent from the pillow. The smell was beginning to fade but was still there.

He put on a pot of coffee and set some bacon under the grill while it brewed. He checked his phone for messages. There was one from Dale. He smiled as he read it.

*Hope you had a good time last night. Have a great day. Can't wait to see you again.*

He keyed a fast reply.

*Suffering slightly this morning. All my own fault. Have a great weekend with Jack. Looking forward to tomorrow night.*

Matt made a bacon sandwich and put it on a tray with a pot of coffee. He carried it to the living room. He turned on the TV and he entered 'Dale Zachary' into the Netflix search field. There were three results. Top of the list was *An Axe in the Dark*. The gory horror movie. Probably not the best choice for Saturday morning breakfast. He added that one to his viewing list for later. The other two were romantic comedies. He selected the most recent, a title from 2013, and hit play.

The movie was dreadful, even to the most undemanding viewer. A young fashion editor was caught in a romantic tangle with a rich designer and a penniless hot dog vendor — Dale. Despite his lowly status and the contrivances of the script, it was obvious from their first scene together that she was going to end up with the hot dog guy.

Who wouldn't? Wow. He was gorgeous. Sometimes the most attractive people can fail to come across that way on film. Dale wasn't one of them. The camera loved him. Especially those sparkling blue eyes of his. They lit up the screen like an old fashioned matinee idol.

Clean-shaven, he also looked a lot younger. The beard he currently wore gave him a rugged maturity, but without it there was something very cute and boyish about his face. He must have been around thirty when this film was made but didn't look anything like it.

It was a strange experience, watching him romance a woman on screen. There wasn't a second of realism in this hokey film but Matt felt an unexpected stab of jealousy when it came to Dale's passionate love scene with the leading actress. He understood what it must be like for the husbands and wives of famous people to watch their spouses pretend to be in love with other people. Weird.

*Stop being ridiculous*, an inner voice warned. He had never been the jealous type and wasn't about to start now with a bad romantic comedy.

The movie was blessedly short at eighty-five minutes. When it was over, he realized he had the whole day ahead of him and nothing planned.

He washed up and changed into his running gear. A decent jog would make up for the workout he had skipped yesterday, not to mention all the booze he'd consumed in the last forty-eight hours. The phone rang as he was fastening his shoes. It was Conrad.

"Guess what?"

"You've got a hangover?" Matt joked.

"Yes, but not the worst ever. That doesn't matter. This is

way more exciting."

Conrad's voice was full of glee. Matt felt happy for him, knowing what he was about to say. His best friend had a tendency to take life too seriously. He admired him for his commitment to the charity work but often wished Conrad would take a time out for himself now and again.

"Don't keep me in suspense."

"I called Danny Taylor. That guy from last night."

"I know who he is. I introduced you."

"I got his number but he didn't get mine," Conrad continued. "So he said he hoped I would call. If I didn't he was going to get my number from you. But he didn't have to 'cause I called him anyway."

"Conrad, get to the point. You're rambling. Are you meeting him this afternoon?"

"No, I can't. Got a committee meeting about our next fundraiser."

"It's Saturday afternoon. Who the hell books a meeting for then?"

"I did," he said, sounding defensive. "It's the only time everyone is free. But I'm not doing anything tomorrow, so Danny and I are meeting for coffee in the afternoon."

"Thank God for that. Shit, Conrad, you need to strike a better balance between your work and personal life."

"Charity isn't work."

"Then you deserve a medal. An MBE. A bloody knighthood."

"That'll do for me." He laughed.

"As long as you get a shag. Man, you're *way* overdue a good time."

* * * *

Matt ran up into the hills above the town, heading in the opposite direction to the boot camp route. He needed variety in exercise to keep it interesting. It was another cold day but thankfully dry. The ground was hard underfoot, making the going a little easier.

He tuned out as he ran, allowing his mind to roam as freely as his body. The stresses of work were forgotten. Even Dale Zachary took a back seat for a while. The time was his own and he enjoyed it.

He paid little attention to the figure in gray running clothes keeping pace behind him, fifty yards down the track. The figure looked like any other runner, hood pulled around their face to keep out the cold. It may just have been coincidence that the runner was using the exact same route.

But the eyes inside the hood were focused intently.

Watching.

Keeping pace.

Following.

# Chapter Nine

Dale put Jack on the five-thirty-eight p.m. train on Sunday. He stood on the platform waving until the train vanished down the track. There was a familiar melancholy feeling in his chest as he watched the boy go. No plans were set for when they would get together again, but it wouldn't be long. It couldn't be. Jack was growing fast, he would soon be a man with no time to spare for his lonely old dad.

It had been a great weekend. Saturday had been fairly packed. After the shops, he had taken Jack to the movies to watch a brainless action film the boy was keen to see. *"Dad, why can't you make movies like this?"* On the way back to the cottage they had stopped for a pizza. It had given Dale another opportunity to spoil his son, ordering a sixteen-inch meat feast and twelve-inch garlic bread with cheese. They had devoured the lot in front of the TV. He had allowed Jack to stay up till eleven. They had talked, caught up on each other's news, then watched a DVD before bed. Sunday morning, they had played football in the garden and Dale had cooked a late lunch. It was a perfect weekend, until the time came for Jack to catch his train.

So that was it. Another visit over too soon. They would stay in touch by phone and Skype but it wasn't the same as face-to-face contact.

Saying goodbye was the worst part. It always was.

Walking from the platform, Dale pulled out his phone and dialed Matt's number.

"Hi," Matt answered straight away. "Good weekend?"

The sound of Matt's voice made the pain of parting a little easier.

"It's been good. Jack just caught his train. I was wondering whether you'd still like me to drop by on the way home."

"You had better drop by. Do you have any idea how horny I've been, waiting for you to call?"

Dale's cock reacted instantly. "Yeah? What made you so hot?"

"I've been watching one of your movies. Pretty hot stuff, even though your death scene was a downer."

Dale groaned. "Don't tell me, *An Axe in the Dark*. That movie haunts me like a ghost."

"You were a hot young thing back then."

He laughed. "As opposed to the old man I am now?"

"Mature, not old. And definitely better with age. So… Are you on your way or not?"

* * * *

The lack of traffic on Sunday meant the drive from the station to Matt's house took less than fifteen minutes. Matt opened the front door as he got out of the car.

*Man, does he look good.* In just a baggy T-shirt and shorts, he was unshaven and his thick brown hair hung heavy and unstyled across his brow. The casual look suited him. With his versatile good looks and *that* body, he could have been a very successful model if he hadn't gone into the law. Back in his own modeling days, Dale had seen plenty of guys who didn't have what Matt did.

As they closed the front door, their passion erupted and they were all over each other.

Up against the wall, locked at the mouth, hands roaming, Dale's hunger for Matt was even stronger than before. He thrust his hardness against Matt's hip. Matt's leisurewear gave him easy access to his body. He slipped his hands down the back of his shorts, grabbing bare ass. *Oh yeah.*

They tumbled into the living room. Matt fell backward onto the sofa. Dale didn't waste any time, tearing down Matt's shorts, tossing them aside. His tumescent cock slapped against his belly. He pulled Matt's T-shirt over his head, getting him exactly how he wanted him — stark naked.

He grabbed Matt's cock and squeezed. Matt groaned, arching his back and spreading his legs. Dale went down, taking him in his mouth. Matt groaned even louder and the shaft thickened. Dale licked the deliciously salty tip and kneaded his balls, hoping to elicit even more pre-cum into his mouth.

"Take it easy," Matt sighed. "I've been waiting for this all day. I could blow at any time."

Dale knew exactly how to handle a man. He sucked long and slow on the shaft, giving his nuts just enough pressure. He listened for the quickening of breath and was alert to the rhythm and pulse of Matt's cock. He edged him toward orgasm and stopped just before the crucial moment, delaying his release time and time again while pre-cum coated his tongue.

But Dale wanted more than his cock. He released him from his mouth and raised Matt's knees up to his chest, giving him unrestricted access to his beautiful asshole. What a sight. That dusky pink opening surrounded by swirls of dark hair. Dale had always been an ass man.

"I'm going to make you feel even better," he said, lowering his head into the crack. Slowly, teasing, he brushed his tongue against the sensitive skin.

"*Oh God*," Matt cried, arching his back farther from the sofa, giving the most intimate part of his body.

Dale was a dedicated ass eater. He could bring a bottom to complete ecstasy with just his tongue. The way Matt reacted to his slow, delicious administrations drove his own desire to unbearable heights. Matt's body responded and lost all resistance. Dale listened to the helpless catch in Matt's breath.

He ate Matt's delectable ass until neither of them could stand the tension any longer.

Dale drew back and undressed quickly. He kept a safe

sex kit in his jacket and hurriedly put the rubber on his quivering cock. Matt watched with undisguised hunger and anticipation. His pupils were wide and dilated, his mouth open. His asshole, wet with Dale's saliva, offered a glistening invitation.

Dale tore into a sachet of lube and hurriedly coated his dick, pushing a finger into Matt's ass, preparing the way. He needed this. He'd wanted nothing else since Friday morning.

He moved over Matt, pulling his hips into position, and looked down at his handsome face as he pushed his cock inside. They let out a unified sigh as one body enveloped another, slow, inch by inch. Matt slid his arms around Dale's shoulders and pulled his face down to his lips.

"Fuck me hard and deep," he said, just before their lips locked.

Dale didn't need much encouragement. The build-up had been too long, too intense. There would be time enough to make love later, but for now, what they both needed was a good hard fuck.

Their passion was equal as they thrust, pushed and clutched at each other's body. Matt grabbed Dale's ass, pulling him deeper. They came together. Dale reached a shuddering orgasm in the tight grip of Matt's ass, while Matt came in a sticky rush all over his hairy abdominals.

"God, that was intense," Matt gasped afterward, wiping his belly with tissues.

Dale murmured agreement, flopping bare-assed on the sofa beside him. His heart was beating fast. He needed a moment to calm down. They both did.

"Like a beer?" Matt asked at last.

"Mmm, that would be good."

Matt located his T-shirt and shorts from the mess of their hastily discarded clothes and pulled them on. While he was gone, Dale found his own underpants and stepped into them. As comfortable as he felt around Matt, it didn't seem right to hang out bare-assed in his living room.

He found his phone and fired off a quick text to his son.

*Everything OK?*

The one word reply came back immediately.

*Yes.*

It was better than nothing.

Matt returned with the beer. They sat side by side and clinked bottles.

"So what have you been up to?" Dale asked. "Apart from watching me being murdered with an axe."

Matt stroked his bare thigh. "At the risk of sounding like a stalker, I watched *two* of your old films. You see, this is something new. I've never been with a guy who I could look up on Netflix when he wasn't around. It beats trolling through Facebook galleries."

"And how was that?"

"A little weird, I'll admit. I can't say I totally enjoyed the movies as much as I enjoyed seeing you in them."

"What was the second movie?"

Matt winched. "You know, I can't even remember what it was called."

Dale laughed. "You should meet my son. You both have an uncanny knack of keeping my ego in check."

"Sorry. You played a hot dog seller."

"Oh, *that* movie! I take it back, that picture sucks. Well done for getting through it at all, that's more than I ever did. They had a screening of that crap for cast and crew. There was no one left by the end. It's difficult enough watching yourself on screen, without watching yourself in absolute shit."

Matt rubbed against him. "I wouldn't say it was *absolute* shit. Just a bit shitty."

"They should've put that quote on the poster. Still, that shitty movie fed us and paid the rent for a few months so it wasn't all bad."

"Like I said, you were good in it. I would never have made it to the end if I wasn't perving over your fine American arse."

After the beers, they were both hungry. Matt fixed them a sandwich — ham and pease pudding.

"Pease pudding? What's that?" Dale asked, watching him spread the yellowy-orange substance across the top of the meat.

"Remember the black pudding I had at the restaurant the other night? This is another local delicacy. Without the blood. Try it. You'll love it. I promise."

"I'll try it if we can have sex again." Dale grinned.

"That's an absolute certainty."

The sandwich, washed down with more beer, was indeed delicious.

"I can't cook," Matt said, clearing away the plates. "But I know my way around a deli counter."

The second bottle of beer put Dale over the limit to drive home. Not that he intended to leave He should really be home, learning his pages for tomorrow, but they could wait. Right now, Matt was far more alluring.

They took it to the bedroom. Naked, beneath the covers, they held each other and kissed. There was so much to discover. Where Matt liked to be touched and how. How tight to hold him. How softly to stroke him. How he shuddered when Dale drew his tongue along the curve of his ear. How he moaned when Dale traced his fingers around the contours of his asshole.

It was a long journey of discovery. And they were just beginning.

\* \* \* \*

Jamie Dench had only been seconded to the Major Incident Team for three days and he loved it. This was the opportunity he'd been waiting for. It was no secret that he wanted to climb the greasy career pole. So what if he was ambitious? He worked hard and did a damn good job.

His new boss, DCI Frank Redgraves, was a hard taskmaster, but Jamie was there to prove that, however hard Redgraves pushed, he was more than up to it.

The investigation into the murders of Conner Welsh and Olly Raymond were important, personally and politically. There were rumors developing, especially on social media, that both the victims were gay and had been killed because of their sexuality. Officially, the police had yet to confirm that they were pursuing that as a serious line of enquiry, but it was true. It was *the* line of enquiry.

No one on the force could accuse Jamie of being out and proud, but his relationship with Matt Blyth was no great secret. His sexuality was probably more accepted by his colleagues than by Jamie himself. As soon as he realized that MIT was looking into *that* aspect of the victims lives, he knew it was also the reason he'd been put forward for the team.

So what if it was? While he didn't want to make an issue of his sexuality, if it opened doors within the police force, he was fully prepared to take advantage of that. He would prove he was the best man for the job, regardless of his sex life.

"Dench, why are you still here?" DCI Redgraves, a small man with thinning gray hair and a powerful voice, looked out of the open door of his office.

It was past nine-thirty on Sunday night and they were the only two officers left on the floor. Jamie had been on duty for over fourteen hours.

"Almost done, sir. I'm just going through the social media contacts of Olly Raymond."

"They've been checked already. Go home."

"Doesn't hurt to check again, sir. A fresh pair of eyes."

"Trust me, we're not going to find the killer through Facebook. Our man is far too careful. Now go. My overtime budget is not infinite."

As reluctant as Jamie was to leave a job half finished, he

was less inclined to piss off the new boss. It was only his third day. While it was good to show a willingness to work, knowing when to back off was just as valuable.

"I'm going, sir. See you tomorrow."

Redgraves peered over the top of his glasses and nodded. It was as good as anything Jamie could hope for.

It was dark and cold as he left the station. Suddenly alone, he found it hard to switch off. He wouldn't show it in the station, but the case and his empathy for the victims had an impact on him. Ordinary, regular boys, just like him, who happened to meet the wrong man. It could have happened to him or any man he knew.

Matt.

God forbid. The idea was abhorrent. If anything happened to him… What? There was nothing he could do about it. Matt wasn't his boyfriend anymore. He'd made that abundantly clear on Thursday night, going on a date with someone else.

Goddammit. How could he even think about another man already? Matt had said it was over but he wouldn't believe it. Jamie had barely looked at another man since their split. Why would he want to? Matt Blyth was the man for him. The only man. He didn't want anyone else. No one else was good enough.

He'd never stopped believing that.

Matt obviously didn't share his faith in their relationship. Going with other men already.

They'd been through a rough patch. It didn't mean they were irreparably broken. Not even close. Jamie was no quitter. He worked hard until he got what he wanted.

He'd proved it in the police force. His personal life wasn't any different. He would keep going till he made Matt see things his way. Perseverance—that's what it took to succeed.

Jamie got in the car and headed along Bowman Road, the opposite direction to where he should be heading. He took the long way home, almost all the way around the town in a circular route — one that would take him past Matt's estate.

He had reservations, of course. He was no masochist. How many times could he listen to Matt telling him they were finished?

As many times as it took until he changed his mind.

Anyway, it was essential that he speak to Matt tonight. If he was putting himself out there dating other men, he had to know the risks he was taking. There was a killer in their community. A killer who preyed on good-looking young men — gay man. Guys exactly like Matt. It was his duty as a cop to make him aware of the danger.

His hands were sweaty as he steered his car onto Matt's estate. It wasn't yet ten o'clock. Not too late. Matt rarely went to bed before eleven-thirty, even on Sundays. There was enough time for Jamie to say his piece, to warn him and show him how much he still cared.

Slowing on the bend to the cul de sac, he suddenly hit the brakes.

There were two cars parked on the drive. Matt's Nissan and another vehicle, an Audi.

He wasn't alone.

Who did he know who drove an Audi? Not Matt's parents. They hadn't changed their Ford in almost a decade. It didn't belong to Annabel either. And the last time he'd seen Conrad, he was driving a Peugeot.

Who then? Was this the guy from Thursday? Was he back already? If not him, who? Another stranger? Had Matt started to put it about? A casual hook-up? No, that wasn't his style. He couldn't believe it. Matt wouldn't screw around for the sake of it. He was better than that.

But if this was the man from Thursday, they had advanced beyond any first date. To be home together at ten on a Sunday night... That was a lot more involved.

Jamie felt an unbearable tightness inside. It gripped his balls, his guts and his heart. It made it difficult to breathe. An overwhelming rush of emotions came through him. Mixed emotions — anger, pain, confusion, jealousy, loss. He ground his teeth and gripped the steering wheel, trying to bring his thoughts together. To clear his head.

He looked at the house again and noticed for the first time there was a light on in the upstairs window — the master bedroom. A place he knew so well. The curtains were closed but the light shone through.

*Motherfucker.* Whoever this guy was — this Audi-driving twat — he was up there. In Matt's bedroom. *His Matt.* In the bed where he used to sleep.

"Bastard. Bastard. *Bastard.*" Jamie slammed his palm against the wheel.

What the fuck could he do now?

He couldn't go in, that was for sure. Matt would never forgive him if he created *that* scene — jealous boyfriend interrupting his tryst with a new guy. But what? He couldn't just drive away and do nothing either.

He sat for a moment, gripping the wheel, his knuckles turning white.

He would fight, that's what. Nothing he'd ever wanted had come easily. He wouldn't let Matt go without a struggle. But not tonight. He needed to calm down. Think rationally. He would win back Matt but not like this.

First, he would find out who this bastard with the Audi was.

Knowledge was power.

He pulled closer to the car and saw the sticker in the back window. Richardson's. A rental company based in Durham. He made a note of the registration plate and the company number. It was enough to go on. First thing tomorrow he would find out *exactly* who was in Matt's bed.

And once he did, God help the bastard.

# Chapter Ten

"Do you have to go?" Matt wrapped an arm around Dale's bare waist. Dale had just silenced the alarm on his phone. The bedroom was in darkness, not a suggestion of dawn came through the curtains.

"Afraid so," Dale answered. "I need to get home before heading to the studio."

"What time is it?"

"Five. I have to be on set by seven today."

Matt groaned. Monday morning always came too soon. The night, peppered with frequent bouts of lovemaking and orgasms, had been too short. He moved his hand lower, fingers grazing the shaft of Dale's hard cock. He cupped his balls and gave them a gentle squeeze, which he'd quickly discovered was one of Dale's favorite things. "Can I persuade you to stay?"

Dale's cock throbbed. "All too easily. But it won't do any good. I'd like nothing more than to stay in bed all day. Screw you in every conceivable way. I feel like we should make up for lost time. I want to be inside you all the time. And if I'm not, I want you inside me. But unfortunately, I have to work today. And so do you." He rolled over, covering Matt, pressing down with his weight, with his dick. He kissed him in the dark. "See you tonight?"

"Yes," Matt said, planting hands on Dale's bare buttocks and pulling him tight. "But it might be late. I'm on call. There's at least one out of hours interview that I know about."

"I'll wait. Even if I have to get up in the middle of the night to see you, I will."

They said goodbye on the drive with a long, lingering kiss. Dale drove home while Matt headed to boot camp. He figured as he was awake, he might as well put the time to good use. Despite the lack of sleep, he felt completely refreshed and invigorated.

He smiled as he drove to the car park. This was crazy. In the very best way. That he should feel like this already. Only a week since he had met Dale at their first boot camp. But what a week. So much emotion, so much sex, so much happiness. It was dangerous, feeling all of this so soon, but it was magnificent too.

*Just go with it*, his inner voice said. *No pressure or expectation. Enjoy it all you can.*

Early March and there was still a hard white frost on the ground. Matt barely noticed the cold. He parked the car and joined the crowd gathering at the assembly point.

Clint Dexter waited with his notebook and pencil. He added Matt's name to his list. "Good morning. Are you on your own today?"

There had been no word from Annabel, not even a text. "It looks that way."

Clint smiled. "Not everyone is cut out for this. But you — you've got what it takes. Inner strength. I'm glad to have you back."

Matt returned the smile. Best not tell him boot camp was well down the list of things he would like to be doing right now. Lying in a warm bed with a hot American between his open thighs — now that was much more preferable.

\* \* \* \*

Dale was in his trailer, partially dressed, when there was a knock on the door. Aaron Oxford entered. Dale hurriedly fastened his trousers and grabbed a shirt.

"C'mon, Aaron, don't you wait for an answer anymore?"

The production assistant smirked. "It's nothing I haven't seen before. Don't be sensitive."

"Well, it's something you won't get to see again, so wait next time. Okay?" Getting involved with Aaron had been a mistake. He could hardly write it off as a location romance—there was no romance. They had infrequent, meaningless sex in his trailer. Nothing more than that. Now that he had Matt, someone he really did have feelings for, the dalliance with Aaron was something he would rather hadn't happened. He couldn't change what he'd already done, but he could draw a very clear line under it.

Aaron shrugged. He didn't seem too bothered. "You're wanted in the production office."

"I'm due on the set at seven."

"Change of plan. They've called a crisis meeting. Johan Turner's come up from London for it. There are a lot of unhappy faces in that room."

Damn. After a great weekend and night with Matt, he'd been optimistic for this new week. That it was a chance for a fresh start. The protestors at the gate were noticeably reduced this morning. Those who remained had a fatigued look about them, as if the fight had gone. He hoped that things would return to normal now.

It was a premature hope.

The meeting room was full when Dale arrived. He saw heads of departments, supervisors and all the main cast members. At the head of the table sat Johan Turner, creator of *Blood Falls on Stone*. Johan was a veteran of TV dramas and had won numerous awards for his writing over the last twenty years. Dale had met him only once before, at his final audition for the show. As one of the most sought-after writers on television, Johan had final approval on all casting.

His talent as a writer could not be denied, but on a personal level, he was less impressive. Heavy set with suety features, his dyed hair was an unconvincing shade of mahogany and he wore oversized tortoiseshell glasses. He always wore a navy blazer with a customary polka dot handkerchief in the pocket. It was a considered, artificial look. Dale suspected the young acolytes and yes-men he was surrounded by had convinced him it was a quirky, individual image.

Johan was a grandiose, ever-smiling figure, but the bonhomie never reached his eyes. He was a carefully constructed character, a façade to hide what lay behind it — a nasty old queen.

Dead eyes watched Dale over the top of old-fashioned glasses as he entered and took a seat between Roxanne and Elton.

Next to Johan, pen poised and watching with viciously tight eyes, sat Edward, his latest assistant. Never smiling, Edward had a helmet of chestnut hair and wore so much fake tan that, for a white, middle-class boy from Surrey, he could pass for Middle Eastern.

"Welcome, welcome, everybody." Johan's southern Welsh accent boomed across the room. He smiled, raising open arms, looking very self-satisfied. "So lovely to see you all, however impromptu this meeting is. Really, really lovely."

Beside him, Dale felt Elton bristle. The director made no secret of his dislike of the writer. "*Overly proud, untalented, fat shit,*" he'd once spat when Roxanne had asked why they were deviating from Johan's dialogue. "*By all means, say the words as written, darling. Dig down deep and drag up every ounce of acting talent you possess. Do all that and more but I can promise you something — you will look and sound fucking ridiculous. Because that's what this script is — fucking ridiculous. It's up to us, all of us, to pull it apart and make something that people will actually want to watch.*"

"Well, you all had quite a time of it last week, didn't you?" Johan beamed as though they had just come back from a summer break. "Quite a time, yes. And very, very sad. But I'm here to do something about it."

"Our fucking savior," Elton muttered, none too quietly.

Dale struggled to maintain a poker face. Stale alcohol fumes were coming off the director in waves. The pong of Roxanne's cloying perfume failed to mask them.

"So," Johan continued, undeterred. "Nicola, Russell, dears, why don't you tell the lovely people what we plan to do?"

Nicola Donahue and Russell Jones, producers of *Blood Falls on Stone*, looked as if they hadn't slept all weekend. Both were in their early forties, with a wealth of experience between them. They showed none of the verve or enthusiasm that had been so evident at the start of filming. Dale had faith in them. He trusted them and enjoyed working for them. If anyone could sort this situation out, he'd put money on this pair.

"Thank you, Johan." Nicola took the lead. A petite, quietly spoken woman, her mannered, businesslike approach was the polar opposite of the writer's oily flamboyance. "Some of you may already be aware of this, but what was predominantly a local issue last week was picked up in several of the national papers over the weekend. To say we, collectively, have been portrayed in a negative light would be a gross understatement."

Dale had been so busy over the weekend that he didn't think to check what was happening in the press. Only now did he remember the newspaper Jack had spied in the coffee shop. *Shit.* Why didn't he check later what that story was about?

"How bad was it?" he asked.

"Most of the papers went with the usual stuff, reporting on the similarities between what we're filming and the recent murders," Nicola said, sounding quiet, calm. "But the *Sunday Sun* obtained an interview with one of the relatives. The sister of the first victim."

"She doesn't even live in this country," Johan said, with a sugary smile. "She's in Portugal of all places, but the dear lady had plenty to say about our show."

"Yes," Nicola said firmly. "That may be so, but the family are grieving and this kind of exposure is very damaging for us."

"She has plenty to say about my scripts," Johan continued

undeterred. "Quite how the paper obtained a copy in the first place, I don't know, but they've blown the whole thing. I'm going to have to rewrite the entire final episode."

"That won't be necessary," Elton spoke up. "I've already made changes to the second half of the series. What leaked is from the original script. It's been much improved since then. What we're going to film bears no resemblance to what the papers are talking about."

Dale looked toward the writer. The smile had finally faltered. Johan looked just as sour and venomous as his pissy assistant, Edward.

"You have no authority to change my scripts," Johan said. The eyes behind the glasses had narrowed to reptilian slits.

"If directors didn't rewrite your scripts, no one would ever watch." Elton grinned. Like a shark sensing blood in the water, he moved in for the kill. Arguing was his favorite pastime.

"That's a conversation to be had later," Nicola said, brusquely. "*In private*. Right now you all need to be aware of what we're doing to address the immediate situation."

Roxanne thumped the table. "You should have done something last week. I told you all but you allowed the situation to escalate."

"I have to agree," Dale spoke up. "A few well-chosen words of support and sympathy would have gone a long way to defuse the community anger. The family might not have gone to the papers if they thought we were listening."

Johan's smile was back in place. "Dale, Roxy darling. I get what you're saying, I really do, but we can't give in to mob pressure. They want to change my scripts entirely. As if they know the first thing about making fantastic television."

"The important thing is that we're doing something now," Nicola said, taking control of the room. She turned to her co-producer. "Russell."

Russell Jones was a nondescript man of forty-two. Like Nicola, his quiet, unassuming manner belied a strong and efficient character. He needed to be, running an efficient production while managing the inflated egos of people like Elton and Johan.

"We've put out a detailed and forthright statement this morning," Russell said. "It should go some way to appeasing the protestors and the press. But that alone is not enough. Later this morning, Johan, Nicola and myself will meet some of the protestors and family members at the hotel. We will do everything in our power to assure them of our good intentions."

"I should be there," Roxanne said quickly. "I am the star after all."

"No," Russell said firmly. "The shoot is already way behind schedule. You're needed on the set today. *All* day."

"But—"

"Hear him out, Roxy," Johan said. "You will be involved. Just listen."

"Tonight," Russell picked up, "at the hotel, we're going to hold a reception. Every person in this room is required to attend. We will be welcoming the journalist Keeley Rank. Keeley is joining the production for the next few days."

A unified groan went round the table.

"Who's the hell is Keeley Rank?" Dale asked.

"A total fucking bitch," Roxanne fumed. "Russell, Nicola, c'mon. What are you thinking? Letting that old cow onto the set."

"Damage limitation. Public relations. Call it what you like, but Keeley will be joining us for the next week to write a behind the scenes feature for next weekend's Sunday supplements."

"What she'll do is a hatchet job," Roxanne warned. "Take my word. That's what she's good at. When I did *Sweet Bird* on stage, the producers thought it would be a good idea to let her chronicle the rehearsal period. She crucified every one of us."

Johan raised his arms and voice. "You're being overly sensitive, Roxy. I know Keeley. She's an absolute sweetheart. I allowed her similar access to the set of *Expose* and she wrote a wonderful piece on us. Besides, she owes me a favor. Trust me, the only stories we'll see in print about this show from now on will be wholly positive. I'll make sure of that. It's my promise to you all."

\* \* \* \*

"Just how bad is this Keeley chick?" Dale asked as he walked back to the set with Roxanne. "I don't like journalists. Never met one I could trust."

Roxanne's high heels echoed along the corridor of the old school building.

"Then you're gonna hate this bitch. Johan might think they're friends but she'd sell him out entirely if she thought he'd make a juicy story. She's not coming to calm troubled waters. If there's a way to aggravate the situation she'll find it."

"Is this not just something personal between the two of you?" he asked hopefully.

Roxanne looked at him sideways. There was a half smile on her glossy lips. "Go ahead then, give her the benefit of the doubt. I just hope you don't have any secrets *in your closet*. Because if you do, and you can take this from me, Keeley Rank will find them. And she'll expose them without a second thought."

\* \* \* \*

Matt's last client of the day was seeking a divorce after sixteen years of marriage. The only man Ellie Coatsworth had ever loved, her schoolyard sweetheart, was no longer the man she had married. Matt discreetly shifted a box of tissues across the desk and listened patiently as she told her story. It was a slight variation on one he'd heard a million times before.

After one too many 'late nights at the office', her husband had come home rolling drunk. So drunk she'd had to undress him and put him into bed. As she had folded away his clothes, Ellie had found a mobile phone in the pocket of his trousers. Not his regular phone. A very cheap pay-as-you-go handset.

"He had the balls to accuse me of snooping on him," she said.

The phone was only used to exchange texts and calls with a single number. Dan Coatsworth had been having an affair with a woman at work for over two years. The affair alone was grounds for divorce but the deception ran deeper than that. There were gambling and credit card debts totaling sixty thousand and Ellie had caught her husband just as he was about to secure a second mortgage on their four-bedroom home.

"His share of the house won't even cover his cards," she said. "I want him out. The bitch is welcome to him and all his stinking debt."

Matt admired her steel. The tissues were not touched. There were no tears from this lady. She knew exactly what she wanted. "I can start proceedings right away," he said. "If that's what you want."

"The sooner, the better," she said, leaning forward in her chair. "I've wasted too many good years on that bastard. I want rid of him ASAP."

The office was closing down as Ellie Coatsworth departed. Matt made a few notes in her file and left it on his desk. He would set the divorce process in motion the following day. It was straightforward enough, as long as the husband's lawyer didn't push for anything more than he was entitled to, which wasn't much of anything, given what he'd done.

He checked the time. Six-twenty-five. He had to be at the police station at seven. So far no other calls had come in for that evening. If it stayed that way he should be home before nine. Enough time for Dale to come over. Matt couldn't wait. He was happy just thinking about him. He'd been like that all day.

Matt headed to the watercooler and checked his phone for messages. There were several texts from Conrad. Trivial stuff, telling him how his day was going and a reminder to ask Dale for help with the charity.

*A donation and/or a personal appearance would be great.*

Conrad was beginning to sound like a broken record. Nevertheless, Matt had promised to ask Dale for something and as yet he hadn't.

He would do it tonight, before they had sex. He couldn't account for anything he did afterward. Dale literally fucked his brains out.

There was also a voice mail. From Dale. He dialed into the account and quietly prayed Dale wasn't calling to cancel. He tabbed through the voice mail options and smiled again as he heard Dale's honeyed tones.

"Hey, sexy. Hope you're having a better day than I am. The only thing making this bearable is remembering all the things we did last night."

It had taken a great effort to think about anything else. From the morning meeting to Ellie Coatsworth's divorce, sex with Dale had never been far from his thoughts, resulting in some highly inappropriate hard-ons.

"I'm just calling to let you know I'll be late tonight. Long story, I'll tell you about it later, but we have to attend some crappy press function at the hotel in Durham. I'm going to blow it off as soon as I can, but that might not be till around ten. I hope that's not too late 'cause I really want to see you." Dale's voice lowered. "Oh God, how I want to see you. I've got a stiff one just thinking about you... But I'll call before I set off. Okay, sexy. See you later."

Whatever time Dale arrived it would not be too late. Matt sent him a quick text to that effect, telling him to come by no matter what the time was.

He went back to his office to retrieve the file on Gary Draper and packed up the rest of his stuff.

There was one thing he'd avoided thinking about until now. It was exactly a week since he'd sat in on Gary

Draper's police interview. Tonight was the follow-up. He'd have to see Jamie again when he went to the station. He didn't want a repeat of what had happened on his doorstep last Thursday. Maybe Jamie was over it. He'd had the weekend to cool off, to move past the idea of them staging a reunion. *Some chance of that.* Three months apart hadn't convinced him. What difference would a few more days make?

There was no point getting into another argument and he wouldn't give Jamie the opportunity. He would keep it professional. No personal chat. No time alone. He was there to discuss Gary Draper. Nothing else.

There was a noticeable difference in the sky when he left the office. The evenings were getting longer. Dusk was cutting in but it wasn't dark, as it used to be. There was enough purple-tinted light left in the sky for Matt to notice straight away that there was something wrong with his car.

The back passenger side tire was completely flat. No, hang on a minute… The front tire was flat too. With a tightening in his stomach, he walked all the way around the car. Fuck!

They were all the same. All four tires deflated.

Stooping to inspect the first wheel, he knew what he would find. They'd been slashed. A clean, inch-wide puncture in every tire. *Bastards!*

Who might have done it? No one obvious came to mind. It could be anyone. In a job like his, there was no way of knowing who you had pissed off. A disgruntled client was the obvious guess, but maybe not. He defended plenty of criminals, and there were always victims and relatives on the other side of the case who blamed the lawyers for the perceived injustice. Or it could be the opposite party in a divorce case. And just because it was his car didn't mean it was a personal attack on him. It could be a grudge against the firm or any one of their lawyers and his vehicle just happened to be the only one left at the end of the day.

There was no CCTV on the car park either, so slim chance of ever finding the culprits.

It must have happened recently, though. Between the others leaving and him coming out. Some people just couldn't help being bad.

*What a pain in the ass.*

Matt headed to the police station on foot. He would report it when he got there. There wasn't much else he could do.

Gary Draper was waiting at the door when he arrived. He had come straight from work. In his suit and tie, he looked a lot more together than when he had been interviewed the previous week.

"I didn't want to go in on my own," he said, stubbing out a cigarette. "Will they put me in a cell again?"

"Unlikely," Matt answered him. "Try not to worry."

"Easier said than done." He popped a mint into his mouth and followed Matt into the station. "I've thought about nothing else all week."

They signed in and were directed to a waiting room.

Matt attempted to keep Gary calm, though he was nervous himself. He wouldn't show it but the prospect of seeing Jamie filled him with dread. It wasn't fair. Jamie had no right to be dredging up the past after all this time. It was unprofessional, for both of them. He had to focus on his client, not an ex-boyfriend who refused to let go.

He'd have to speak to him. It was unavoidable. They had to reach a compromise that meant, when moments like this arose, they were able to deal with it professionally. They still had jobs to do. Responsibilities other than themselves.

His anxiety was unfounded. When DS Sophie Talalay came through to speak to them, she was accompanied by a young female officer. Talalay's smile was wide, her manner soft and friendly. Matt knew immediately that Gary was safe. She was over-compensating—being too nice. She had no case.

The Detective Sergeant confirmed it moments later. "Mr. Draper, I'm happy to inform you that Mrs. Smith has withdrawn all allegations against you, and after investigation, I can confirm that there will be no further action in this case.

Gary stared at her, open mouthed. "What does that mean?"

"It means you're free to go. The case is closed."

He looked at Matt and then at DS Talalay. "I don't get it. I've been accused of rape. And now you say it's over. Just like that?"

"That's right. All the allegations against you have been withdrawn."

"So Victoria is now saying I didn't rape her? That we did have sex and she did consent to it?"

"That's right."

"And she lied about me. She told an absolute lie, accused me of a despicable crime—one of the very worst—and that's it. She can get away with that?"

"This case is over, Mr. Draper." Talalay was already heading out of the door. "Go home and forget about it."

Alone again, Gary looked at Matt, his face dejected. "They're going to let her get away with that? What's to stop her saying something else about me? Or some other poor guy? All my friends know what I was arrested for. My family. Everyone is talking about it. You know what they say—'No smoke without fire.' How can she get away with that?"

"They won't prosecute her unless you make a complaint."

"What will happen then?"

"Well, she could be charged with perverting the course of justice."

"What does that mean?"

"If found guilty, she could go to prison. More likely she would get probation."

"Then I want to make a complaint. I don't want that bitch getting away with this. She'll do it again if no one challenges her."

Gary was angry. Understandably. Matt persuaded him to do nothing right away. "Go home and relax. You've had a terrible week. You need time to come down from that. Give yourself a few days to take it in. If you feel the same way after that, come see me at the office and I'll talk you through your options."

After calming Gary down and sending him on his way, Matt went to the front desk to report the criminal damage to his car. It was merely a formality, for his insurance claim as much as anything. They were never going to catch who was responsible. But it was better to have the incident logged in case of further damage.

Finally done, tired and hungry, he called a taxi and headed home. At least he would still see Dale tonight, which was something to look forward to.

The phone was ringing as he entered the house. Instinctively he answered, regretting the decision straight away.

"It's me, Jamie. Are you all right? I heard you filed a report about your car."

Good news had a way of getting around.

"I'm fine. It was the car that got damaged, not me. Look, Jamie, I appreciate your concern and all that, but I just walked through the door. I'm tired. I haven't eaten yet." He kept his voice calm. Better to get rid of him gently. The last thing he wanted now was a fight.

"I just wanted to know you were all right. We might be finished but that doesn't mean I stopped caring about you."

"I know." He sighed. His determination to keep Jamie at arm's length was weakening. He didn't have it in him. "Where were you tonight? Sophie Talalay did the follow-up interview on Gary Draper."

"I'm in the city. Seconded to MIT to investigate the murders."

"Congratulations." His enthusiasm was muted. It was the promotion Jamie had always wanted but if Matt gave him too much encouragement he would exploit it. "I really need to go now."

"Wait. Matt, I just want to say something."

*Oh no, here it is again.* "Jamie, don't."

"It's not what you think. I want to tell you to be careful. These murders we're investigating, well, both of the victims were gay and it's looking like the most obvious connection between them. Someone is preying on young gay guys. We don't know how he chooses them or why. Until we do, I just want you to take care."

"I will."

"I mean it. Don't take any risks with strangers."

"You know I'm not like that," Matt said. He knew what Jamie was doing. Trying to control him through fear. It wouldn't work. "Good night, Jamie."

"I don't want yours to be the next body we fish out of the river."

*Enough.* Matt hung up.

# Chapter Eleven

There was no time to go home and change after the shoot. Dale didn't wrap until after seven. If he went home he would not be back for the press party. Not that he wanted to be there, the pull of seeing Matt was too strong. But the directive to all major cast and crew members was very clear—attendance was mandatory.

And that was okay for those staying at the hotel. They could go back to their rooms and freshen up. Dale didn't have that luxury. He showered in his trailer and the wardrobe department arranged for him to borrow some clothes for the night. Dark jeans, a gray jersey and a sports jacket. Everything in his size. Not bad. It was better than wearing the rumpled sweatpants and T-shirt he had arrived in that morning. Boy, that seemed a long time ago.

He considered leaving his car at the studio and taking a taxi to the hotel so he could have a drink. But that would make it difficult to get away easily and find his way to Matt's place. The freedom of a quick getaway was worth the aggravation of a sober evening. He could kill for a drink, but seeing Matt was so much more important.

The party was already swinging when he arrived. The function room was full while smartly dressed waiters catered to the needs of the crowd with trays of champagne and canapés. Dale suddenly realized he hadn't eaten since noon and was starving. He grabbed a napkin from a passing waiter and loaded it with mounds of unsatisfying bites.

He was stuffing them into his mouth when Edward, Johan Turner's odious assistant, took hold of his elbow.

"Finally, you're here. Good. Come this way. Johan will

introduce you to Ms. Rank."

Dale resisted his clawed hand. "Can I finish eating first?" He shoved two more canapés into his mouth. They were dry and difficult to swallow. He should have stopped for food on the way here.

Edward folded his arms and watched him disapprovingly. The assistant had squeezed his chubby figure into tight black trousers and a pillar-box red shirt, which stretched unflatteringly across his man boobs. It was profoundly unattractive. Dale found it hard to look at anything other than his squidgy rack.

With some effort, he swallowed the last mouthful. "All right," he said. "Take me to court."

"Huh?"

"Never mind. After you."

Keeley Rank was a short woman in her early fifties. Her hair, a mixture of severe blonde and scrappy roots, had been teased into a huge nest around her head. If the look she was aiming for was 1980s rock chick dragged through a bush backward—she had totally nailed it. Her powdery makeup failed to conceal a crêpey top lip and soft jowls.

Surrounded by Johan, Nicola Donahue, Russell Jones and a group of nodding yes-men, she was the queen bee surrounded by her swarm.

Johan, spotting Dale's arrival, bustled forward. "Here he is," he sing-songed loudly. "Dale Zachary, our American stud. Isn't he gorgeous? Be careful with him, Keeley. He's a real lady killer, this one."

Dale shot the writer a filthy look. What the hell was he playing at? Presenting him like a piece of meat. Maybe Elton had the right idea about this asshole. There wasn't much to like about him.

Keeley considered him with cool gray eyes and extended a bejeweled hand. "Keeley Rank."

She presented the back of her hand, as though she expected him to kiss it. Dale took it in a firm grip, turned it over and gave her a traditional handshake. "Glad to meet you. Your arrival has caused quite a stir."

She returned a weak smile. "When Johan told me what was happening here, I just had to come up and find out for myself. Pitchforks and flaming torches." She laughed at her own joke. "You really have pissed off the yokels. I do love *the North*. So earthy and basic. It's like another country. Another era. Talk about stepping back in time."

"It *is* another country for me," he said, successfully keeping the edge from his voice. "A really beautiful country."

"Really? Since your ex-wife returned to the UK it seems you spend more time here than in the States these days. Isn't this your home now?"

He didn't rise to the bait. "I'm an actor. Home is where I find work. I try to see the best of everything, whereever I go. Places, people, culture. Approach it without prejudice and you'll see Durham is as beautiful as anywhere else."

"Except you won't find angry mobs at the gates of Pinewood," she said smartly.

"Oh, I don't know. When you travel as widely as I have you see that anger gets into most places, if people let it."

"A philosopher, eh? I'm going to enjoy finding out all about you, Dale."

"I thought the whole point of your visit was to highlight the hard work and good intent of this amazing crew."

Keeley sipped her champagne. "It is. But I'm a journalist first. I report the stories as I find them. How about I do an in-depth interview and feature on you? I'm sure it will be something special. All the tales *you* could tell."

Dale felt nervous under her merciless gaze. He didn't do personal interviews. He was an actor. Not a celebrity. Exposing his secrets to the pen of a tawdry tabloid journalist—nothing in his contract said he had to go for that. He would do this to promote the show but personal stuff was off limits. "There are far more interesting people to write about than me. Roxanne, for instance. She is the star after all."

"*Roxanne.*" Keeley threw back her head in an exaggerated

laugh. "No one wants to read about her. We're heard it all before. But you—you're new. You're fresh. You're exactly what we want."

Johan grinned inanely and nodded at every word she said. Dale wondered whether he was wired. There was a coked-up look in his eyes. "Yes, Dale is a real angle for your story. Your readers are going to love him. I'll make sure you two get plenty of time together."

Dale gave him a dangerous look. *That's what you think, asshole.*

First thing tomorrow, he would speak to the producers, Elton, his agent if he had to. No way was he granting any kind of personal interview to this pen-pushing piranha.

Edward returned, this time with Adrian Nelson in his vise-like grip. As the other actor was pushed forward to meet the journalist, Dale took the opportunity to step away and take Russell Jones aside.

"How long is she staying?"

"Till Thursday. Friday maybe. I'm not sure," the producer said. "Most of the week. It depends how it goes. If the protests die down she might get bored and leave."

"You're out of order, you know," Dale said. "Thinking you can turn me over to her. I'm not selling my private life to save the show."

"You're contractually obliged to carry out promotional work."

"I've got no problem promoting the show. *The show.* Not me."

"Dale, please." Russell put a hand on his forearm. "You know how bad this situation has got. Our show will be dead on arrival if we don't do something to turn the tide of publicity. We need a break. Just play along for a few days, please."

"You're selling me out."

"No, not a bit. You've been around. You know how this shit works. Just throw Keeley a few tidbits. Make it up if you want to, but please give her something."

Dale sighed. He didn't like it. He hated it. But he would play the game. For a while at least.

* * * *

Aaron Oxford watched from across the room. Dale was trapped in the inner sanctum with Johan, the producers and the visiting journalist. Drones like him wouldn't be invited to that scene. He was here to make up the numbers and fill the room. He didn't mind so much. Not if it meant he could get close to Dale, away from the studio.

Dale had been distant with him for over a week now. He was uptight and aloof. Hopefully this party and a few drinks would loosen him up and help them get back to where they were before.

It had started so well. Aaron had fancied Dale the first time he saw him. God, who wouldn't? The man was to die for. He had a great look—the all-American boy grown up to be one fucking hot daddy. And with the beard he had grown for the show... *Woof.*

Aaron had sensed Dale was on his side as soon as they met. He'd read his IMDb profile. He'd known all about his marriage and divorce, his kid. But a deeper trawl of the forums had turned up the rumors. Suggestions that the hunky actor was more interested in guys than girls. Though he'd checked them all of course, Aaron had taken the stories with a grain of salt. Read the IMDb forums for any sexy, remotely successful actor and the gay question always appeared on the first couple of pages.

But when they had been introduced at the rehearsal studio in London, Aaron *had known* the stories about Dale were more than rumor. His body language, his smile, the way his gaze lingered for a fraction too long. Telltale signs, imperceptible to anyone not looking for them, but a sure giveaway to anyone in the know. Aaron's gaydar had never been wrong.

He was not in the habit of seducing actors on the shows

he worked on. There had been the odd short-lived traveling affair but nothing as major as blowing the star. The more time he had spent alone with Dale, Aaron had got a sense that Dale wanted it as much as he. And he had been right. It had been the briefest of seductions. Three days into shooting and Dale was his.

There was nothing like it. Taking a man in your mouth. Rendering him helpless. Feeling his body react, listening to his desperate breathing, taking him to the ultimate release. Aaron prided himself on his skill. Untroubled by a gag reflex, he could deep throat without effort. He gave the very best blow jobs.

Everybody said so.

No teeth. No hands. He could get a man off with the skill of his mouth alone.

Dale hadn't been able to get enough in the beginning. Aaron had offered to mix it up, making his juicy ass available, but it was his blow jobs that had driven Dale crazy.

Maybe it was stress-related. Or guilt—not uncommon with sexually confused guys—but Dale had gone cold on him lately.

Not for much longer. It had been over a week. Aaron needed cock and he needed it tonight. One way or another, Dale would give up that hot ejaculate.

"God, is there nothing decent to eat?" asked Jess, the wardrobe assistant, as she knocked back her third glass of champagne. "They force us to come to this butt-kissing party but don't bother to cater for the little people."

"Looks that way," Aaron said.

The waiters with the canapés attentively circled the upper echelons of the company but didn't come near the unimportant people.

"Let's get out of here," Jess said. "We've done our duty and put in an appearance. I want a pizza. There's an Italian place five minutes from here. What do you say?"

The rest of the group nodded in agreement.

"This will be done by nine," Aaron said. "We should wait."

"Stuff that. I've got to be up at five-thirty. I want food and an early night."

Aaron helped himself to a fresh glass of champagne. His fourth. "Go ahead. I might catch you up later. I'm not really hungry yet and, you know... Free booze."

Jess and a group of ten left him alone. Aaron didn't mind. He could hardly make a move on Dale with that lot around. Discretion was key with the closeted types.

He bided his time around the edge of the party, never letting Dale out of his sight, careful not to get drawn into another group of colleagues.

Time moved slowly. Dale looked as bored as Aaron felt. Roxanne and Elton had yet to put in an appearance, so Johan and Edward guarded Dale, not letting him wander too far from their cherished reporter, dragging him back into her orbit whenever he looked as if he were making an escape.

Aaron was happy just watching. It had been a long time since he'd fancied a man as much as this. Dale was perfect. Ridiculously handsome and funny, with a lovely big dick and meaty ass. Aaron had to be careful. He wouldn't fall in love, tempting as that was. Falling for Dale, an actor with a ton of emotional baggage, could lead to a lot of heartache.

But if they kept it light, fuck buddies with a bit of spice... The end of *Blood Falls on Stone* was being kept open. If the show was a hit, they would all be back to film a second series. Who knew where their on-set romance could go from there?

And if it didn't develop, the sex alone made it worth the effort.

Patience finally paid off. Roxanne Maxwell and Elton Weaver made a grand entrance together. Roxanne looked amazing. She had really gone to town with the glamour. Big hair, overstated makeup, a dress that showed plenty of bronzed and toned flesh. For a woman approaching fifty, she was an absolute knockout.

The entire room stopped to watch, then burst into rapturous applause. Even Aaron was entranced, taking his eyes off Dale to cheer the leading lady. This party had been all about the journalist Keeley Rank. Not anymore.

Roxanne, often so aloof on the set, greeted runners and third assistants like her dearest friends. Smiling beatifically, she crossed the room, shaking hands, flashing jewelery. The photographer assigned to accompany Keeley rushed forward then began to walk backward in front of Roxanne, cameras flashing to capture every moment. It was some spectacle.

Dale took advantage of the distraction to slip from Johan's grip and head to the men's room.

At last it was Aaron's chance.

Dale was at the urinal when he followed him in. He went right up beside him. "I was beginning to forget what that thing looked like," he said, staring at Dale's pissing cock.

Dale started. "Jesus, Aaron." He shook and shoved his dick back into his pants.

Not the reaction Aaron had hoped for. "You should relax. You look tense."

"I could do without all this," Dale said, washing his hands. "I feel like I've been pimped out to the press."

"Roxanne is here now, so relax. She's a natural at this kind of thing. You saw how she came in. No one will notice if you and me slip away. What do you say? Back to your place? It'll be nice to do it somewhere other than your funky little trailer."

Dale shook his head. "Don't you get it? That's not going to happen. Nothing else is ever going to happen between us."

"Why not? I give great blow jobs. You said so yourself."
"No."

"C'mon, Dale. I'm damn horny. Slip me some meat. I want you to fuck me."
"Forget it."

Dale headed to the door. Aaron beat him to it, blocking his exit. "Why not? You were all over me a week ago. What changed?"

Dale looked him straight in the eye. His mouth was set in a tight, angry line.

"C'mon," Aaron pleaded. "What did I do to piss you off? I know you enjoyed the things we did. Why are you being so cold to me now?" It took a lot of restraint not to grab Dale right then. To force a kiss upon him and prove just how hot he was.

Dale closed his eyes and took a deep breath. "I've met someone else, okay? It's nothing you have or haven't done. The truth of the matter is I've met someone and I really want to give it a go. So that means no cheeky blow jobs or whatever else you had in mind."

Aaron looked at him incredulously. "Who is it?"

"Nobody you know."

"It's Mike from carpentry, isn't it? I knew he'd been making a move in your direction."

"What? No. *Mike?* Of course not. It's no one involved in the show. You really don't know him. He has nothing to do with the industry. Aaron, you're a great guy and you do give incredible head. In other circumstances, I'd accept your offer in a heartbeat, but not anymore. I want to give this my best shot."

Aaron slowly deflated, accepting defeat. "When did you meet this guy?"

"Last week. It's early days."

"Monday?"

Dale nodded.

"That makes sense." Aaron sighed, stepping away from the door. "It was after Monday that you started to go cold on me. Okay. I won't push it. Good luck. Tell him he's a lucky man."

"No, I'm the lucky one," Dale said as he left.

*Shit!* He felt like an idiot now, making his stupid passes. Why hadn't Dale said something before, instead of letting him play up like this? Despite what people sometimes thought about him, Aaron always had complete respect for other people's relationships. He wouldn't have interfered with that, however much he wanted Dale.

He wondered who the other man was, this rival. Someone young and gorgeous no doubt. The very best. Aaron wouldn't be able to compete, however great his blow jobs were.

There was nothing else for it. He would forget about Dale. Get drunk and find someone else to blow.

It was a short-term solution but better than nothing.

* * * *

Dale's plans for an early exit came to nothing. Johan Turner intended to wring every ounce of publicity from the paid talent. The photos seemed to go on forever. It was worse than a wedding — solo portraits, two shots with Keeley, group photos and every variation in between. With Elton already steaming drunk and Roxanne well on her way to joining him, he began to regret his decision to stay sober and drive.

It was almost ten. Damn it. Next time Johan took his beady eyes off him, he was out of there. He wanted to be with Matt. More than ever. All of this was bullshit. Unnecessary bullshit. If they had only taken charge of the situation last week and put out an appropriate statement then.

Keeley Rank made him uncomfortable. She was a crazy lady and kind of creepy.

It may be paranoia, but she spent a lot of time looking his way. Not in an obvious way either, kind of slyly. Like a cat with the canary in its sights.

Roxanne's words came back to him. *'I just hope you don't have any secrets in your closet.'*

Was that a direct warning?

Dale wasn't out to anyone in the crew. Not officially anyway. There was Aaron, but that was a private matter.

As an actor, he wasn't out at all. He didn't want to be. There were rumors, he'd heard them all but said nothing to confirm his sexuality.

Except that wasn't true either. He played up the fact that he'd once been married, that he was a dad. Suggesting, without ever saying as much, that these gay rumors were nothing more than bitchy gossip. He couldn't afford to be an out actor. Maybe if he was more famous, or acclaimed for his acting rather than his looks, he could take the risk. But when the bulk of his work came from playing heroes and boyfriends, he couldn't be a fag actor.

Rightly or wrongly, he *was* a closet case. And that was how it had to stay, at least for now.

He should find out more about Keeley Rank. Was she a serious journalist or a gossip hound? *Know your enemy.*

He saw Aaron across the room. He was with some of the other production assistants. He looked as if he were getting steadily drunk, along with everyone else. At least he'd had the good sense to come on to him in the privacy of the bathroom and not here in front of everyone.

But how much could he trust him? What if he decided to get his own back and tell everyone what they used to do in his trailer? And he'd just confessed to being serious about another man. How much would Keeley pay for *that* exclusive? God, what an idiot. Could Aaron be trusted? He barely knew him. He'd been careless this time and allowed his dick to get the better of his brain.

Roxanne left the group that had gathered around Keeley and sauntered to the bar. Dale followed.

"She's quite something, this Keeley," he said, coming up behind her.

"*Something?* Oh, she's that all right." Roxanne signaled the waiter and ordered a large vodka and tonic.

"Still not a fan?"

She licked her glossy lips. "I can't stand the woman. But that's all right because she detests me. I can't believe they were stupid enough to bring her on board. As if we weren't in deep enough shit already."

"Why does she hate you so much? Have the two of you got history?"

"No. She hates me because I'm a woman. And a successful one. There's no sisterly solidarity with her. Other women are the enemy. All women."

"I can't say I got the warmest reception from her myself."

Roxanne dramatically closed and opened her long lashes. "You're a handsome man, Dale. If you can muster a hard-on to fuck her with, you might do all right. She'll go easy on you. You might even come out of it okay when she writes her story. But if not..." She mimed a bullet to the head.

"Now I'm worried."

"You should be. That article she wrote about my play — complete character assassination. Not just me. The director, writer, my co-stars — she trashed us all. Affairs, drink, drugs, attitude, there was nothing that didn't make it into print."

"Fuck, the worst kind of hack."

Roxanne laughed softly. "She gives hacks a bad name. Most of them would be mortified by the comparison."

"Why the hell did Johan invite her?" he asked angrily.

The waiter brought Roxanne's vodka. She took a long, grateful drink. "For some bizarre reason they seem to like each other. I don't know why. I can tell you right now how her article will go. She'll dish the shit on all of us, then conclude by saying that, despite all of our failings, and incompetences, the strength of Johan's writing means that we've still managed to produce a great series. But how much *better* it would be if they had cast Rosamund Pike and John Hamm instead of us. She'll spread it over eight pages or so, but that is basically what she'll say."

Dale laughed bitterly. "So we're fucked."

She shrugged. "Who gives a shit? She's tried to stitch me up so many times in print. It hasn't done me any harm. No one really takes any notice of her columns — only those in them. *Sweet Bird* was a hit at the box office, despite what she wrote. It might not seem that way now but we're making a good television show. I know it. I've got a sense for these things. I've acted in real crap before and I know this isn't it. The elitists who take any notice of Keeley's column don't watch this kind of TV. She won't harm our ratings in any way. Trust me."

Dale was reassured but it didn't stop him worrying. Maybe Keeley couldn't do much to harm the fortunes of the show but she could sure as shit do some damage to his reputation. To his career. He would have to play her very carefully.

"Have a drink. Relax," Roxanne said. "You look like you're at a funeral."

"I just want to get out of here. I might make a move now. Where is Johan?"

Roxanne glanced over her shoulder. "Still kissing Keeley's arse. You know, I've often wondered about him."

"Johan?"

"Hmm. He's fruitier than a fruit cake, and I know he's a fan of the cock, but even still... I don't think he's sniffing round Keeley's fanny for the good of the show. There *could* be something going on between them."

"Johan and Keeley? No way."

"It's a ghastly idea, I know. And once you've got the image on them going at it in your mind, you can't get rid of it. But I don't think it's that far-fetched, do you? He's a funny one. They both are."

"You're right." He laughed. "That's not a picture I want in my head. On that note, I think I will split." He leaned in to kiss her cheek. "I'll see you tomorrow."

Roxanne put two very strong hands on his waist.

"Don't rush away so quickly," she said.

"I really need to go."

She moved in closer, moving that tight body of her against his, pushing her tits against his chest. "Don't you think it's time we got to know each other a little better?" She swayed her hips against his.

*Oh God. Please tell me this isn't happening. What's got into everyone tonight?*

"I'm staying right here in the hotel," she drawled. "Why don't we go up to my suite and get better acquainted? You've got a mighty fine arse that I'm just dying to see in the flesh."

"Roxanne, stop." He tried to remove her hands but her grip was tight.

She moved closer, reaching up so her face was close to his. Her warm breath on his face. "C'mon, Dale. Don't be so shy. I like to screw all my leading men."

Her lips covered his and she shoved her tongue into his mouth. *What the fuck is happening?*

There was a sudden flash and the awful realization that Roxanne's stolen kiss had just been caught on camera.

*Could this nightmare evening get any worse?*

# Chapter Twelve

"You interfering bastard." Brian 'Lugz' Mosley was waiting on the steps of the courthouse when Matt came out. Lugz was a six-and-half-foot wall of muscle, fat and attitude—bad attitude. He had a large football-shaped head with Toby jug ears and no discernible neck, just a colossal set of shoulders. A serpentine tattoo slithered from the open neck of his shirt to twist around his left ear. His face was distorted into a mask of demonic rage.

Matt was in trouble.

It had been an arduous morning in Crown Court. He had been defending Akram Khan, a post office manager. Akram's wife had been working on the counter of their family business when Luke Mosley, the seventeen-year-old son of Lugz, had held up the counter with a large ax. Akram had come to the assistance of his wife, tackling the teenager to the floor while getting in a few well-placed punches, breaking Luke's nose and two of his ribs in the struggle.

As well as an assault conviction for the post office manager, the Mosley family was hoping to claim a hefty compensation payout. It wasn't to be. At this morning's plea and directions hearing, ahead of a trial, Matt and Devon Morris, the barrister acting on their behalf, had managed to convince the judge that there was no case to answer against Akram Khan.

His case had been dismissed while the trial of Luke Mosley for aggravated robbery would go ahead regardless.

Matt, in a hurry to get back to the office and prepare his next case, thought nothing of leaving the court on his own. A big mistake.

Lugz's bald head was red with anger, his huge ears, one of which had a partially chewed lobe, was even more livid. "*You Paki-loving bastard.*" He came closer, clenching his tattooed fists. "No fucking case to answer. No case to answer. Did you see the state of my boy when that Paki bastard had finished with him?"

"Mr. Khan was acting in self-defense. Luke held up his store and threatened his wife. With an ax!"

"The dole had sanctioned his benefits. He had no money. What was he supposed to do? He was desperate."

On the day of the robbery Luke Mosley had been desperate all right. For a fix. The seventeen year old had huge drug debts — heroine, amphetamine, cannabis — most of which were owed to his own father and his associates. Lugz was one of the biggest dealers in the area. The beatings he had dealt his son in the past for failing to pay up made Akram Khan's assault look like slap and tickle.

"It's over, Brian. Case dismissed." The dealer took a menacing step toward Matt.

"Over? Nothing is over. Not for you or that Paki scum you represent."

Matt had heard threats like this before. They were nothing new, just part of the job. But with a hulk like Lugz in your face, threatening to do some damage, you had to take it seriously.

He took a step back toward the door. It was time to involve security. And prevent Akram Khan, and his wife Feeza, from coming out the same way.

"Don't walk away from me, you cunt." Lugz suddenly lunged at him.

Matt had speed and agility on his side. He was through the door and into the court foyer before Lugz reached the top step. Two uniformed security guards stood beside the body scanners. Beyond them, the waiting room was full of defendants, their relatives and lawyers, waiting for their cases to be called. All heads turned toward the commotion.

The guards were quick to recognize Matt and realize

what was happening. One was already on his radio, calling for back up, while the other let him straight through the gate, before closing it again.

"Get outta my way, you fuckers," Lugz Moseley roared.

Matt turned in time to see him strike one of the guards straight in the face. The second guard tried to tackle him but Lugz brushed him aside like a five year old. Across the waiting room, Matt spotted Mr. and Mrs. Khan and waved frantically at them to stay back. The sight of them would only infuriate the drug dealer and send the situation further out of control.

Black-uniformed reinforcements came pouring out from the courtrooms. Lugz was big but he was no match for their numbers. He shouted and swore but soon he was down and cuffed.

Matt jumped as a hand was placed on his shoulder. It was Danny Frost.

"Are you okay?" The lawyer's eyes were full of concern.

Matt slumped, suddenly relieved and grateful to see a friendly face. "Shit, Danny. Yes, it was hairy for a moment there."

Danny put a hand on the small of his back and led him toward a bench. "You're ghostly white. C'mon, sit down. You've had a shock."

Lugz Mosley was marched out of the foyer, toward the holding cells.

"Get off me, you twats. I know where you all live. I'll find you. Fuck your wife. Fuck your kids. I'll break your kneecaps. *You cunts.*"

The doors closed behind him, though they could still hear his poisonous rants, slowly growing distant.

Danny brought him a coffee from the vending machine. "I know you don't take sugar but I got you one loaded with it. Drink it, you need it for the shock." He sat beside him. "Feeling okay? God, Matt, that was a lucky escape."

Matt nodded, sipping the hot, sweet drink. If Lugz had had the brains to tackle him away from the courthouse, the outcome would have been very different. His car was in the garage today, being fitted for new tires and he had come to court on foot. Lugz could have attacked him at any point on the route and there'd have been no security to help him.

"Could he have been the one to trash your car?" Danny asked when Matt told him about the slashed tires.

"Maybe, I don't know. Why would he bother? The damage was done last night, but at that stage none of us knew the judge was going to throw out the case. The Mosleys thought they were in for a nice compensation payout."

"Someone has it in for you. You really know how to make friends and influence people."

Matt laughed. It sounded flat. "It's not funny. But if I didn't laugh…"

"You would go crazy."

"Already there. Thanks, Danny."

Matt's hope of an early exit were dashed. One of the security guards came over to tell him the police were on their way. They wanted him to wait until they arrived and make a statement. He called the office to let them know what was happening and that he wouldn't be back for a while. By the time he finished the coffee Danny had bought, he felt a lot better, despite the sugar coating it left in his mouth. He went to the vending machine to get another, minus the sugar this time.

There was a discarded newspaper on one of the waiting room tables. A photograph caught his eye. It was Dale — on the front page. One of his smiling, staged publicity photos. The production on Dale's show seemed like a never-ending saga. What was it now? He picked up and unfolded the paper.

*Kissing Co-Stars* exclaimed a bold headline. Beneath there was a new photograph. Dale and Roxanne were locked at the lips. It was a blurred paparazzi-style picture rather than a staged publicity shot. Roxanne had a diamond-decked hand on the back of Dale's head, pulling him into the kiss.

He scanned the article. The photograph had been taken

last night, at the production party Dale attended before coming to his place. *'The party was boring,'* Dale had told him. It didn't look that way.

*Sexy co-stars Roxanne Maxwell and Dale Zachary can't keep their hands off each other,* the article boasted. *Maneater Roxanne, forty-seven, currently filming the controversial serial killer series, was all over the American hunk at a reception in Durham. Sources from the set say that Dale, thirty-four, is smitten with his foxy leading lady. If these two can steam up the screen in the same way they steamed up the party, then we're all in for a treat when the series airs later this year.*

*What the fuck!* Red heat rose from Matt's chest, creeping up his neck and envelope his face. What the hell was going on? Dale had said nothing about this. The article was full of hype and speculation – probably all made up – but there was no way he could ignore that photograph. Fuck, look at their mouths. That was a proper French kiss with tongues.

Matt was overwhelmed by emotions. Anger. Disappointment. He read the story again and a sense of hurt replaced his fury. Was any of it true? Was Dale stringing him along? Using him for a convenient fuck, when he couldn't be with his glamorous co-star? The story in the paper was plausible enough. They had been at that party together.

Dale said he had no interest in women. Could he believe that? The photo told a different story.

Matt felt desolate. He'd been drawn into an intimate relationship with a man he didn't know at all. Jumped in with both feet. Had he made a stupid mistake?

\* \* \* \*

If the purpose of Keeley Rank's presence was to bring a sense of hope and optimism to the set, then the opposite had been achieved. On Tuesday, Dale was more unsettled than ever. Keeley lurked around the old building. When she wasn't trying to ingratiate herself with members of the crew, she was out front talking to the protestors, whose numbers had at least diminished.

Last night's party had had an unsettling effect on the cast too. Roxanne was pissed at him over the knock back he gave her. Though she'd latched on tight for that damn kiss, he'd eventually managed to break her hold and told her very clearly that he wasn't going to join the list of guys she toyed with on location.

Unfortunately, that was not borne out in today's newspapers. Several of them had run the photo of the kiss, together with stories of their torrid behind-the-scenes affair. Dale had been oblivious to the headlines until mid-morning, when an assistant director had shown him one of the offending front pages. His blood boiled. Damn. He had to pay more attention to these frigging papers.

"Have you seen this?"

Roxanne was having her makeup retouched at the side of the set. She barely glanced at the paper and her expression didn't change. "Yes."

"And it doesn't bother you? It doesn't piss you off? It's bullshit."

"It's publicity. People are talking about us. We're trending online. It's good for the show."

He couldn't believe what he was hearing. "Mismanaged publicity got us those crowds at the gate."

She raised a weary brow. "And now they have something else to write about. Surely this is better than associating the show with the murders? Give the press a bit of spice and all that other stuff will go away."

Was he hearing this right? *A bit of spice.* "Did you engineer this?" He waved the photo of their kiss in her face.

"No, Dale, I didn't engineer it. But I'm not sorry about it. So what if it's not true? We can still use it to our advantage. It's show business. Don't be so naive."

He was called for his next scene. There was no time to get a message to Jack or Matt. He didn't want either of them seeing these crappy stories before he had a chance to warn them. Neither would believe what the press were saying, but he'd feel better about it if they heard it from him.

The morning was a drag. A lot of the crew were nursing hangovers from last night. Work-night parties were never a good idea. Aaron hadn't even made it in yet. Dale hoped it was because he'd had too much to drink and not because of their confrontation in the bathroom. Aaron had nothing to be embarrassed about. Dale took full responsibility for their brief affair, but it was over now. They had to put it behind them.

When lunch was finally called, he hurried to his trailer to retrieve his phone. He keyed in a brief message that he copied to Jack and Matt.

*Take no notice of the stories in today's press. I am NOT involved with Roxanne M.*

Surely Matt was sensible enough to realize the story, despite the corresponding photo, was crap. Then again... Matt was so removed from this crazy world, maybe he didn't understand the way it worked. Roxanne's attitude was pretty standard within the industry. There was no such thing as bad publicity. They knew well enough that the papers would write about someone else in a few days' time. Hot stories soon became old.

But, to an outsider, maybe that entire concept sounded as ridiculous as it was. From Matt's point of view, his boyfriend was on the front pages kissing a woman. For a regular guy, that was a pretty irregular situation to be in.

Dale picked up his phone again and dialed Matt's number. It went straight to voice mail.

"Hey," he said to the answered phone. "You might have seen the papers today. I just want to let you know you have nothing to worry about. Roxanne kissed me at the party and that one photo is all that kiss amounts to. There's no affair, no on-set liaison, nothing. I'll tell you all about it later. I'll pick up a takeaway and see you around eight. Okay? Don't worry about this. I love you."

*I love you.*

The words came out of his mouth before he even knew he was saying them. *I love you.* Holy shit. He'd said it out loud. And it was true. God damn him if it wasn't.

He suddenly felt light inside. He was in love with Matt Blyth. Why'd he have to say it for the first time to a fucking answering machine? *Idiot.*

Still, he *had* said it. The words were out there. Dale laughed nervously. He just hoped Matt felt the same.

\* \* \* \*

Jamie bought the coffee while his new partner, Detective Constable Shona Long, went outside to take a call from HQ. Unlike him, Shona was a permanent member of the MIT. A fact Jamie had yet to get over. It wasn't anything she had said, done or even implied, to make him feel like a spare part of the team, it was just the way it was. He was one of a number of officers seconded to the unit, but those placements would be short-lived. When the case grew cold and the budget tightened, they would go back to where they came from.

Jamie had a very short window of opportunity to make an impression. That window would close soon. He had to shine before it did.

The only problem was he couldn't stand his partner.

Shona was in her early forties. Tall and slender with shiny auburn hair. She wore trouser suits and expensive silk blouses, and despite her glossy appearance, she might as well have had *Fuck You* tattooed across her forehead. Getting ahead in the police force was as tough for women as it was for queers. Shona came from a common breed of policewoman. There were women like her in every station he'd worked at. Dressed to the nines with a mouthy attitude. They swore louder and talked dirtier than any of the men. He didn't blame her for the chip on her shoulder. He carried a bigger chip of his own. Shona had fought, bitched, clawed, fucked and ass-kissed to get to where she was. Jamie was prepared to do all that and more to join her there. Permanently.

Shona, he knew instinctively, was not a team player. She would use anyone, steal their ideas and initiative to make herself looked good.

He carried the coffees over to the floor-to-ceiling glass front where he could keep an eye on her while scoping the large open car park. The coffee shop was located on an out-of-town industrial and shopping estate. Warehouses and factories nestled side by side with designer outlets and home furniture stores.

Shona, still on her phone outside, tossed her hair and laughed. In his personal life, he'd run a mile from her. She was not the kind of bitch he could ever be friends with. Her career was her best friend already, and she would tear down anyone who got in the way of it. But she also had the ear of his new boss, DCI Redgraves, which made her someone to keep on the right side of.

That was how police promotion worked. Fuck merit. It was all about who you knew and what you could do for each other.

At his first briefing on the team, before they were even paired together, he noticed the rapport Shona had with the boss. Her devotion to him crossed the fine line of respect and ass kissing but while her banter with the boss made Jamie cringe, Redgraves appeared to appreciate it. Because of that, Jamie was quietly delighted when instructed to accompany her on this afternoon's investigation.

He caught sight of a silver BMW pulling into the car park. Its plate was obscured by other vehicles but Shona immediately terminated her call and jerked her head for him to join her. They were on.

"Triple shot cappuccino with Sweet'N Low," he said, handing her the takeaway cup.

She took it without thanking him. "Our guy has just arrived."

"I saw that," Jamie said. "So how are we going to do this?"

"Save it for Grindr, pretty boy." She laughed unpleasantly. "Guys like you are what got him into this mess. You'd better leave it to me."

Bigoted bitch.

The man who got out of the BMW wore a dark gray suit. The color suited his grim expression. He was in his late twenties with a pleasant but unmemorable face, short blond hair that was going thin on top. Despite the ignorance of idiots like Shona, not all gays had an uncontrollable attraction to every guy they met. He could appreciate the man wasn't bad looking but didn't fancy him.

Especially not with the gold band on his wedding finger.

"Paul Goss?"

The detectives approached, displaying their ID. The man nodded, glancing at the badges before looking nervously around the car park.

"Would you like to do this inside?" Shona jerked a thumb toward the coffee shop.

"No," Paul Goss replied hastily. "I don't want to go anywhere we can be overheard."

"Over here then," Shona said, indicating a grassy area to the side of the building, far away from the outdoor smoking area.

"Are you going to arrest me?" Paul asked, glancing anxiously between them.

"We just want to ask you some questions, that's all." Jamie smiled.

Shona shot him a look. *I do the talking, fuck wit*, it said. "Right now, we're trying to put together a picture of Olly Raymond. His lifestyle. That kind of thing."

"I hardly knew him," Paul said.

"We've got his Internet records," Jamie said, ignoring Shona's deathly stares. "Emails, Facebook. We know that's not true, Paul. You knew him rather well. So let's not waste time. Tell us what your relationship was."

Paul nibbled at a fingernail. "All right. So I did know him, but not that well. We weren't friends or anything like that. We would hook up now and then, nothing more."

"Hook up?" Shona said. "Does that mean sex? I can't keep up with all these queer terms."

Jamie shot her a filthy look. She was trying to get a rise, from him as well as Paul.

"Yes," Paul hissed.

"How often?"

"Once or twice a month, that's all. Since last October. Like I said, we weren't close or anything. I liked him. Olly. He was a really nice guy. Nicer than most I've met."

"What does that mean?"

"He was nice. Just that. He was honest. If he arranged to meet me, he stuck to it. He wouldn't cancel 'cause someone better came along. I...have to be discreet. He appreciated that. He didn't push it or ask too many questions. What we had going on, well it was what it was. An afternoon here, an hour there. I didn't want anything more than that and neither did he."

"Did anyone else know about your...affair?"

"No one."

"What about your wife?" Shona pushed.

"No," Paul snapped. "She doesn't know about *that*. And that's how it's got to stay."

"When did you last see Olly Raymond?" Jamie asked softly. Shona's challenging attitude was going to lose Paul's patience.

"About three weeks ago. We were planning to get together again last week. That was before all this."

"Where did you meet?"

"Grindr."

"No, I mean where did you get together?"

"At his place. I won't take guys home with me, and I don't like hotels. But Olly had his own flat and didn't mind taking me there."

"Did you ever see anyone else at Olly's place?"

"No. He was always alone."

"Did he ever tell you about other guys he was seeing? Or do you think you were the only one?"

"No, of course I wasn't. He saw other guys. Why shouldn't he? He had no ties. He could do what he wanted. It was none of my business. I didn't ask and he didn't tell."

"Tell us about your sex life," Shona said.

Paul blanched. "Why?"

"It's relevant," she insisted. "Did you ever do anything kinky?"

Paul glared at her with undisguised hostility. "What do *you* consider kinky, Detective? Isn't two men fucking enough for you?"

Jamie stared incredulously at his partner. She was behaving like a bull in a china shop. Like a bully from a 1970s cop show. How was this helping anyone?

"I don't like your tone," she continued. "So wind your neck in and answer the question. Did you ever tie him up?"

"No. Nothing like that."

"What about choking? Did you ever tie anything around his neck? A belt? A rope?"

The interview continued in the same, disastrous vein for another ten minutes. Shona pursued an aggressive line of questioning, which to Jamie's way of thinking bordered on harassment. Paul, quite naturally, went on the defensive and answered in monosyllables. It was obvious he had nothing to do with Olly Raymond's death. Unfortunately, on the night of Olly's murder, he had been at home with his wife.

"I'll check out the alibi," he said to Shona when they were in the car, heading to back to the station.

She looked sideways at him with an unpleasant grin on her face. "Afraid I'll upset the little lady? Maybe it will do the poor cow some good to know what her pathetic little man is up to."

"That's not our call," he said firmly. "We can ascertain his alibi without compromising his domestic situation."

She laughed. "What cabbage bush did they find you

under? Listen, soft lad, you need to toughen up and grow a pair if you want to get anywhere in this job. The gentle approach won't cut it. I'm surprised you ever got out of uniform with that limp-wristed attitude."

Jamie bit his tongue. He was equally surprised that Shona's brash approach hadn't taken her right back to the uniformed beat. Today had made him realize something — he would not stoop to her level to get ahead. He would bide his time, then, quietly and carefully, he would stomp all over her.

* * * *

When Dale arrived at Matt's place, laden with takeaway pizza boxes, food was the last thing on either of their minds. They could barely contain themselves, kissing and tearing at their clothes until they reached the bedroom. They fell on top of each other in a passionate heap, limbs entangled, mouths locked, hard cocks dueling.

"I do love you," Dale groaned between fervent kisses. Saying it to Matt's voice mail meant nothing compared to speaking the words directly to him.

Lying beneath him, Matt gripped him tight. "I love you too."

They sealed the deal with their most passionate lovemaking ever. All over the bed, they rolled and clung to each other. Taking turns to fuck, switching it up, both coming twice until they collapsed in a delightfully breathless and sweaty heap.

Dale felt drunk and he hadn't touched a drop. It had been an exhausting day. Sometimes exhilarating, sometimes terrifying. The film set was a pressure cooker already, without the uncertainty of knowing how Matt would react to his declaration on the phone. Not just that, but the ridiculous photo of his kiss with Roxanne and the press stories that accompanied them. But all of his fears were unfounded. When he was in Matt's arms the words came freely. He could say *I love you* without the fear of rejection, knowing he meant it and Matt felt the same.

"Your smooch with Roxanne is all over the net," Matt teased.

Later, they lounged on the living room sofa in just their underpants, bare feet on the coffee table, eating cold pizza and drinking beer.

Matt was checking out the news on his phone.

"It's the top story on *Digital Spy*," he continued with a grin. "And you're all over my Twitter front page."

"Knock it off," Dale said. "I hate all that Internet gossip."

"Surely this must be better than what they were writing last week. They were out to crucify your show. Now they want to hear all about the backstage drama."

"That's what Roxanne said too. But you can't fool the press or the public for long. As soon as they suspect the romance is a sham, the knives will come out again. I don't like any kind of personal publicity. PR for the show is one thing but I don't want it to be about me. When you draw that kind of attention to yourself, people start looking for more."

Matt put down his phone. "Must be hard. Trying to keep that balance."

"You have no idea."

Matt looked at him earnestly. "I have a favor to ask you. I won't be upset if you say no. But my friend Conrad bugs me every day about it. I'll never hear the end of it if I don't ask."

Dale patted his bare thigh. "You can ask me anything you like."

"Conrad volunteers for a charity. He's doing work for this theater that supports kids with disabilities. They're in real financial trouble and need to raise some serious cash."

"Great cause. I'd love to make a donation."

"It's a little more than that," Matt said. "They are having a fundraiser next Saturday. Conrad was hoping you would attend. The publicity would be invaluable to the group."

Dale's immediate reaction to public functions was no. He always felt like a shit for saying so, but public appearances were not his strength. Despite the good intentions, you were putting yourself out there, drawing attention and inviting the world to come snooping.

"How big a function is this?"

"I'm not sure. It's at the theater but I don't know what he has in mind."

"Can I say *maybe* for now?" The coward's way out. "I'm working this weekend and I don't know how much good publicity I could bring them right now."

"No problem at all. I told him I would ask. I didn't make any promises."

"I'd like to but… Well, we'll see. It's not a no. If I can't attend I'll arrange some great prizes your friend can give away. I might even be able to fix up a visit to the set once things calm down a little."

Matt moved closer, pressing against Dale's bare thigh. "Can you fix a prize for me right now?" he said lasciviously.

Dale's body reacted instantly, cock coming up hard. "Now that's something I can commit to."

* * * *

Paul's alibi checked out. Jamie managed to get hold of his wife on the phone, earlier that evening, at the department store where she worked. He took a very soft approach. Telling her a man matching her husband's appearance had been involved in an incident the week before and they just needed to rule him out of their inquiry. Not a complete lie. It was not his role to expose her husband for the cheat he was. Despite Shona's insistence to the contrary, extra-marital affairs were not against the law and not a matter of police business.

Julie Goss made a clear statement. "You must have the wrong man. Paul was at home that night. I had the evening off and we stayed in to watch TV. *Masterchef.* I'm thinking of applying for the next series and we never miss it."

Jamie thanked her for her assistance and wrote up his notes. Paul Gross was no longer under suspicion. Though Shona had enjoyed giving him a hard time, he was never a serious suspect. What he had told them about Olly Raymond checked out too. Paul was not the only man he had slept with. He wasn't excessively promiscuous by modern standards, averaging one, random hook up per week, usually on his day off.

Most of the men he met were strangers. Olly saw them once and never again. He was a normal, very regular guy. He didn't appear to be into anything heavy or kinky and there was no evidence on his phone or computer to suggest he'd made arrangements to meet anyone on the night he was killed.

Jamie wanted to be thorough in his investigation but it looked increasingly unlikely that Olly had met his killer through a hook-up app or chat room.

Still, these things couldn't be ruled out.

He signed off his report and checked the time. It was past nine. It had been another long day. He was starving. He would grab something to eat on the way home and get to bed early. With a good night's sleep he could be back here by seven a.m.

Jamie was heading for the door when DCI Redgraves came racing from his office. The older man's face was ashen. He looked around the incident room and saw Jamie was the only member of his staff still on duty.

"Dench," he barked, grabbing his jacket from the hook and marching for the door. "Come with me."

Jamie followed. Something was up. "Yes, sir. What is it, sir?"

"The university rowing club have just called it in. Their team have spotted a body on the banks of the Wear. A young man in his twenties. It looks like our bastard has done it again."

# Chapter Thirteen

Keeley Rank was a great believer in being in the right place at the right time. She owed the greatest successes of her career to just that. She had a knack, maybe it was instinct, or even clairvoyance, for arriving at a location just before a story either broke or developed further. When Johan Turner had called to offer her exclusive behind-the-scenes access to his latest TV series, she felt that uncanny sense, prickling, urging her to take the job. Given free rein on the set of a very troubled production was incentive enough, but instinct told her a bigger story awaited.

And those instincts had proved right again. How fortunate.

Keeley was in her hotel room, raking through various old stories about the handsome leading man, Dale Zachary. The gay rumors that surrounded Dale seemed a little more vehement than the usual speculation or wishful thinking which plagued most good-looking actors. Few Hollywood men were immune to them, even the notorious womanizers were accused of screwing those bit part bimbos to disguise their true selves. But the gay question cast a long shadow over the career of Dale Zachary.

Maybe this was the story her instincts were nagging her to reveal.

It was more than just speculation. Keeley had it from several sources, who had been close to Dale at one time or another, that he was very definitely into other men. But so what? Outing a B-list actor was no big deal. Who would give a shit? She needed more than that. The story required an angle.

He was playing a sexually ambivalent sex killer in this hokey TV series. So it wouldn't be a stretch to make links between the man and the character. Again — so what? No one would care unless the show was a huge ratings hit. And there were plenty of hack gossip column writers who could make that connection with just a few minutes of Internet research.

That couldn't be the story. She hadn't dragged herself to the fucking North just for that. Keeley needed more.

And, boy — she had got it.

Just as she was finishing her research into Dale, a call came through on her mobile. A subdued voice said quickly, "We've found another body. On the bank of the river, down from the castle. Right now." The caller hung up without saying more.

Keeley had only been in Durham a couple of days, but she worked fast. It was more than enough time to make important contacts within the local police force. To grease a few greedy palms.

She leaped up, grabbed her phone and camera and headed for the door.

Another murder. *This* was the story. The reason she was here. In the heart of the action as the killer claimed a third victim.

She left the hotel and set out on foot. Durham was a small city. It was easier and much faster to get around on foot than by car. She had a good idea of the geography, how the river curved around the peninsula upon which the ancient castle was built. She knew which way to go.

Across the old cobbled streets, she strode with the fixed purpose of a journalist after a story.

There was an eerie stillness about the city at night, a trait it shared with many other historic cathedral towns. She would come out another night with her camera and take the pictures that would make a colorful backdrop to the whole series of articles she now envisioned, about the beautiful city and the evil that lurked within it.

Down the steps and under the bridge, she followed the course of the river downstream. Though the path was dark, it wasn't far. Ahead there were lights, a scattering of people. Keeley quickened her step.

Two sober-looking police officers held back the small crowd. Keeley smiled. She really had got here before the action developed. There were just a handful of uniformed officers. No MIT. No SOCO. The plods had barely secured the scene yet. Keeley raised her camera and fired off a succession of shots.

"What's going on?" she asked the nearest member of the crowd, a young man in T-shirt and shorts. He looked as if he had to be freezing — a member of some sports club, too afraid of missing the action to go and get dressed.

"They pulled another body from the water," the young man said in a soft, southern accent.

"Who did?"

"Not me, but a couple of my buddies. I was in the boat that spotted him. Stu and Rossy, they jumped in. The river isn't deep here in this weather, they could wade right up to him."

"Him? Another young man then? Just like the others?"

He nodded, looking past Keeley to the torchlights of the police officers farther along the bank, securing a wide area around the corpse. "A young guy. Yes, that's what it looked like. He had no clothes on."

*This is it. Right place, right time. Another sex murder. Nice one, Keeley.*

"What else did you see?" she asked eagerly.

"Nothing much. The guys dragged him to the bank but there was nothing they could do except call the police. It was awful. I've never seen a dead body before."

Keeley scanned the line of watchers. "Where are your friends? Stu and Rossy — the guys who went in the water."

"The cops put them in their car to wait for an ambulance. They were both soaked through."

"Did you talk to them before they were taken away? Did

161

they tell you anything?"

The boy suddenly looked at Keeley more closely. His brow furrowed. "Who are you?"

"Never mind," she said, stepping away from him. He had nothing more to offer. There were a couple of others guys farther along the bank, dressed in the shorts and T-shirts of the college rowing team. She approached them next. "Did either of you get a look at the body?"

"Yeah, we both did," answered the taller of the two, a good-looking blond with strong shoulders. He spoke with a foreign accent, Dutch, maybe Norwegian. Keeley couldn't quite place it.

The moments straight after a traumatic event were the best time to ask questions. Witnesses were usually still in shock and willing to tell someone, anyone, what had just happened. Their natural suspicion of a person asking questions—worse, journalists—was forgotten and they were only too happy to unburden themselves.

"I don't think he could have been in the water for long," the blond continued. "He looked too normal, if you know what I'm saying. There was no bloating or swelling to suggest the body had been in the water for long."

"Did either of you recognize him?"

"No."

"Know of any guys missing around the college? Anyone not show up in the last day or two who should have?"

They both shook their heads.

"Are you a copper?" the second boy asked. He was dark with an upper body that was even more defined than his buddy's.

"No. A journalist."

"Oh." Neither of them was fazed.

"Did you get a good at the body? Notice anything wrong? Stab wounds, for example?"

"No. There was no blood. Nothing like that."

Both the previous victims had been strangled. This was soundeding increasingly like the Durham killer had struck again.

More police officers began to arrive. There were sirens and flashing lights on the bridge behind them. The crime scene was about to get a lot busier. Keeley raised her camera and began to fire off more shots. She wouldn't learn much more out here tonight, but she was already thinking ahead, to the morning. To the breaking news that the killer had claimed another victim. To the effect it would have on the already troubled production of *Blood Falls on Stone*.

\* \* \* \*

Morning was bright and cold, with a frost on the ground, but a cloudless sky bode well for the day ahead. After a long winter, this morning held the promise of spring.

Somehow, Dale and Matt managed to drag themselves from the warmth of the bed and each other's bodies to attend the mid-week boot camp. It was easier than it had ever been. Once they were up, buoyed on by the light in the sky and their feelings for each other, they arrived at the park laughing and in high spirits.

*Everything seems easier when you're in love.*

Even Clint Dexter was smiling. Almost. There was a slight upward turn at the corners of his mouth as he ticked off their names in his notebook. His icy-blue eyes looked coolly from Matt to Dale. "Good morning, gentlemen. Nice to see you both again."

Dale stiffened. Was that a dig? What was he trying to suggest in that comment about the two of them? And what was that look all about? *Knock it off*, he warned himself. Clint wasn't getting at anything. It was his own paranoia. He'd always been hopeless when he was out in public with another man. Imaging that they were the center of attention. As if everyone were looking at them, and whispering things. *Faggy things.*

He had to get over it. That kind of obsession would only hold them back. Matt deserved better from him.

They took the course together. Matching each other all the way. Being with Matt made him better. They spurred each other on. He was lighter and faster than he'd been before. Being in love could do that. But he should really give credit to Clint. His boot camp did get results. In just over a week there had already been an improvement in his fitness. If he kept it up, he would be a machine after a month.

Dale told Clint as much as they reached the end of the course. He had pushed them to the point of collapse and it felt so damn good. "Man, you're amazing." He was bent over, hands on his knees, gasping for breath. "Don't know how you do it, but where other trainers promise results, you actually get them. One hour, three times a week. That's truly remarkable."

"What matters is how you use that hour," Clint said flatly. "Work to the max and an hour is all anybody needs."

"In times of trouble that's the kind of man you'd want on your side," Matt said as Clint walked away. "Nothing fazes him. He'd bat your enemies aside like a fly."

"Yeah, he's a real terminator."

They both laughed.

They said goodbye in the car park. Dale wanted to lean in and give Matt a passionate parting kiss on the mouth. He sensed Matt wanted it too, but couldn't bring himself to do it. A lifetime of repression could not be undone in a few short days.

Instead, he softly said, "I love you."

\* \* \* \*

Dale drove directly from the park to the studio. He would shower there and get straight into costume. He was expected to give face time to Keeley Rank today, but even that could not spoil his mood as he drove along the quiet country lanes in the welcome haze of a low morning sun. Despite all the shit in the last two weeks, there was a lightness in his heart, because through all of that he had found love in a most unexpected place. He was no romantic — quite the opposite — but, like the song says, love changes everything. It changed everything for the better.

The happy vibes lasted exactly as long as it took him to drive to the studio. There was the usual crowd of placard-carrying protestors at the gate, but their mood was subdued. Dale immediately saw why. The car park was filled with police cars.

"What's going on?" he asked the first officer he encountered, a serious-looking WPC who looked swamped by her uniform.

"Do you work here?" she asked.

"I do. Dale Zachary, I'm one of the actors."

The WPC consulted a list of names on a clipboard before directing him inside. The narrow corridors were teaming with police. What the hell? Had one of the protestors broken in overnight? Sabotaged the set? Even if they had, the police presence seemed excessive.

Dale pulled out his phone and called the producer's number. Nicola Donahue's phone went straight to voice mail. He tried Russell Jones next, who answered immediately.

"Russell, I just got to the studio. There are police everywhere. What's going on?"

"We're in the production office. Come straight away."

"I just got back from boot camp. I'm a sweaty mess, should I wash and change first?"

"No," Russell said anxiously. "That doesn't matter. Come as you are."

He found Russell in his office with Elton Weaver. They stared at him, grim-faced, as he entered. He knew, just from the look of them, that something major was afoot.

"What the hell is going on? What are the police doing here?"

Elton opened a window, lit a cigarette, and dragged fiercely on the stick. Russell, who would normally go apeshit over such a blatant breaking of the rules, seemed not to notice. Dale had never seen the producer in such a numb state.

"Haven't you heard the news? It's all over the TV and radio."

"What? No. I left early to work out. I haven't seen any news today."

"Oh," Russell said slowly, looking blankly at Dale. "Sit down then."

"Tell me what's going on."

"They dragged another body out of the river last night," Elton said, making no attempt to blow his smoke out of the window. "Our killer has done it again."

"Shit," he said, finally taking the seat. "But what does that have to do with us? Why are the police here? They can't seriously think there's a connection between our show and the murders. This is all make-believe."

"That's just it," Russell's voice was hollow. "This time, there *is* a connection — a real connection. It's Aaron Oxford." His voice cracked. "The body they pulled from the river. It was Aaron. Our production runner. The murdering bastard has killed one of our own."

The room around Dale seemed to shrink. The walls and ceiling were caving in. He repeated what Russell had told him in his mind, changing the order, trying to make some sense of it. Aaron — dead. The only words that mattered. It just couldn't be.

Then he remembered... Aaron didn't show for work yesterday. An invisible fist seized his insides in a ruthless grip. "Aaron... He did call in sick yesterday? Didn't he?"

Russell shook his head. "Everyone assumed he had a hangover but he hasn't been seen since the reception at the hotel on Monday night."

"Oh my God." Dale clung to the armrest of his chair as a surge of dizziness came over him. This could not be happening. Aaron couldn't be dead. No. It wasn't possible. Except he knew with agonizing certainty that it was very possible. "Has he been identified? Is it definitely him?"

"They're waiting for his sister to arrive and do that formally, but Nicola has been to see the body and given an informal ID. There's no doubt about it, it's him."

Dale didn't know Aaron had a sister. He didn't know much about him at all. Why would he? They didn't have that kind of relationship, didn't share personal information. Whose fault was that? Shit. If he hadn't spurned Aaron at the party on Monday, he might still be alive. It was a devastating conclusion.

"Are you all right?" Russell asked. "You don't look good."

"Shock. I can't get my head around it."

"Ironic, isn't it?" Russell said sadly. "We spend our days talking about and creating murders in front of a camera, striving for authenticity. But when we're confronted with the reality of it, we are ill-equipped to cope."

"He was only thirty-two," Dale said, wringing his hands.

"Was he? Oh, that's right. He was your assistant too, wasn't he? You probably knew him better than any of us."

"What happens now?"

"The detectives will want to speak to everyone. You included, Dale, given that you knew him so well."

Elton threw his used cigarette butt out of the window and immediately lit another. "What will happen to the show?"

Russell gave a small shrug. "Can't say."

"Will they close us down?"

"I don't know. I can't see us shooting anything else this week. We should close production down out of respect, if nothing else. Maybe we can pick up again next week."

"What's this *maybe* crap?" Elton said harshly. "Are we picking up on Monday or not?"

"I don't know."

"You're the fucking producer. You ought to know."

"Elton, please. I don't know. It's not my money. We've had enough problems already before any of this. Maybe they'll decide it's just not worth it and close us down for good."

"They can't do that."

"They can do whatever they like. We're not talking about a minor disruption. Bad weather or a temperamental fucking director. A boy is dead."

"One boy — one employee out of hundreds. It's a tragedy, yes, but you can't put all those other people out of work because of it. We have to keep going."

Dale stood up angrily, staring at the pair of them. "I don't believe what I'm hearing. You assholes. How can you even think about money and your fucking careers when a member of our team has been killed? You're a disgrace. Both of you."

He stormed out of the room, letting the door crash behind him. He couldn't stand it. The heat, the arguments, the oppression. He couldn't breathe. He had to get out.

\* \* \* \*

Dale Zachary. Jamie finally put a face to the name. After seeing the Audi parked on Matt's drive Sunday night, Jamie made a casual enquiry to the rental company on Monday and learned that the car had been rented to a man called Dale Zachary. The name had meant nothing at the time. He had not paid much attention to the news that linked the Durham murders with the TV drama. Why would he? The idea was ludicrous. Nothing more than a coincidence. Until now.

With the murder of Aaron Oxford, the connection was very real.

Jamie stood in Dale's trailer. The actor was in jeans and a loose checked shirt. His dark blond hair was still damp from a recent shower, while he searched the trailer for his socks and shoes.

Could this really be the man who was parked up at Matt's place the other night? It sounded unlikely. How did they even know each other? A small-town solicitor and a visiting American actor. Where would they ever have met? Grindr? Cruising the Internet? That wasn't Matt's style. Maybe there were two Dale Zacharys. Again, it sounded unlikely. It was hardly a common name for this area. And both men driving rented Audis? Not a chance.

This was him.

He was good-looking enough. Very. Looking at him now, with his damp hair and open-necked short, had Jamie feeling, well, horny. Yes, *horny*. That was not the typical reaction he had to suspects.

Not that Dale looked happy about the situation. Right now that handsome brow was drawn into a pretty intense scowl. Dale located a pair of socks in a dresser and sat to pull them on.

The TV crew had been stood down for the rest of the day, though DCI Redgraves had given instructions that no one was to leave the studio until they had been spoken to by his team. Jamie, intrigued after seeing Dale's name on the list of crew members, made sure that he bagged this one.

"Aaron Oxford was your personal assistant?"

Dale looked at him with wide blue eyes. *Jesus, this guy's a knockout.* "I can't believe you have to say *was*. Sorry, this is all still such a shock. No, Aaron wasn't a PA. He was a production runner. It's more general than PA. He worked for the whole crew, not just me. But he was assigned to help me out when I needed anything."

"So you must have known him pretty well?"

Dale looked away, paying an unusual amount of attention to his socks. "I wouldn't say well, no."

"Did he know anyone in the area?"

"I don't think so. He didn't mention anyone if he did. Most of the crew are strangers to Durham. I don't think Aaron was any different. It was work."

"Girlfriends?"

"Aaron was gay."

"Okay," Jamie said, sensing an opening. Something he could exploit. "You see, you knew him better than you thought. What else can you tell me? Did he ever talk about any boyfriends? Did he ever go cruising?"

Dale signed. "Is that what you think happened? He picked up the wrong man?"

"We don't think anything yet," Jamie said. Suddenly he was no longer keen on Dale. He was holding something back. An unpleasant image of Dale and Matt formed in his mind. He could see how well they would complement each other. Matt, so tall, dark and handsome, and Dale, the blond all-American hunk. He knew intuitively that this *was* the guy whose car had been parked outside Matt's on Sunday. "We didn't even know Aaron was gay until you told me just now."

"It's not like it was a secret," Dale said. "Everyone knew."

Now he was being defensive. They stared each other straight in the eyes. Jamie no longer felt horny about Dale. He was a *'good-looking nothing'*, as his mother would say. Dale looked away first.

Inexplicably, Jamie wished that Shona were with him. He couldn't stand the pushy DC but she wouldn't give a man like Dale an inch of maneuverability. He might be the big man on set but Shona would twist him so tight, he would divulge everything.

"It sounds to me like you knew him pretty well," Jamie pressed. "What else can you tell me?"

Dale stared at the floor, clasping his hands together. "All right," he said quietly. "This has no relevance to your case but I'll tell you now because it's better to be upfront than have it come out later and be misinterpreted. Aaron and I had a little bit of a thing going on."

"A *thing*? Does that mean you were seeing him?"

"Not as such. It wasn't really anything, just a couple of guys away from home and keeping each other company. Do you know what I mean?"

"Spell it out for me," Jamie said slyly.

"We were screwing," Dale snapped. "Is that clear enough for you? Aaron was a nice guy. I won't talk bad about him, but it didn't amount to anything. I never saw him outside of work. We just…fooled around a little in here. In the trailer.

That's all it was."

"Two minutes ago you told me you hardly knew him."

"I didn't know him. We're guys, you know? We don't have to be in a committed relationship to help each other get off. That's all it was. I even put a stop to that last week."

"Why did you do that if it was so meaningless and convenient? It seems to me that you have nothing to lose. You were on to a good thing. Why spoil it?"

"Because I met someone else. Someone I am serious about."

*Matt? It had better fucking not be.*

"When did you last see Aaron?"

"On Monday."

"Here?"

"No. Monday evening. There was a reception at the hotel in town. It was a press thing. We were all there. The whole cast and crew."

"Monday? The night he went missing?"

Now there was anger in Dale's eyes. "If you say so."

"What did you do afterward?"

"I stayed at the hotel till around ten. Then I went to see my friend. I was there all night."

"The name and address of this friend?"

"Oh, come on. He has nothing to do with this either. He didn't even know Aaron."

"But you knew him, Mr. Zachary. Very well, it sounds like. And you claim to have ended a relationship with him the week before he was murdered. So you'll understand that we have to check out this alibi of yours very carefully." Jamie couldn't deny the callous pleasure he got from watching this smarmy American squirm, though he dreaded the answer to his next question. "What's the name of the man you spent Monday night with?"

"Damn," Dale said, wrenching his fingers through his hair. "All right, his name is Matt. Matt Blyth."

The words went through Jamie's heart like a knife.

# Chapter Fourteen

When Clint Dexter closed his gym at ten p.m. he had been at work for over fifteen hours. That was the way he liked it. Clint didn't believe in downtime or days off – that only led to laziness and apathy. Soft minds and, even worse, soft bodies. Hard physical work – that was the best form of stress relief and relaxation.

Clint wasn't superman and he couldn't be in two places at once. He'd hired a full-time manager, Jimmy Richards, to run the gym while he was engaged in other activities – his boot camp, personal training sessions and seeing to his own fitness regime. Jimmy finished work at seven p.m. and Clint took care of the gym for the last three hours each night. He ran a tight business, a hangover from his military career, and didn't tolerate bad attitudes, poor gym etiquette or any kind of drug misuse. If the meatheads wanted to abuse their bodies with steroids and illegal supplements they could do it on someone else's premises.

Clint Dexter didn't want trouble of any kind.

John Armstrong, a heavyweight boxer, was emptying his locker as Clint made his final check of the building. John was the last customer.

"How's it going?" Clint asked.

John was the very image of a beat-upon boxer. At forty-two, he should have retired from the sport at least five years earlier. He had a square head, bull neck, cauliflower ears and a nose that was every shape of broken. Despite his knackered appearance, John was still a winning fighter.

"Not too bad," he said, pulling a hoodie over his head. They patted each other's shoulders. "I'm trying to get my weight down. I've got a fight in Liverpool next week and could do with shifting about eight pounds. They just won't come off."

"Cardio?"

"That's what I've been doing. Two hours straight tonight."

Clint told him about his morning boot camp. John had time to attend four sessions before his next fight. "So long as you don't finish off with a gut-busting breakfast, my course will get the weight off."

Encouraged, John signed up for the next week. "Those early mornings will probably kill me, but it will be worth it."

"All effort is rewarded," Clint said stoically.

John waved good night. Clint locked the door behind him. He loved the stillness that came over a busy building when all the people had left. The uneasy, almost spooky quiet. He felt right at home there.

Alone, the forced smile he struggled to keep up in front of the customers faded.

Clint went to the reception desk and tapped the computer screen. He closed the program Jimmy had installed to manage membership plans and logged onto the local news pages. The bold headline on the opening page made him smile again.

*Durham Strangler – Latest Victim Named.*

At last. They had given him a title. The Durham Strangler. This was new. He liked it. Simple and to the point. No mistaking its intent. Though strangling was only a minor part of what he did – the final, most crucial part. He was so much more than a that.

*Aaron Oxford has been named as the latest victim of the predator now known as the Durham Strangler.*

Predator. Now that was a more fitting description for him. He was an apex predator.

*Aaron, thirty-two, from Brighton was working in the North East as a production assistant on the crime series* Blood Falls on Stone. *The controversial TV show has come in for much criticism from local groups for the chilling similarities between the crimes it depicts and the recent, real life murders. In a tragic twist of fate, the fictional killings of the series have become intrinsically linked with the crimes of the Durham Strangler.*

It was no accident.

Clint hadn't intended for Aaron to become his next victim, not until last weekend. But adaptability had always been one of his strengths. It was a poor twist of fate for Aaron, but once Clint had made up his mind, it had all gone to plan.

He turned off the computer. There was nothing more of note in the story. The press and the police were clueless. Nobody knew what motivated the Durham Strangler. How or why he operated. That was the way it would stay. It was time to switch things up again. The riverbanks around the city would be too well patrolled now. He couldn't risk grabbing another boy from within the city or dumping them in the river. Didn't matter. He was ready to take his campaign to another level. While the police were looking one way, he would seize them from another.

Clint turned out the lights and locked up the gym. His four-by-four was parked in the deserted car park behind the main street. He sat behind the wheel and ate the beef sandwich he'd picked up earlier. It had been a long day and it was not over yet. He ate slowly. Thoroughly chewing before swallowing each mouthful. The bread was stale and dry and the beef was tough. It didn't bother him. Clint took little pleasure from food. It was merely fuel.

Finished, he started the engine and got on his way. Driving carefully and observing the speed limit. The Durham Strangler would not be one of those incompetent killers the police caught on something as mundane as a traffic stop.

The press had claimed Aaron Oxford was Clint's third victim. A fact that was far from true. The police had only made the connection between Aaron and the previous victims because he had wanted them to. The parallels between the three killings were deliberate. They thought

Connor Welsh was his first but Clint had killed before Conner, many times. None of those deaths were ever connected or attributed to a single killer. He liked killing. But as with all things he enjoyed, moderation and variety were key. Together with a considerable will and steely determination. Clint was confident in his abilities. He would not be caught. The murders would only stop when he wanted them to.

And that would be never.

He had been twenty-five when he had taken his first life. Serving in Germany, he'd picked up a skinny blond boy in a leather bar. The kid had been all for show, posturing around the club, telling everyone how much he had wanted an older top to fuck him hard. Going back to the boy's grimy apartment, Clint had done just that, fucking the boy harder than he'd ever expected or wanted. He had cried like a bitch and begged him to stop. When he'd begun to cry rape, the only way to silence him had been to break his neck.

It had been a spur-of-the-moment loss of control. He'd reacted on instinct, foolish instinct that could have landed him in prison, but he hadn't been able to deny how much he'd enjoyed it. The power of that control. Of exercising his strength over the boy's weakness. Feeling those bones crack. He had cleaned the apartment as best he could. There would always be traces he could not eradicate, but thankfully he had used a condom to screw the kid, keeping DNA evidence to a minimum.

The murder had not made the news. He had followed the local papers and bulletins, but seen nothing. He had been deployed to Ireland four months later and considered himself lucky.

He'd always known there was something wrong with him. Being queer was bad enough but his issues went deeper than that. Sex alone was never enough, even before that night in Germany. He liked to punish his lovers. Fuck them without lube, hit them, mark them, take them by force. He craved total domination over other men.

But he didn't know what that truly meant until he broke the German boy's neck in that depressingly small apartment.

For the first time he'd experienced real power. Total control.

Having tasted it, nothing else would ever be enough.

He tried to keep those urges at bay. He had struggled for years to deny them. Making do. Humiliating his lovers. Punishing them. The men he met in leather bars and on hook-up sites were submissive. Willing victims who got off on the cruel punishments he devised for them. Clint could take no pleasure from their masochism. There was nothing he could do to hurt those men, short of ending their lives. But he wasn't ready to take that step again. Not yet. He'd left the Army and was living permanently in the UK. It would not be as easy to get away with it on home turf.

For a while, rape provided the solution. Taking other men by force satiated those passions.

He had to be careful. Always. He had no intention of going to jail for raping some faggot's ass. He was no opportunistic sex offender. He chose his victims with tremendous care. It was the only way to control it.

It could sometimes take weeks to make a selection. He would travel far on weekends, just looking. In the small towns and villages around County Durham, going south to North Yorkshire, or up into Northumberland. Always looking, discounting hundreds of men until a suitable victim emerged.

Supermarkets were his favorite hunting ground, prowling the aisles, seeking the perfect one. There was no particular type. His selection was based on the feelings he underwent when he saw a certain man. He seldom found them attractive. It was the excitement they triggered that he found most electrifying.

Straight men were the best. Married men even better. They had so much more to lose when he exerted his ultimate power over then. Straight men were less likely to report it when he raped them. They couldn't admit it when another guy took their ass. Out of dozens of attacks he'd carried out, Clint was only aware of three that had been reported to the police.

He was never questioned about any of them.

He thanked his carefully planning for that. Once he chose his victim, he spent weeks stalking them. That's where supermarkets proved so fruitful. Most people doing their weekly shopping went straight home afterward. Which made finding out where these men lived so effortless. He would return several times, always in disguise, learning his victims' routines, who they lived with, where they worked, when they were alone. Compiling a picture. Formulating a plan. People were creatures of habit and that made his task so easy.

The plan and the anticipation of executing it could be delightfully drawn out for weeks. He was rarely in a hurry and always in complete control of his emotions. The murder in Germany had been the one time he'd lost control. He made sure that it never happened again.

For many years, stalking and sexual abuse was enough. The thrill of taking another man and exerting control over him satisfied his darkest needs. He wasn't too prolific either. One or two men each year, that was all he needed.

When they cried and begged him to stop — that was when he liked it best.

New Year's Eve 2013. Clint had been invited to a party at the home of one of his gym regulars. He hadn't planned on going but had changed his mind at the last minute. He had been unusually optimistic about the coming year. As he'd stood in the kitchen, talking to the husband of another gym member, he'd realized why he'd been looking forward to the new year. It had been time for him to kill again.

Once the decision had been made, he'd begun to enjoy it.

Yes, he would kill a man that year. He had decided then to start with the man he'd been talking to at that very moment. His name had been Anthony and they had only met that night. Anthony had been an electrician, almost thirty and still hanging on to the prettiness of his youth, despite having been married for four years with two kids. His hair had been receding and he had the beginnings of a beer belly.

*Yes*, Clint had thought. *I'll kill him this year before he loses his looks completely.*

It had been a great liberation as he'd made the decision, all he'd done till then was suppress his natural instinct. The urge to kill again had been with him ever since Germany. He wouldn't deny it any longer. Now he was free to do what he wanted.

Free did not mean careless. He had planned the murder of Anthony more minutely than any of his other crimes. He had to. It wasn't going to be like before—choosing a random stranger in a nowhere town. He would be acting out his fantasies here, in the city where he lived, among people he knew.

Keeping tabs on Anthony hadn't been an easy thing. As an electrician, he had no set routine. His job had taken him all over the county and his hours of work had been erratic. Clint had taken care not to mention him when his wife Laura had attended the gym. Once the deed had been done, he hadn't wanted anyone making even the most tenuous connection between him and his victim.

He had bided his time. There had been no rapes elsewhere that year. He hadn't needed them. They had been a coping mechanism, to stop him from killing, and he hadn't required that anymore.

He had made his move in August. For some reason, an upcoming family holiday he guessed, Anthony had taken up jogging after work, three nights a week, heading up into the lonely hills outside the town, following the same route each time. It had been too perfect.

Clint had been waiting in the deepest part of the course. Anthony hadn't even seen him when he'd stepped out from behind and smacked a rock against his head. Clint had dragged him unconscious into a deeply shaded gully and had taken his time with the rest.

The body hadn't been found for two days.

Despite a major investigation and tearful appeals for witnesses by his wife, no arrests had been made and Anthony's murder remained unsolved.

* * * *

Clint parked his car in a quiet residential street, a mile from the estate where Matt Blyth lived. He had used this spot only once before, several weeks back and would not come this way again. There was no CCTV coverage in the area and there was nothing about his car to make it stand out from any other on the street. But twice was enough. People were naturally nosy and nosy people noticed things.

He got out of the car and pulled a scarf around his neck, high enough to cover his lower face. It was a cool night and he would not look suspicious dressed as he was. Sticking to the shadows, he took a circuitous route through the estate, down narrow pathways, between the houses, avoiding the brightly lit open spaces that were popular with late night dog walkers. Like a soldier, under cover of darkness in enemy terrain, he was the ultimate professional stalker.

Matt Blyth had been his target for almost a year. Before any of the most recent killings, Matt had been on his radar. Matt was something special. More special than any man he'd pursued before. There always came a point for Clint, during the long process of choosing a victim and following him, when the urge to kill became too great, when it couldn't be denied any longer. That hadn't happened with Matt. So far, he drew more pleasure from the slow pursuit and manipulation of his prey than the idea of killing him. Toying with him, playing with him, fucking with his mind. Like the other night when he slashed the tires of his car.

With Matt, he was playing a longer game than usual.

The more recent killings, indeed the creation of the Durham Strangler, were a diversion, a side project that allowed him to draw out the chase. It was considerably more rewarding.

Matt was a curiosity. Clint didn't fully understand why this man piqued his interest more than any other. He was a handsome bastard — nice body, nice ass — but that wasn't it. His body would be even better soon. If he kept up the exercise. Luring him to boot camp had been inspired. And easy. Clint dropped fliers for the course at all the houses on the estate and then a week later to all the businesses in the area of Matt's work. He was prepared to wait. Do it all again in a few week's time. But that hadn't been necessary. The bimbo from Matt's office had called to book a session after the first drop.

Of course if he hadn't come to boot camp Matt would never have struck up a romance with the cheesy American. But even that had the potential to amuse him. Especially since Dale was mixed up in that stupid TV show, the one they claimed Clint was copying. How was he supposed to mimic something he hadn't seen? Still, it struck him that he could delay Matt's murder and make it a lot more interesting by killing Dale first.

What a blast that would be.

Watching from afar as Matt dealt with his grief. Playing a long game of mental torment before the inevitable end.

Cutting between two houses, he came up on Matt's place. The American's rental car was parked on the drive. That Yank spent so much time here, he should pay rent.

Clint crossed the street then ducked into the shadows. He crouched low and waited. Silence. No twitching curtains or faces at the windows. No one to see him. He waited another five minutes, just to be sure, before edging toward the gate, opening it and disappearing around the side of the house. He was used to operating in complete darkness and maneuvered without making a sound.

For someone who worked with dangerous criminals and

lived alone, Matt was hopelessly lax about security. There were no outside lights or cameras. Not even a dog. The house was not alarmed and he often slept with the windows open. The upstairs windows were easily accessible from the roof of the kitchen porch.

Clint had been in the house several times. Tonight he was only here to look. He hadn't intended on coming at all. Not until the news about Aaron broke. The fact that his latest victim worked on the American's TV show would bring his crimes into their world.

The murders were no longer taking place on the news, happening to other people. They were right here on their doorstep. It was someone they knew.

That notion alone gave him a big hard-on.

He raised his head above the kitchen sill. They were in the dining room, facing each other across the table, both in profile. There were two glasses between them and a bottle of red wine, almost empty. He didn't need to hear what they were saying. He understood the serious tone of their conversation from their expressions. Furrowed brows, soulful eyes, downturned mouths.

Death had entered their perfect lives. It had been there all along, they could only see it now he had chosen to offer a glimpse.

*Look at them talking it over, trying to make sense and comfort each other. Sweet. Enjoy it while you can.*

Clint grinned.

Matt Blyth and Dale Zachary had no idea. They were living on borrowed time and the end would come soon enough.

# Chapter Fifteen

They stayed up talking late into the night. Dale told Matt everything. Not just about Aaron, but his whole life. His anxiety from being in the closet and the fear he felt should he be outed. The impact it would have on his son. The ruin it would bring to his career. The fear he'd felt for so many years, of himself, of being gay. The panic that had driven him to marry Laura.

Matt listened. Without comment or judgment.

It was difficult for Dale to open up like this. He could see it in his face. Hear it in his fractured speech. But gradually, as his story unfolded, the strain began to ease.

"So that's everything." Dale sighed, sharing what was left of the wine between their two glasses. "Every damn, complicated, fucked-up facet of my life. What a crock of shit."

Matt reached across the table, putting his hand on top of Dale's. "Thank you. You didn't have to tell me any of that. But please know how much I appreciate it."

"Really?"

"Honestly." He squeezed his hand.

"The shit is gonna hit the fan, you know. Over Aaron. There's no way I'll be able to keep my name out of the press. Shit, listen to me. That alone should tell you what a fuck-up I am. A man is dead and I'm worried about how the press might link my name with his. What an asshole."

"Sssh," Matt said softly. "So what if they out you? Big deal. We're not in the 1970s or 80s. It's not going to ruin you. Your role in *Blood Falls* proves that you've moved on from the pretty-boy phase of your career. This is a serious role. A dark role. I can't imagine they'll want you for more teen romances on the back of it."

"It's not just my career that I'm worried about. There's Jack."

"Does he know you're gay?"

"Of course not," Dale said with wide eyes.

"Are you sure of that?"

"He's twelve years old."

"And twelve year olds today are a lot wiser than we ever were," Matt said. "They're not hung up on things in the same way earlier generations were."

Dale laughed thinly. "No kid wants to think about their parents' sex life. I doubt things have changed that much. It's gross."

"Grosser still to have to read about it on Facebook, or in the school yard."

Dale looked up. "What are you saying? That I should tell him first?"

"It would be better coming from you, wouldn't it?"

"I...don't know."

Matt felt for him. He was hurting badly. Watching the bottom fall out of his world. "Look, if you ask me, I think there's a pretty good chance he knows already. I'd be amazed if he hasn't asked Laura about you. Give her a call in the morning. Find out. But I think you should speak to him soon. If the press is going to keep a lid on the story, it won't be for long. You'll have until Sunday, I would say. The British press—they love running scandal stories on Sunday. It's a tradition."

"Some tradition." He drained his wine.

"Come on." Matt emptied his glass too. "It's late. Let's go to bed. There's nothing you can do until the morning."

"I couldn't sleep. I've got too much going through my mind."

Matt leaned in closer. "I said let's go to bed. I didn't say anything about sleeping."

He wanted to be close to Dale, to assure him and prove

he was there for him. Dale had been so worried. Telling him about Aaron and the relationship that ended just as they met. Matt wasn't the jealous type. Everyone came to a new relationship with some kind of past, bringing their emotional baggage with them. It wasn't enough to put him off. The only thing they had together was a future. There was nothing to be gained dwelling on what had happened before they met.

Dale went up first while Matt cleared away downstairs. He rinsed the glasses and placed them in the dishwasher, then put the empty wine bottle on the bench by the back door. The recycling bin was outside. He would take it out in the morning.

Just for a moment, through the kitchen window, he thought he caught sight of something pale. A face on the other side of the glass. It was gone as quickly as he saw it. A face? It couldn't be. Could it? He turned off the kitchen light to make it easier to see and leaned in close to the glass. The darkness outside was almost absolute. He could barely make out the borders of the garden. There was no one there. It must have been a trick of the light. Or a cat. There were plenty of those around the estate.

Or just his imagination.

It was running away with him. Hardly a surprise. It was late, and with all this talk tonight about the Durham Strangler and poor Aaron… Well, he had a right to be jittery.

He went up to bed.

Dale was finishing in the bathroom. Stripped to just a tight pair of white briefs that were a perfect showcase for his beefy butt, he rinsed toothpaste and spat into the sink. Matt came up behind and slid his arms around his waist, leaning the side of his face against Dale's shoulders. He squeezed, enjoying the warmth and hardness of his body.

"We'll get through this," he said, kissing the golden skin of Dale's shoulder. "I love you. And I'm going to be there for you. It's Aaron and those other boys we should worry about. We're alive. We've got our health and each other.

Everything else we can deal with."

"What did I do to deserve you?" Dale said, pressed his bountiful ass back against Matt's hips.

Matt kissed a slow trail from his shoulders to the back of his neck. Dale shuddered. His skin broke into gooseflesh beneath his lips. "You'll get everything you deserve," he said, rubbing his hardened crotch against Dale's ass.

They separated and Matt finished in the bathroom, washing his face and brushing his teeth. He stripped to his underpants and followed Dale to the bedroom.

Dale was waiting in the doorway with open arms. They wrapped around each other, mouths and bodies coming together. Matt was overcome by the instinct to protect him. He wanted to hold him, cover him, keep him safe from the storm that was brewing outside these four walls. His hands moved down Dale's spine, to the small of his back, to his ass, pulling him even closer. Dale surrendered to him, giving in, wanting and needing that protection.

Matt moved him toward the bed and lay him down carefully. He slipped his briefs over his hips. Dale raised his legs, yielding to Matt, looking up at him with wide, trusting eyes.

Matt went down on him with complete tenderness. He drew his tongue slowly around his balls, attuned to Dale's reactions, feeling his sac tighten and retract, seeing the hard shaft of his cock surge and jolt. Dale groaned and spread his thighs wide. Matt took his tongue lower, beneath his balls, tickling the seam of skin with just the tip of his wet tongue.

"Oh God." Dale sighed. He put his hands around the back of his knees and lifted his hips higher, leaving Matt in no doubt about where he wanted him to go.

Matt kissed him. Soft, warm, intimate kisses. As intimate as two men could be. With a light, darting tongue, he teased the sensitive, opening and listened to Dale's helpless gasps of ecstasy. He put his hands on Dale's ass and spread him wider. He could have stayed down there all night, driving his lover crazy.

"I want you," Dale said desperately. "I need you inside me."

"Anything you want," Matt said. He shoved off his underpants and scooted around the bed, hard dick bouncing. He took condoms and lube from the bedside cabinet and lay on top of Dale. Dale wriggled into position, lying on his back, between Matt's knees. With his thighs wide open and lifted, his asshole offered a wet, glistening invitation. Matt squeezed lube onto his fingertips and carefully smeared it around Dale's hot opening. Dale threw back his head, exposing his throat. Total surrender.

Matt put on a condom and palmed his dick with even more lube. He wanted this to be perfect — painless. An act of love and commitment rather than lust.

He entered slowly, pushing just enough to feel him give, then pausing, in complete control until Dale was ready, before easing in another centimeter. Deeper and deeper, he sank into Dale's welcoming body. Dale reached for him, drawing him down into a kiss. Now Matt was thrusting into his mouth and ass. Their two bodies joined as a single unit. Dale wrapped his legs around his hips, digging his heels into Matt's butt, drawing their bodies even tighter.

Matt began to lose that mannered control as the sheer pleasure of his lover's body consumed him. His thrusts became longer and deeper, feeling Dale with every inch of his dick. His whole cock tingled. Sweet, sweet torment — the most pleasurable itch that he didn't ever want to scratch.

"I love you so much," he whispered, burying his head into Dale's shoulder. He slid his hands beneath Dale, gripped his ass, pulled it higher and screwed him harder and deeper. Dale clung on tightly, taking everything he could give. Urging him further with animalistic groans.

"Come inside me," Dale sighed. "Let it all go. Come in me."

It took an exquisite age. Matt felt as if he were on the perpetual verge of orgasm. Each languid thrust took him closer without ever reaching end. It was like a roller coaster before the drop, teetering on the edge, suspended in time. Then suddenly the pull of gravity was too much. He was falling hard, coming fast. Blood roared through his ears as he spilled everything into the man he loved.

Dale clung to him. Slowly, Matt pushed back onto his knees, leaving his dick inside. Dale gripped it tight and held on as he stroked his cock to rapid release. His body trembled violently, his ass even tighter and forced Matt's cock out as orgasm racked his body.

They collapsed together afterward. Laughing. A hot, sweaty, spunky heap.

They rolled onto their sides and gazed at the ceiling, taking in huge chestfuls of air.

"You're right," Dale said at last.

"About what?"

"Me. Jack. I'm going to call Laura in the morning. If she's okay with me talking to him, I'll speak to Jack when he gets home from school. Tell him exactly what his old dad is."

"His old dad is a great man. But he knows that already." Matt rolled back onto his side, slid his hand across the flat hairy plane of Dale's belly. He stared at his profile in the dim light of the bedroom. It overwhelmed him at times, just looking at Dale. He had never known what the man of his dreams would look like, but knew with certainty that he was looking at him now.

"Hmm. I'll have to think of how I'm going to explain to him about Aaron. That's one thing I don't want him learning second-hand."

"Tell him the truth. Aaron is a man you used to go out with and someone has done something very bad to him."

"That's not exactly true," Dale said, placing his hand on top of Matt's, entwining their fingers. "Aaron and I never went out. We never went anywhere except my trailer. I'm not about to explain the concept of a fuck-buddy to a twelve year old."

"Tell him you liked him. That's all you have to say. It's enough, isn't it?"

"I guess it will have to be."

"What was he like? Aaron, I mean."

"He wasn't you."

"That's not what I asked."

"Sorry. I can't help feeling guilty. Angry too. He was a nice guy. Really. He was sweet, cute, funny. Some fella would have been very lucky to have him. He would have made a great boyfriend, I suppose. I never took the time to get to know him."

"Did the police say anything about what happened? Or what they *think* might have happened?"

"Nah. I'm a suspect. They want me to tell them how I killed him, not the other way around."

"You won't be a suspect tomorrow. Not after I tell them you were with me all night."

"That depends on what really happened to Aaron," Dale sighed. "On when he was taken. When he was killed."

Matt leaned against his side, holding him tighter. "It's frightening, isn't it? Someone is out there killing young men. Men like us. It's unreal even talking about it. Like we're discussing one of your movies rather than something real."

"Oh, don't," Dale said. "It's bad enough already without bringing up the connection between ours scripts and the killings."

"There is no connection."

"It doesn't feel like it. I'm playing a serial killer, then my buddy is offed in a very similar fashion."

"Sssh," Matt said. "You don't know that."

He sighed. "You're right. I don't know anything anymore."

Eventually they got under the covers and turned out the lights. Dale lay on his side and Matt spooned into his back, holding him, still feeling protective.

"Try to get some sleep," Matt said, pressing a soft kiss against the back of Dale's neck. "We'll get through this together."

Dale snuggled against him. "Together. That sounds

good."

Despite everything that had happened, they both drifted into an easy sleep, safe in each other's arms.

# Chapter Sixteen

Jamie did not waste any time. When Matt came out of the morning meeting, the phone in his office was ringing.

"DC Dench is here to see you," the receptionist told him.

"Thank you, Monica. Send him up."

He should have known it would be Jamie. Seconded to the murder team, he would not pass up the chance to dig the knife into Dale and hinder their relationship.

Through the open door, he saw Jamie come up the stairs. Annabel did a double take at the sight of him. He saw her greet him. Jamie returned the gesture with a non-committal nod and headed for his office. He closed the door behind him.

"Is this really appropriate?" Matt asked. "Couldn't they send someone else to take my statement?"

"How do you know what I'm here for?"

"Oh come on. Don't waste my time. You're here to check on Dale's alibi. Can we just get on with it?"

He looked rough. Sallow-skinned, with eyes even darker than usual, as if he wasn't looking after himself. Though Matt didn't buy it entirely. Jamie was the master of emotional blackmail. There was a message behind his appearance. It said, 'Look what your new relationship is doing to me.'

He took the seat across the desk.

"Dale Zachary. What can you tell me about him?"

"Besides what you can find out on Wikipedia? We've been seeing each other for a couple of weeks. But you know that much already, don't you?"

"A couple of weeks?" he sighed. "So that night I came

round your house and you wouldn't see me…?"

Matt nodded curtly. "Yes. I was meeting Dale. It was our first date, if you really want to know. Does that make you feel better?"

Jamie tutted. "You let me make a fool of myself."

Matt shook his head. This was typical of Jamie. He'd always had selective memory and a flair for painting himself as the wronged man. "You did that without any help from me. In case you don't remember, I tried to stop you but you wouldn't listen. You insisted on making a scene."

"I didn't know I'd been thrown over for a movie star. Shit, it's pretty hard for a regular guy to compete with that."

"Except you weren't thrown over for him. We were finished months before I met Dale. You came round under your own steam that night. I didn't invite you. Why would I? I've moved on, Jamie, it's time you got that through your head. Now, I've got a busy day ahead, can we please get on with this. I know it's just another false pretense for you to come here, but I'm sure you want to rule Dale out of your inquiry."

His brows came together angrily and he pulled his notebook from his jacket pocket. "What do you even know about this guy?"

Matt banged his fist on the desk. "That's not police business. So ask me a relevant fucking question."

"Was Dale Zachary with you on Monday night?"

"Yes."

"From when?"

"He came round after ten. When he got finished with the reception at the hotel. And he stayed until the following morning. He was with me all night. Okay?"

Jamie didn't look at him. "He's been staying over a lot."

"Is that a question or a statement? Not that it has any relevance to your case, but yes he has."

Matt wanted him to go. He was sick of the anger that resurfaced whenever they were near each other. Jamie got off on provoking him. Matt had done his best to let him down gently and support him after their split, but he saw now what a mistake that had been. Jamie wasn't the kind of ex-boyfriend you could remain friends with. He took every sign of friendship as a hint to try again, and every rejection of that led to a personal attack.

"You know your movie star was involved with one of the victims? Sexually involved with him."

"Yes, I know that."

Jamie's eyes widened. "Really?"

"Yes. He told me all about it last night."

"Last night? Don't you think that's strange?"

"No."

"He never mentioned him before?"

"Why would he? I haven't told him about *you* either. I don't care who he knew before me or vice versa. He told me about Aaron because of what has happened to him."

"Matt," Jamie spoke very slowly, as if he were talking to a child. "Did he ask you to cover for him? To say you were with him on Monday night when you weren't?"

"No. And I think you know me better than that. Like I'm going to make myself an accessory to murder for anyone. Dale was with me on Monday, all night. Now if you expect me to give you a minute-by-minute account of the time we were together, you're badly mistaken." Matt stood up. "I think we're done here, Jamie. If your boss wants more information than I've given he can send another police officer to interview me. And when he asks why it's inappropriate for me to talk to you, I'll tell him exactly why."

Jamie put away his book but made no attempt to leave.

"I'm only looking out for you," he said softly. "I wish you would realize that. You're at risk. Don't you see? You're exactly the killer's type. Do you really think it's a good time to invite strange men into your home? Especially one who was the lover of the latest victim."

He was like a damn terrier. He didn't give up. "I'm not inviting men into my home. Just one man. And, as I've clearly proved, he is not the one throttling these boys and throwing them in the river." Matt came out from behind the desk, crossed the room and opened the door. "Your time is up. I've got work to do."

Jamie rose angrily. "You can be a real bitch, you know that?"

Matt closed his eyes and took several deep breaths before saying. "Goodbye, Jamie. Don't come back. If you try to question me again I will speak to your inspector. You'll find yourself off the investigation pretty quickly."

With his eyes still closed, he felt the draught as Jamie thundered out.

He hadn't made it back to his desk when Annabel hurried into the office. "What did he want?" she said excitedly. "More to the point, what did you say to him? I've never seen him look so angry. I thought he was going to punch the wall as he went out."

"Long story," Matt sighed. "He overstepped the mark."

"I don't have to be in court until eleven." She grinned, slipping into the chair Jamie had just vacated. "So give me the slightly condensed version of that story."

* * * *

Keeley Rank snapped impatiently at her lighter until the cigarette caught and she paced the pavement in front of her hotel, sucking in smoke. It was downright ridiculous that you couldn't smoke inside, not even in the privacy of her own room. She'd been tempted to open the bathroom window and light up there, but they had installed bloody detectors in the toilet too. There were signs all over the hotel stating smoking would not be tolerated. She considered doing it anyway, just to see what would happen, but it wasn't worth the hassle. There was too much going on right now without trying to find another place to stay.

In a royal-blue trouser suit, with her customary nest of lacquered hair, she was a striking sight as she stalked back and forth, frequently checking the time on her chunky gold watch.

Her mobile phone rang. She threw her cigatette butt into the gutter and answered with a curt, "Keeley Rank."

Pressing the phone tight against her ear, Keeley listened carefully. Her heavy scowl began to relax. Her eyes softened and very slowly the corners of her mouth curled into a smile. When she finished the call she was beaming.

*Yes*. Brilliant. Fucking brilliant.

She knew she'd made the right call, listening to her instincts and hanging in there, waiting for the story to emerge.

And what a story it was turning out to be.

Her police contact, a hard bitch called Shona, had not only come through, but had struck gold. So much gold she owed her a nice backhanded bonus. Ha.

She had to act fast. So far there were no other journalists on the story like she was. Right there, with intimate access. It wouldn't stay that way for long. There was no honor among thieves or coppers. Their story would be leaked to other hacks for a price.

Keeley strutted back into the hotel and waved at the concierge. "Get me a taxi," she snapped. "Now."

Ten minutes later, she was at the gates of the TV studio. There were a couple of uniformed cops keeping vigil beside the regular security team. The studio staff waved her through.

"There's not much to see today, Ms. Rank," said Alan, an ex-engineer, eking out his pension with a bit of casual security work. "They've shut down filming until Monday in view of what's happened to that production guy."

She cast her gaze over the car park — fewer than half the usual vehicles. "Who's around? The producers, I suppose."

"Yes. Mr. Jones and Ms. Donahue are in there. Want me to let them know you're here?"

"What about the cast? Is Dale Zachary in?"

"No. All cast members have been stood down till

Monday."

*Damn*. She should have checked that before allowing her taxi to leave. "I'm supposed to be interviewing Dale today. I don't suppose you know where I can get hold of him?"

Twenty minutes later she was in another taxi winding its way up the narrow roads to a development of new houses built on old farm land. She gave the driver an extra ten-pound note on top of his fare and told him to wait. She had a feeling she wouldn't be here long and didn't want to get stuck in the middle of nowhere with no way back.

She knew which house was Dale's from the rental car parked in front. He was home. Fantastic.

Keeley strode purposefully to the front door and rang the bell. A middle-aged woman with thin mousey hair answered. The housekeeper, she assumed — very Northern.

"Can you let Dale know Keeley is here to talk about the show," she said confidently.

The woman looked unimpressed. "Mr. Zachary is not expecting anyone today. He gave clear instructions that he doesn't want to be disturbed."

"He's expecting me," Keeley said firmly. "He must have forgot."

"I don't think so. You must have made a mistake, Keeley, was it?"

The audacity of the bitch. Beneath that mousey exterior was a lion. "Just tell him I'm here. And tell him it's important. *Very* important."

The woman looked her up and down. "Wait here," she said at last, closing the front door and leaving Keeley on the doorstep.

For a few moments her fury at being treated this way threatened to overcome the malicious pleasure she took from the news she was about to impart. Keeping her on the doorstep indeed. Not for much longer. Dale Zachary would soon be kissing her ass and begging for journalistic mercy. And there was no chance of that. Not for anyone. If it made good copy, Keeley would trash her own mother in print.

Eventually, after five long minutes, the door opened. Dale was dressed in casual shorts and a checked shirt. He didn't invite her in. Didn't even smile.

"Keeley, what are you doing here? Johan gave you access to the studios, not to our private lives. We didn't have anything planned for today and I'm not in the mood to talk."

Typical man, thinking he could dictate terms.

"I think you will be in the mood to talk to me. Especially as I'm such a sympathetic listener. Some of those other hacks, they won't be so kind-hearted when it comes to writing up your story. At least I can get to the real truth." She stepped forward.

He leaned into the doorframe, blocking her entry. "All right, stop with the shitty insinuations and get to the point. What do you want?"

Charming. He was hardly the smooth heartthrob now.

"All right. How does *Shamed TV Star's Gay Affair with Murdered Assistant* grab you? Quite a snappy headline, don't you think? Especially when it's spread all over the Sunday front pages. I can turn that around for you. I can tell your real story instead of the closet-busting crap those other journos will run with."

Well, that hit him where it hurt. He looked as wounded as if she'd punched him in the balls. A real crushing blow.

"C'mon," she continued. "Just think about it. This story is going hit big in the next few days. You can't hide from it anymore. But you can handle it in a controlled, dignified manner. I promise everyone will be on your side when they read my version of your story."

"That's never going to happen," he said angrily. "You can tell whatever shitty version of events you like. Try the angle you got from the police. I'm sure you paid enough for it."

"Think about this. C'mon, Dale. Don't be a fool. You're making a big mistake."

"No. Talking to you would be a mistake. Now fuck off."

He slammed the door in her face and turned the lock.

\* \* \* \*

Dale balled his shaky hands into a fist and breathed deeply. The shit had hit the fan. He'd known it was coming, but that didn't lessen the impact of the inevitable. He'd been lucky, getting away with it for so long. To get to thirty-four, as a working actor, and preserve his private life. This wasn't the 1980s and journalists didn't routinely make a big deal of outing anymore, not even the low-life tabloids. But if there was a newsworthy aspect to unmasking someone's sexuality, then all moral obligations were waved. And boy, was there a newsworthy story here.

Mrs. Butterworth was moving the vacuum cleaner across the hall to the living room. "Did I do the right thing?" she asked.

"Oh, yes. Thank you, you did great."

"A newspaper woman, was she?"

Dale nodded.

"Thought so," Mrs. Butterworth said, chest bristling. "She had an untrustworthy look about her." She carried on vacuuming.

Dale headed to the kitchen. There was coffee brewing. He was usually a decaf drinker but today he'd made a strong pot of Arabica coffee. He needed the caffeine hit and poured a large mug.

So what was he going to do now? He didn't have a plan. Neglectful really, when he'd been dreading this moment for the whole of his career. He should have had *something* planned. Unlike a major Hollywood player, he didn't have a team of lawyers, agents and publicists to call upon when the heat was on. The story was about to be written and there was nothing he could do to stop it.

So what? There were more important things to agonize over. Poor Aaron for instance. The man was dead along with two others. What did it matter if Dale Zachary, who most people in the UK hadn't heard of until last week, was a fag? The news was hardly going to break the internet.

The people in his life, they were the ones he had to worry about.

He picked up his phone and dialed his ex-wife's number.

"Hi, Dale," Laura answered after a couple of rings.

"Hi. Can you talk?"

"Not long. I'm working. Is something wrong?"

"Oh," he stalled. "Well, maybe I could call you later. At a better time."

"Tell me now. Just a second, I'll step outside. Okay, good. Now, quickly, what is it?"

*Oh, boy.* His insides contracted. His throat was tight. The words wouldn't come out. "It's... It's erm..."

"You're scaring me now," Laura said softly. "Is there something wrong? You're not ill, are you?"

"No, no. I'm not. It's not that."

"Then what is it?" she pressed.

"Okay." Deep breath. "You know we're getting a lot of heat from the press about this show?"

"I'd have to live on Mars to miss it."

"Well, the heat is about to be turned up higher. There's this journalist, well, she's barely that, more like a glorified gossip columnist. She's going to write a story about me. Outing me."

"Shit. Dale, I'm sorry. Can't you put a block on it somehow?"

"I have neither the money nor the influence. To tell you the truth, I don't think I want to. I've been in hiding far too long. I'm in my mid-thirties and still living a lie. I think the time has come. No more hiding."

"That's very brave.

"Not really," he said honestly. "If Keeley wasn't about to out me, I wouldn't do it myself. But that's not the issue. It's how it's going to unravel. It's not going to be pleasant. It serves me right, in a way. If I had come out myself I could have avoided headlines. Unfortunately, now, I think it's going to be front page news. No, I don't think, I know. The story is big."

"What are you talking about?"

He told her about his casual relationship with Aaron Oxford. "Keeley is going to portray me as the secret gay lover of the latest victim. That'll make one juicy lead story, don't you think?"

"It's offensive. The boy's grieving family doesn't want to read that."

"Exactly," he sighed. "And I don't want my family to read it either. That's why I'm calling, Laura. I want to speak to Jack before the story breaks. Listen, we've been stood down on the production until Monday. If I drive down this afternoon, I could speak to him tonight, put him in the picture before the headlines turn ugly. I don't want him to find out his old man is gay from someone else."

Laura gave a soft laugh. It was not unkind. "You're a little late to that party, I'm afraid."

A fresh wave of shock came over him. Dale sat down as his legs began to weaken. "He already knows? Who told him?"

"Nobody. Well, I did. Kind of. But Jack had already figured it out when he asked me. He's a bright boy, Dale. And a modern boy. Kids today, they don't have any hang-ups about that kind of stuff. And they're better for it."

"Oh my God." What an idiot. How could have waited so long to do this? He'd been living in a protective bubble, blindly believing that everything was okay. "What did he say?"

"Dale, relax. He's totally fine about it. He's got a lot of questions, naturally. Stuff I couldn't answer for him. But, as far as having a gay dad goes, he's completely chilled."

"Really?"

"Honestly. He's a great kid. You have nothing to worry about."

Relief flooded through him and suddenly there was a lump in his throat, a hard ball of emotion. "I want to see him."

"Of course."

"Can I still come tonight?"

"Yes. You don't have to ask."

"I think it's best, don't you? He might be okay about me but I don't think anyone is going to be fine with the headlines that are about to drop. I'd like to tell my side of that story before he reads a distorted version."

When he ended the call, Dale laughed. A nervous, uncertain sound. He was still trembling. The world felt like a completely different place from the one he was in before picking up the phone. It was a lot less frightening. Hopeful.

Maybe it would be all right.

He could only hope.

# Chapter Seventeen

The bedroom was small and dark. Dirty net curtains hung across a tiny window, blocking a nondescript view of the alley behind. There were two twin beds with mismatched, over-washed covers. The dark blue carpet was worn right through to the floorboards beside the door and probably responsible for ninety-five percent of the bad odors in the room.

Jamie couldn't imagine spending one night in a shithole like this, let alone the three months *Blood Falls on Stone* was scheduled to film for.

Nigel Perigrew, a sound engineer who had shared the room with Aaron Oxford, stood against the wall with his arms folded. He was a heavyset man in his early forties, with thinning ginger hair and a red face. "It's a toilet, I know, but I've stayed in worse. It's cheap and that's what counts. We can't afford to spend our wages on fancy hotels."

Jamie nodded understandingly. "That's for the stars, eh? Dale Zachary?"

"Too right it is. They can afford it. That guy, Dale, he's renting a posh house in the country. The rest of us go for the cheapest digs we can find."

"Did you always room with Aaron?"

Nigel nodded. "Since we've been here, sure. I never met him before then but we've had this room since getting to Durham. To be honest, I wouldn't mind something cheaper myself. I don't care how shitty it is. What I've got left in my pocket at the end of the week, that's all I care about."

"How did you get along with him? Aaron? What kind of man was he?"

He shrugged. "Didn't have a lot to do with him if I'm honest. You try not to spend too much time in a place like this. The bathrooms are so bloody dirty we've taken to showering at the studios. Breakfast is better there too. This was just a place to get our heads down, that's all."

Breathing in the fetid air, Jamie said, "It's a miracle you could do that much."

"I'm telling you, man, I've stayed in worse. And no doubt will again, but neither Aaron nor me spent much time in here."

The two men kept their possessions on separate sides of the room, though neither appeared to have made much effort to unpack. Aaron's stuff was stored in an open suitcase, with a handful of personal items spread across the dresser on his side of the room. There was a can of deodorant, a small plate for loose change, a phone charger and a trial gym membership card. No effort had been made to settle in. His clean clothes were folded neatly in his suitcase rather than stored in the wardrobe. His mobile phone and tablet computer had already been taken to police HQ for analysis. They had failed to yield anything of use so far.

"Did Aaron ever bring anyone back here?" Jamie asked. "Lovers? One-night stands?"

Nigel rolled his eyes. "Would you? It's not exactly the kind of place to make romance."

"I guess not. Did he ever talk about anyone? Tell you if he was meeting someone? Going on a date?" *Like with Dale Zachary?* He left the last question unsaid.

"I hardly knew him. He wouldn't tell me that stuff anyway. We shared a room. Some days we didn't even see each other. Just a lump beneath the covers as we went to bed late or left early. Don't get me wrong, he was a nice lad and all that. I wouldn't have a bad word said against him, but we weren't good friends or anything."

"How did you come to be sharing together?"

"There's a young girl in the production office, she sorts all that out. She puts out a list of cheap local accommodation and we all go in for it. It's pot luck. Find someone willing to go in with you on a penthouse like this one and you're made up."

The room had already been gone over by a specialist team. Jamie was not going to find anything here that hadn't been discovered before. The identity of Aaron's killer would not be found in this rundown bed and breakfast. But he wanted to see the place. To get an insight into the kind of man Aaron was and what his life here in Durham had been like. There wasn't much to be learned. Aaron was a transient worker, passing through with no intention of setting down roots.

The trial gym membership said everything. Temporary. No commitment.

"Okay, then." He smiled at Nigel. "Thanks for letting me look around. I know our boys have already been through this, but you never know what a fresh pair of eyes can find."

"Happy to help," Nigel said. "I just hope you catch that fucker soon. Before he hurts anyone else."

Jamie left the B and B — feet sticking to the stair carpet — and headed back to his car. The mental picture he was beginning to form of Aaron was of a regular, hardworking guy. Quite unremarkable. He fit the killer's brief in so much as he was of similar age as the earlier victims, slightly older but not so much you'd notice. A good-looking boy-next-door type. *Gay* boy next door. But, unlike the others, Aaron wasn't a local. It was a cruel twist of fate that brought him to work in Durham right when the strangler was hitting his swing.

But what was it that brought Aaron to his attention? Or any of the other boys?

That was the thing the police were struggling with. The boys were all gay. Sure. And they were handsome. But there was nothing else to connect them. They didn't know each other or go to the same places, or frequent any of the local cruising areas. They all had social media profiles — but who didn't? They had online dating accounts but none of the boys were overly promiscuous or risk-taking in their behavior. They weren't cruising for dick twenty-four hours a day or touting for anonymous sex. There was nothing to connect them.

Except the fact that they had all caught the deadly eye of a serial killer.

* * * *

"What'll you have?" Conrad asked. "Wine?"

"Not tonight," Matt said, shrugging off his jacket and hanging it over the back of the chair. "Vodka and tonic. Make it a strong one."

"Bad day?"

"Get the drinks and I'll tell you about it."

They met in town, straight from work. Matt had been working late when Conrad had called to say he was in the area and asked if he fancied a drink. He'd jumped at the chance. Dale had called earlier to tell him about the incident with Keeley Rank on his doorstep. "I don't think she knows about you. Not yet anyway. But it'll only be a matter of time. I just want to forewarn you."

Dale was on the motorway, heading south to see his son. He didn't know how long he would be gone. It could be the whole weekend.

"I'm gonna miss you like crazy," Dale had said.

Matt felt the same way. The notion of being apart for just one night was bad enough, but three or four—it was unbearable. "Just do what you have to do," he'd told Dale. "Your son is the most important person here. You're doing the right thing. And don't worry about me. I can take care of that tit-witch journalist if she does come knocking at my door."

They both had laughed but it was a bittersweet gesture, masking the pain of separation.

Conrad returned from the bar with Matt's vodka and a large glass of white wine for himself. They sat at a table by the window. The sky outside was steadily darkening, casting an ominous aspect over the tranquil river. The water here, which had always been so peaceful and safe, was tainted by the recent killings. Matt wondered if he would ever be able to look at the river and feel anything other than sadness again.

He took a long swallow. The vodka was pure and strong. The fiery heat as it went down was most welcome.

"So what gives?" asked Conrad, sipping his own drink.

"Dale," Matt answered, giving him a brief update on the last few days.

Conrad listened quietly, without any remark or judgment. He'd always been a good listener. Matt appreciated it. He couldn't tell anyone else about this. Certainly not Annabel. She would widen her eyes and gasp and smile all the while then post a Facebook update to share the story. Conrad wasn't like that. Matt could tell him anything and he would respect his confidence.

"It sounds like it's getting serious between you."

"It is." Matt smiled. "He told me that he loves me."

"Wow, already?"

He nodded. "And I love him too. I know we've only known each other five minutes but I've never felt anything like this. Not with anyone. I've been in love before. I loved Jamie for a while. But it was nothing like this. This is...so strong, so all-consuming. I think about Dale all the time. When I wake up the first thought I have is about him. And all through the day, when I should be concentrating on my cases, I just look at my watch and count down the time until I see him again."

"I'm happy for you, Matt."

"Even with all the shit that is going on, it makes me happy just to think about him." He told Conrad about the visit he'd had from Jamie. "He's working on the case now. Of course, when the boy from the studio was murdered, Jamie took it as an opportunity to put some pressure on Dale and me. Even had the nerve to suggest Dale might be the killer. He was none too happy when I provided Dale's alibi."

"Shit. He won't take that well."

"He didn't. It doesn't matter what I say, he wants to get back together."

"He'll find someone else soon. Once he realizes there's no chance of you making up."

"I hope you're right."

Matt finished his drink and went to the bar for another round. The place was starting to get busy. He was in the mood to stay out and get drunk. With Dale down south, it was a good way to blot out the lonely night ahead. But it was only Thursday. He still had to work tomorrow and he had a trial lined up at Crown Court. No way he could do that with a hangover. No, this would be his last drink. He would get up early and head to boot camp for the last session of the week.

Conrad gave him an update on his charity fundraiser.

"Damn," Matt said, suddenly remembering. "I was supposed to ask Dale to get some autographs and stuff from the studio for your prize fund."

"Don't be daft," Conrad said. "You two have far too much to worry about."

"No, I said I would help and I completely forgot. It's too late now. I don't think Dale will be home until Sunday evening."

"It's not a big deal, honestly. You can fix up a prize for next time instead."

It was a shitty thing to forget. These charity nights were a big deal to Conrad and the kids at the theater. "I'll be there though," he said. "Feel free to sting me for as many raffle tickets as you like."

"You're on." Conrad smiled.

Matt suddenly had an idea. It wouldn't make up for the missed celebrity autographs but it was better than nothing. "I'm going to boot camp in the morning. Why don't I ask the instructor if he'd like to help out? You know, donate a prize or something. He runs a gym as well as the morning groups. Maybe he could provide a free membership or something along those lines."

"All donations are gladly accepted. You know that."

Matt grinned, pleased with his idea. "Clint's all right. A bit intense, but I think he means well. I'll speak to him. I'm sure he'll be happy to help out."

* * * *

It took six hours to complete a journey that would usually take a little over four. Heavy traffic and frequent roadworks all down the motorway meant Dale rarely got above fifty miles per hour. He pulled off south of Nottingham to use the bathroom and sent Laura a text to say he was running late. After driving all this way, he didn't want her to put Jack to bed before he arrived. Now that he'd decided to be open with his son, he couldn't wait another night. Who knew what kind of stories they'd wake up to in the morning? He had a suspicion that Keeley would keep a lid on her scoop until the weekend. Scandal played so much better in the Sunday editions, but the murders in Durham were major news. Maybe she would go straight to press before another journalist got a lead on her exclusive. Only one thing was certain—the story was coming out. There was nothing he could do to stop it.

He'd been a jerk. Six hours on a dreary motorway had given him ample time to assess the situation. It was a mess entirely of his own making. Matt had been right, no one gave a shit about gay actors these days. They assumed the pretty ones were all gay anyway. Why the hell hadn't he come out when Laura divorced him? Or when he had followed her to England? A new beginning in a new country, it was an ideal chance to start over. No more lies or covering up. It would have been so easy.

Better than becoming a scandalous footnote in a murder enquiry.

Thinking about the murders, and Aaron, only made it worse. His problems were nothing compared to what those boys had gone through and what their families must be suffering now.

If he could only get to Jack before the shit hit the fan. If Jack was okay, he didn't care about anyone else.

Eventually he reached the modest three-bedroom house where Laura had settled with her new husband. A large white Qashqai was parked on the drive and Dale pulled in behind it. He left his luggage in the trunk. He'd look around for a hotel once he'd seen his son. He saw movement behind the living room window and the front door opened before he raised a hand to knock.

Henry Kinnear, Laura's second husband, greeted him with a warm smile and a handshake. A heavyset, balding man, Henry made up for what he lacked in looks with a friendly personality, kind eyes and a wicked sense of humor. When they'd first met, Dale only had to spend a few minutes with the guy to totally get what Laura saw in him. If another man had to be a father figure to Jack, Dale couldn't have chosen better.

"Don't look so serious," Henry said, welcoming him inside. "You have nothing to worry about here."

The house was in its usual state of habitual chaos. There were children's toys all over the floor, laundry on the radiators, the TV blasting to an empty room.

From above, came the thunder of footsteps across the landing and Jack's excitable face appeared at the top of the stairs.

"Dad," he squealed excitedly, rushing down to meet him.

"Hey, take it easy. You'll fall."

Then the boy, dressed for bed in pajamas, was wrapping his arms around Dale's waist and pressing the side of his face into his stomach. The worries that had plagued him all the way here were forgot in that moment. He put his arms around his son's shoulder. Jack was warm and his damp hair smelled of shampoo. Dale cherished each second. The six-hour drive had been worth it.

"Have you eaten?" Henry asked.

Dale shook his head.

"We made you a pizza," Jack said excitedly. "Ham and mushrooms."

"Wow, my favorite. Did you make it yourself?"

Jack nodded. "Mum bought the base but I put all the toppings on. We've already had ours so it's all for you."

"All for me? That's great. I'm *starving*."

Jack giggled. Taking Dale's hand into two of his own, he dragged him toward the kitchen.

Laura met them halfway, carrying Emily, her wide-eyed little girl, in her arms. She leaned in, turning her cheek for a kiss. Laura had blossomed into motherhood in the years since they'd separated. Her face and figure were fuller than before, but there was a contentment about her that he couldn't ever remember in the years they were together. She was finally happy. It was only through distance and time that he was able to see how wrong they had been for each other. Laura had fooled herself about him just as much as he'd fooled himself.

"She's grown so much," he said, planting a soft kiss on the baby's chubby cheek and stroking her blonde hair. "How old is she now?"

"Nineteen months," Laura said, stepping back to look him over. "You look tired."

"Long journey. The traffic was a nightmare."

"Mum," Jack wailed. "Let's put the pizza on."

"Why don't you and Dad do that?" she said. "Henry and I are going to put Emily to bed." She looked at Dale with understanding eyes. "Go ahead. We'll see you in a while."

Dale followed Jack into the kitchen. The oven was already preheated and on the counter, ready to go, was the most top-heavy pizza he'd ever seen—tomatoes, mushrooms, ham, onions and a ton of cheese. Jack pulled on a pair of oven gloves.

"Let's go, Dad, you get the door and I'll put the pizza in. It's gonna be delicious. I know it."

Dale smiled. "If you ever decide to make a living of this

you may need to cut back on the toppings. You'll be out of business before you get started."

"Mum says you're too skinny," Jack said, sliding the tray into the oven.

"She does, does she?"

Jack nodded, pressing the buttons for the timer. This kid was a real pro.

"How come you don't cook like this when you come to visit me?" Dale asked.

"'Cause you like to live off takeaways."

Dale laughed. He suddenly felt very calm and sure of his future. Jack was a great kid. He didn't know why he'd been worried for so long.

"C'mon, let's sit down. While this monster pizza of yours is cooking, your old man needs to tell you something."

\* \* \* \*

Matt got home around eight-thirty and ate a solitary supper at the kitchen table before watching television. He went to bed at eleven. Clint Dexter saw all of this through the kitchen windows. It was remarkable how much could be seen by a stranger hiding outside a well-lit window, especially when it was dark outside. Because the house was not directly overlooked at the rear, Matt rarely closed his curtains or blinds.

Clint watched, expecting the American to show up at any time. When Matt turned off the downstairs lights and went upstairs alone, Clint smiled. No Yank in the bedroom tonight. Good. It was a comforting thought, knowing Matt was alone in the house. He could go in there if he wanted. It would be easy. Creeping around the house while its occupant slept. Standing over his still, softly breathing form.

The idea made him hard.

He could end it all tonight if he wanted to. Slip silently in and take what he wanted. Destroy the younger man in the most depraved manner. Ravage him. Hurt him. Matt was strong but Clint was stronger. One punch would take him out, long enough to tie him down. And once he was bound... Clint could do what the hell he wanted. Make use of that heavenly body—corrupt and defile it. Torture and fuck him.

God, how badly he wanted that.

But not yet.

He was playing the long game. The time was not right.

But it would be soon.

# Chapter Eighteen

For most people, as the week reached an end, the urge to exercise weakened. The turnout for Friday's boot camp proved the theory. Dale was not the only regular who was absent that morning. Matt made it through habit rather than willpower. A mindless autopilot kicked in when his alarm went off, getting him from his bed to the park without too much effort.

Thinking about Dale was the biggest incentive. He wanted to look good for his return and intended to work out every day till he came back. He wanted to be in the best possible shape to please him. Thighs, bum, abs, chest — he would be the best version of himself he could be. Dale deserved it.

He missed him so much already and he'd only been gone a night. He'd been sleeping on his own for months now, for far longer than he'd known Dale, but going to bed alone, he felt his absence enormously. Without him in the bed, the sleepy smell of his hair and beard in the night, just didn't seem right. He was like a child, denied his favorite teddy bear or comfort blanket. He woke several times, reaching into the empty space, rolling onto Dale's pillow to breathe the scent that still lingered there.

He understood Dale's reasons for going away — it was a massive moment in his life — but selfishly he hoped he would come back soon.

So he'd decided to exercise. Boot camp this morning and maybe a run or a session in the gym after work. He would make himself so exhausted that he'd have no option but to sleep tonight, however lonely and unwelcoming the bed felt.

These were intense feelings. Especially for such a short relationship. But they didn't scare him, he embraced them. He loved Dale and wanted to be with him. There was nothing scary in that.

Matt pushed hard along the course. Clint barked orders from the front, blowing his whistle. "Thirty squats. *Now.*"

Matt dropped into the squats without a pause, performing them with steely determination. His thigh muscles screamed their protest but he didn't break form. He took all of his frustration out on his body. Off again, running hard, embracing the pain. It was insignificant compared to being without Dale.

Dale had sent a text before bed last night. Everything was okay. By all accounts, Jack wasn't fazed in the slightest by his dad coming out. No reason why he should be. Kids were often a lot more relaxed than their parents when it came to issues like that, but it was a big deal to Dale and he appreciated that. With Jack on side, Dale was ready for anything.

He hoped Dale was wrong about the oncoming media storm. Surely an actor's sexuality wouldn't cause much of a scandal these days. He would like to think so, but if Dale was right, they would know soon enough.

He warned him it wouldn't be pretty. If the press got wind of their relationship, they would drag Matt into it. *Big deal*, he thought. Bring it on. He had nothing to hide. He'd already made up his mind to handle any press intrusion with quiet dignity. They'd get nothing from him because he had nothing to give. If it was scandal they wanted, they would have to source it elsewhere. Matt's slate was clean.

"You pushed it again this morning," Clint said at the end of the course. "Well done, my friend. I like to see commitment like yours. You have everything it takes."

Matt was knackered. *Shit.* He fell forward, gripping his thighs, sucking in air, the coldness of which was painful against the back of his throat. He'd pushed it harder than he'd thought. The muscles in his legs trembled. But despite the exhaustion it felt damn good.

"Take it easy," Clint said, a hand on his shoulder. "Get your breath back. It's good to work it hard, but not if it kills you."

"I'm fine," he gasped at last. "But maybe not quite as up there in terms of fitness as I thought."

"You're getting there." Clint squeezed his shoulder.

Eventually Matt straightened up. Clint was looking straight at him. Matt laughed. "Don't worry, I'm not going to have a heart attack. It just looks that way."

"I'm not worried about you. You're one of my best men."

What was it about Clint this morning? The vibes he was giving off were very different to his usual no-nonsense demeanor. The way he was looking at him and how he'd touched his shoulder just then, sustaining the contact for longer than necessary. Did old Clint fancy him?

Matt laughed at the idea as soon as it occurred. No way. Clint having an eye for him — it was ridiculous. There was just no chance. He'd never met a guy who was so determinedly straight in body and character as Clint. He made guys like Gerard Butler and Colin Farrell look effeminate.

Maybe it was him. With Dale away, he was horny. Seeing sex in the most improbable places.

"Clint, before you go, can I ask a favor? I've got this friend, Conrad. He does a lot of work for charity. He's got a big event this weekend and he's looking for prizes that can be raffled or auctioned off on the night."

"Prizes?"

"Yes. Anything. I wondered whether you'd be in a position to help out. It doesn't have to be much. A free month's membership to the gym, or a couple of free boot camp sessions. Anything you can afford, really. I wouldn't ask but it's a great cause and it means the world to Conrad."

He looked Matt carefully in the eyes. "Tomorrow, did you say?"

"Tomorrow night, yes. It's short notice, I know."

He smiled. It looked uncomfortable on him. "I'd love to."

"Brilliant. You're a great guy, Clint."

"Why don't you call round later and I'll see what I can come up with? Can you stop by the gym tonight?"

"Absolutely," Matt said. "I'll call on my way home."

Clint slapped him on the shoulder again and walked away.

Matt chuckled. Clint fancying him — the idea was insane. Maybe he'd pushed it too hard after all. His head was cracking up.

* * * *

Clint watched him walk away. There was no trace of the excitement he felt inside visible on his face.

Matt's jogging bottoms clung to his sweaty ass, dark and damp in the cleft between those firm mounds. His T-shirt was soaked, clinging to the contours of his torso like a second skin. His hair was also wet, plastered in delectable curls to the skin of his neck. *What I wouldn't do to that body.* If he allowed his iron control to waver for just a second, he would drag that ass into the woods and brutalize it. Fuck it without mercy. Piss in it, come in it, make it bleed.

Clint turned away from the stragglers in his group before any of them could see the protrusion of his massive hard-on.

Matt was coming by the gym tonight. It was too good an opportunity to pass up. He'd been playing the long game, teasing himself with the belief that he would take Matt sometime in the future. By why wait? Plans could change and he was adaptable. It was a skill that had kept him at large and functioning all this time.

No, he couldn't let this one go. Matt was coming to him tonight. He would be ready.

* * * *

That morning, Dale had a rare opportunity to experience

215

what it was like to be a regular dad. He was there for breakfast with his son, over which he helped Jack complete the homework he'd been too excited to do the evening before. He got to nag him gently about loading the dishwasher afterward and about brushing his teeth properly. The icing on the cake was Laura asking him to run Jack to school.

"You'd be doing me a big favor," she said, getting her youngest ready for the child minder. "I've got a meeting at nine. There's no way I'll make it."

Dale was delighted. "Go ahead. I'd love to do it."

In the car, Jack jabbered excitedly about the football match he was due to play that weekend. "Can you come to watch, Dad? It would be so cool if you could."

Dale was overwhelmed with love for his son. Last night he'd made the big announcement, telling Jack just who he was, and the kid had taken the news without a trace of misgiving.

"*I knew that already,*" Jack had admitted. "*I've been waiting for you to tell me.*" All of this time he'd been worrying — for nothing.

"I can't make any promises," Dale said regretfully. "I'd love to be around to watch you play, but the truth is, I don't know what today is going to bring. If things kick off, like I suspect they might, then I want to get as far away as possible from you guys. I don't want awful reporters stalking out your house, or your soccer game. You understand, don't you?"

"How many times, Dad? It's football," Jack said with a playful groan, "*Football*. Nobody calls it soccer over here."

"When I get off this show, I guess you'll just have to take me to a few games and educate me all about *football*."

They both laughed.

Dale's good mood lasted for all of five minutes. Until he said goodbye to Jack at the school gate. His phone rang as he navigated the traffic back to town. It was his British agent, David. A straight-talking Londoner who'd been in the business over forty years.

"Where are you?" David barked through the car's speakers.

"On a school run. Heading back to my ex-wife's house."

"Well, I guess you probably know this already but the shit has hit the fan. I've had reporters on the phone since I got in at seven. All they want to ask about is you."

"Fuck!"

"It's a fucker all right. But what do you want to do about it?"

"They're asking the obvious question?"

"Obviously," David drawled.

It was finally happening. The moment he'd dreaded for his entire career. Surprisingly, Dale was okay about it. There was nothing to fear. No humiliation. He'd cleared things with the people who were important to him. What was the worst that could happen now?

"Okay, tell them the truth. Let's put out a statement. Tell the world Dale Zachary plays for the other team." He laughed. "Wow. It feels good to say it after all this time. I am gay."

"Want me to do it? All official."

"Shit, no. I'll do it myself. Is there anything in today's papers?"

"No. But there will be tomorrow," David said.

"Okay. I'm going to head back to Durham. If they come chasing me for a picture or a story, I don't want my family caught up in it. I'll decide how I want to word it and make a statement on Facebook this afternoon. Do you mind holding them off until then?"

"Not a bit. If you ask me, you should have done this years back," David said confidently.

"Why are you telling me this now?" Dale laughed.

"'Cause you never wanted to hear it before."

* * * *

*"Someone must have seen something."*

What was wrong with these people? Didn't anyone have eyes? Keeley had never encountered a film crew so short on gossip, so oblivious to what was going on right beneath their noses.

She met with Donna Bradey and Luisa Capaldi, two of the main makeup assistants on *Blood Falls on Stone* at the Honest Lawyer Hotel, a couple of miles south of Durham. She had promised them a full three-course lunch with wine in exchange for a shitload of gossip from the set. Two courses into the meal and the painted dollies had failed to deliver anything she didn't already know. These bitches had better sing before lunch was over or they'd regret it.

Donna was in her early fifties but dressed like a woman thirty years younger and five stone lighter. Her hair was a dyed red-brown color and bolstered by dozens of hairpieces in shades that no way matched. She put her orange foundation on with a trowel, before caking various shades of red, purple and gold on top. Spidery eyelashes and glossy purple lipstick completed the look. The average drag queen would think she had gone too far.

Next to her, Luisa looked like full-on tranny road kill. Her hair was white blonde, with cheap extensions that had also been embellished with awful hairpieces to create a shoddy bird's nest look. Her makeup comprised of shades of red, white and blue. With an emaciated frame and horsey features, she looked like a juvenile Russian hooker.

Keeley surmised they had made the effort to look *nice* on her account. If they turned up for work looking like this, no sane actor would let them near their face with a makeup brush.

"Well, I guess, like, Aaron did spend a lot of time in Dale's trailer around lunch," Donna said in a ghastly Geordie accent.

"He was Dale's assistant," Keeley pointed out. "Was there anything unusual in that?"

"Suppose not."

"Did anyone ever comment on them spending time

together?"

"Not really."

*Jesus. What a fucking waste of time this was turning out to be.* "Did either of you know Aaron personally?"

"I worked with him before," Luisa piped in. "Couple of years ago on a movie. *The Passion of Rosemary.* Did you see it?"

"Never heard of it. Tell me about Aaron."

"Oh," Luisa said vaguely, pouring the last of the second bottle of wine into her glass. "He was all right. A nice guy. He was seeing one of the department heads back then."

"A man?"

"Yes, a fella."

"You never told me that," Donna said, wide-eyed, as if she'd just been privy to a huge revelation.

"Well, there was nothing much to tell. They came to a couple of crew meals together and the wrap party and that was about it. I didn't have anything to do with them."

"Ladies," Keeley said firmly. "This isn't enough. I'm writing about Dale Zachary and you're not giving me the slightest scrap to go on."

She saw the sudden panic in their eyes as they realized a refill on that empty bottle of wine might not be forthcoming. They looked at each other, searching their tiny minds.

"What was it Jess from wardrobe said the other day?" Donna asked Luisa.

Luisa chewed an acrylic nail, thinking hard. "Oh, erm… What was it again? Something about Aaron."

"Yes," Donna said brightly, eyes suddenly very wide. "That was it. Jess said she'd thought for a while that there might have been something going on between Aaron and Dale. She was friends with Aaron, you see."

"Did he confide in her?"

"Not so much. He never came out and *told* her he was shagging Dale or anything, she just got the impression that there was something going on."

"Yes," Luisa said, waving a taloned finger. "And Jess said

Aaron had been down for the last few days, before he, you know, died. She thought that whatever might have been happening had come to an end. You know, like Dale had finished it or something."

"Why did he do that?"

"Dunno."

These idiots were useless. Keeley had had enough. "All right. It sounds like I need to speak to this Jess. Where can I find her?"

"You can't. We've been stood down till Monday," Donna said. "As soon as she heard, Jess went home. She's got a kid, you see. It was a nice chance to spend some time with it. She won't be back till late on Sunday."

Keeley took a deep breath. *Control, Keeley, keep a lid on it.* "Do you have a phone number? Some way I could reach her?"

The makeup women pulled out their mobiles and swiped through their contacts.

"I haven't got it," Donna said.

"Me neither," Luisa replied.

"Do you think you could get it?" Keeley asked carefully.

"Let's order desserts and then we'll ring round a few people. I'm sure someone can get it for us." Donna reached for the menu. "Could we get a dessert *and* a cheese board?"

* * * *

Jamie drove to Bishop Auckland, a rural town twelve miles south of Durham. Like many places, the old market town was clearly divided into the haves and the have-nots. When he'd first joined the force, Jamie was stationed here for a while and got to know the have-not areas very well. From the market place, a visitor would see it as a picture-perfect rural town, but they would only have to travel a mile up the road to encounter the rundown estates that housed the drug dealers, the addicts, the wife beaters, alcoholics and professional criminals who resided there.

Jamie hated the place. Every minute he spent working there, he counted time to his next assignment. He always remembered the words of an old detective he used to work with. "When the UK takes a shit, it eventually washes up in Bishop Auckland."

Fortunately today he was heading toward Durham Road and the affluent side of town. Four and five-bedroom detached houses, set back behind high hedges and long drives. The only time he'd had cause to visit this area when he was stationed here was when one of the mansions overlooking the golf course got knocked off. The incompetent thieves were caught three days later trying to offload their goods at the pawnbrokers.

Jamie was in a better mood today.

Matt was moving on. He didn't like it but it didn't hurt as much today as it had yesterday. The fact that Matt was fucking the American actor stuck in his throat, but there was nothing he could do to stop them. He'd been involved in enough late-night calls when ex-partners refused to believe things were over. It almost always ended in violence and certainly in bitterness. He didn't want to go there. It would be fruitless and likely to fuck up his personal and professional life. No. It wasn't easy, but when he woke up that morning he finally realized it was time to draw a line under the whole relationship.

It was history.

Maybe when this case was over, and he had a little more free time, he would think about dating again. Getting back out there. Perhaps join a dating site — a decent one, not one of those sleaze-fests for sluts and cheating married men. He wanted to find a nice guy. Someone with an understanding of what he did. Another copper would be an idea, but there were far too few of them out at work ever to make that viable.

Still, it would be nice to get out there, go on a few dates and hopefully meet someone new.

Jamie arrived at the address, pulling on to the drive of a

nice-looking property on the modest end of Durham Road. It might not be as grand the neighboring houses but it sure beat anything on the other side of town. He killed the engine and got out just as the front door was opened by a good-looking, slightly heavy, bearded man in his thirties.

Jamie approached with his ID raised. "Barney Kilofer?"

"It's Barney Kilofer-James," the man answered. "Tony and I are married."

Married! Jamie would never get used to *that*. "Detective Constable Jamie Dench."

Barney Kilofer-James looked him over, seemed to decide he was nothing to get excited about and invited him in. The hallway had a beautiful dark wooden floor and a staircase that rose to large airy landing. The house was tastefully decorated. There were fresh flowers in a vase on the dresser and the aroma of strong coffee. Jamie was impressed. It was exactly the kind of house he used to imagine Matt and him living in one day.

Shit. There he was again. Matt, creeping into his thoughts. He must stop that.

"Come through to the kitchen," Barney said. "I've made cheese scones and coffee. I hope you're hungry. Tony is at work. It won't be a problem with just me, will it?"

"No problem at all. All I'm here to do is take a statement from you. If we have any questions we can contact your, er...husband later."

"I can't see how he could tell you anything more than I can. We barely got to know the guy." He poured two cups of coffee. "Cream? Sugar?"

"Both please." Jamie sat at the breakfast bar while Barney set out the coffee and a plate of freshly buttered scones. "Help yourself. They're still warm and that's the best time to eat them."

Jamie thanked him and took a bite. Delicious. When he eventually signed up to that dating site he would look for a man who could cook too. Matt had been a horror in the kitchen. Every meal they ever ate came from a tin, jar or takeaway.

"So," he said, washing the scones down with the expensive-tasting coffee. "You called to say you knew Aaron Oxford."

Barney looked suddenly bashful. "We didn't *know* him exactly. We didn't even know his surname name was Oxford. But when it came up on the news, Tony and I realized that we might be among the last people to see him alive. We thought we'd better come forward, if only to rule ourselves out."

"So when did you see him last?"

"Sunday afternoon."

"And that was…where?"

"Here. Aaron came here. Well, not strictly true. We picked him up in Durham and brought him here, but it was all arranged in advance. He didn't drive, you see, and these country bus routes are such a drag, especially on Sunday. So we thought it best if we went to meet him."

"I understand. So Aaron came here for…sex?"

Barney grimaced and looked into his coffee. "It sounds tacky when you put it as bluntly as that, but yes. He came round for a shag."

"Had he been here before?"

"Only once. About three weeks ago. He hadn't been in the area long and was trawling around online, looking to meet new people. He caught our eye and we sent him a message. It was Tony's idea. I didn't think we'd stand a chance, if I'm honest. He was too good-looking for us, but, I don't know, maybe he was lonely. He sent a nice reply and said he'd love to come round."

"Did he tell you he was lonely? That he was looking to meet people?"

"Not lonely exactly. That's more like the impression I got of him. He told us he was in the area for work and didn't know anyone outside of that. We didn't know what he did. Didn't even ask, which is terrible really. Taking someone to bed without knowing anything about them. I think we might have been the first guys he met round here, you know, for sex."

"He told you that?"

"I think so. Can't remember the exact words, but it was something along those lines. Again, this was just an impression, but I felt he wasn't the type to go whoring round. Not like some of these pigs. We've brought guys back who've been searching for their next shag before they're even out the door. But I think with Aaron, the Grindr thing was just a way to meet new people. It wasn't all about sex."

Interesting. Everything they had learned suggested that Aaron was not the typical, promiscuous risk taker. He was having his fun but not in any excessive way. Nothing that should bring him into the path of an opportunistic predator. But somehow it had.

"Did he tell you anything about his lifestyle? About men he might have met, or was planning to? Any unwanted attention his profile attracted?"

"Absolutely nothing. Nothing I can remember anyway. We didn't do a lot of talking," Barney said bashfully. "The first time we met, we picked him up from outside a gym in town. He'd been working out and wanted to use the shower before, you know. Then the next time, he was waiting at a bus stop along by the university. He was alone both times and didn't mention anyone else. I'm sorry, Officer Dexter, but I think I might have wasted your time in coming here. There's really not a lot I can tell you about the poor man."

\* \* \* \*

Everything had happened too quickly today, Matt barely had time to catch his breath. Work had been nonstop. Rushing from court, to meetings, to client appointments. In between he took several short phone calls from Dale, who was on the motorway heading back to Durham after just one night away. What a night though. Everything had changed, including Dale. His joy was infectious.

"I can't believe how happy I feel," he said. "No more secrets or worrying about what people will say. I'm free. Free to be with you. I want you to be a part of this."

Even though he couldn't see it, Matt's smile was a mile wide. "I'm going to be there for you, you know that. We're in it together. What time will you get here? I can't wait to see you. Want to come to my place?"

"Maybe you should come to mine," Dale said. "I might be overestimating the press interest in this, but just in case there are any reporters or photographers looking for me, I don't want to bring them to your door. What would the neighbors say?"

"Oh, my neighbors would love it. They don't need much excuse to get their curtains twitching."

"Well, I've got something else that's twitching."

They laughed. "Okay, I'll come to yours." It suddenly occurred to Matt that in their short but intense relationship he hadn't ever been to Dale's place. "Hey, I don't know where you live."

"I'll text you the postcode. Come as soon as you can. Straight from work."

"I'll go home to change first."

"No. Don't do that. I want to see you in your smart lawyer suit. Then tear it off you."

It was only later, as he hurried his last client out of his office, dying to get to Dale's, that Matt remembered he had another commitment. Clint was expecting him at his gym for his raffle donation. Conrad's charity function was tomorrow night. He needed that prize. But even if he collected if from Clint, how was he going to get it to Conrad in time, especially if Dale's doorstep was under siege by photographers?

Hurrying from the office to the car, he called Conrad. His friend answered straight away.

"Hey you," Conrad said, "if you're looking for another drinking companion, I can't tonight. I've got so much to do."

"That's not it. Can you spare ten minutes to collect a prize?" He explained about Clint's offer. "He said if I called into the gym after work he'd have a donation ready for you. Only I don't have the time tonight. Any chance you could swing by yourself? Just explain that I sent you, I'm sure it'll be fine."

"Not a problem," Conrad said. "I'm heading to the theater in the next half hour. I can stop at the gym on the way. Dexter's, isn't it?"

"That's the one," Matt replied, fastening his seatbeat. "Give him your best charity pitch. You might get more out of him than I can."

"Is he handsome?"

"He's not ugly. But you shouldn't be looking. I thought things were going well with you and Danny Frost."

"They are," Conrad said. "But I can still look. After all, a handsome man is a handsome man."

"I'll let you be the judge of that. Tell Clint I'm sorry I couldn't come in person. I'm sure you can sweet talk him."

"I'll give it my best."

Matt hung up and swung the car into the stream of traffic. He'd already programmed Dale's address into his sat nav and let the system guide him. His mind was full of other things. Of Dale Zachary and the night they had ahead of them.

The future they had ahead of them.

Nothing could spoil it.

Everything was going to be perfect.

# Chapter Nineteen

Things were coming together nicely. Very nicely. Tickets for tomorrow night were ninety-five percent sold and Conrad had already pre-sold a whole load of raffle tickets. It was shaping up to be one of the company's most successful fundraisers ever. The autumn production of *Fiddler on the Roof* was a certainty now. But this was not the time to sit back and bask in achievement. That would come on Sunday. Right now, there was plenty of work to be done.

Such a pity about Matt's boyfriend. Ordinarily, having a star like Dale Zachary onboard would have brought the kind of publicity that money couldn't buy. But right now, the timing was wrong. Aside from the personal drama Matt and Dale were caught up in, *Blood Falls On Stone* was generating the kind of attention that no one wanted to be associated with, much less a children's charity. Hopefully there would be other opportunities. Matt was smitten with the American actor. If their relationship worked out, then Dale would still be around to help with their next fundraiser.

Conrad hoped things did work out. Matt deserved some luck in love. Especially after Jamie turned out to be such a dick. Morose and uncommunicative, he was a drag. It was no secret that he didn't like Matt's friends and hated Matt spending any time with them. Conrad never understood what Matt saw in him. He was decent-looking but so what. Matt was in a different league and could take his pick of the hottest guys. Why saddle himself with a misery like Jamie?

He hoped Dale turned out to be different. It was hard to judge. Without ever having met him, he could only go on what he'd read. He was a hottie. No denying that. When it came to looks, Dale and Matt were perfectly matched. But looks weren't everything. What was he really like? It was hard to see what Matt could have in common with a closeted American actor. A deeply closeted actor it would seem. There was plenty of gossip about his sexuality, but not one comment from Dale. In interviews he trotted out the same bland, pre-prepared lines about the importance of family and how he'd like to settle down again someday. Always guarded, always careful. A man with something to hide.

So unlike Matt, who'd always worn his heart on his sleeve. There was no artifice or deception. He was confident in his sexuality — always had been — and sure of himself.

Maybe that was what Dale needed. A guy like Matt to support him as he crawled out of the closet. He couldn't imagine it working the other way. Matt wouldn't lurk in the background for the sake of appearance.

They would see. Conrad had resolved to ask them both out next week. Once his obligations were out of the way tomorrow night, he'd have time on his hands, at least for a couple of weeks. A double date. That was how he would pitch it. Things were developing nicely between him and Matt's lawyer friend, Danny. What better way for them all to get to know each other than dinner in a nice restaurant?

Of course, if it did blow up over Dale's outing, as Matt seemed to think it would, they could stay in. Conrad loved entertaining and could knock out a pretty good three-course dinner. Homemade pate, a nice lamb and potato stew and a chocolate mousse for dessert. Perfect. He'd call Matt on Sunday with the invitation. It would be nice to give something back to his friend.

He arrived at Dexter's gym. There was no parking out front, so he had to drive around the block and find a spot in the back street. He'd never been a gym bunny — life was too short to spend it on a treadmill going nowhere — but plenty of people were. If this guy Clint could offer up a nice incentive, it would shift a few more raffle tickets. That's all that mattered.

He walked back to the main street and tried the front door. It was locked. The lights inside were all off. Eh? What time was it? Was he too late? Matt had said Clint would be waiting. Then he noticed the handwritten sign taped to the window. *Closed Temporarily – Plumbing Fault – Reopens Tomorrow.* Then, in smaller print, written beneath was *Plumber and Other Emergency Contacts, Use Back Door.*

Okay. That implied that Clint or one of his assistants was still in there. Maybe they'd left the raffle prize at the back door. It was worth asking. He hadn't come out of his way to leave with nothing.

The back door was located farther down the alley from where he'd parked. There was an open gate in a high wall, leading to a small backyard. A sign stating Dexter's Gym was fixed to the door. Conrad knocked hard. And again.

The door was opened by a huge guy with a gray crew cut. He looked exactly how he imagined the customers of one of these places would look. Handsome all right, but in a kind of threatening way. As his mother used to say, "*You wouldn't want to meet him on a dark night.*"

"The gym is closed," the man said bluntly, pale eyes glaring down at Conrad.

"Hi. Are you Clint? My name is Conrad. My friend Matt Blyth sent me. He said you'd kindly offered to donate a prize to our raffle."

The man stepped out into the yard and looked up and down the alley. "Is Matt with you?"

"No. He's very sorry and all that. Something came up at work and he can't make it. He asked me to drop by instead. I hope that's all right. I can try ringing him if you like, he'll confirm that I am who I say I am."

There was something very strange about this man. He was rude and unmannered and had yet to crack a smile, but it wasn't just that. The sheer size of him was intimidating enough, but there was something else. Something animalistic. There was an aura about him. It was threatening. Frightening. Conrad's flesh prickled. Suddenly a deep primal instinct kicked in. It was telling him to flee. He needed to get out of there. *Now*.

"I'll tell you what," he said. "I'll just go. Matt can contact you in the morning and make his own arrangements to collect your donation. I really should be going."

"No." The man's mouth stretched into what could be interpreted as a smile. It had the shape and look of a smile but was devoid of any warmth, humor or humanity. "That's fine. I was expecting Matt, that's all. I have the prize. It's in my office. Come inside. You might as well take it while you're here."

*Don't go in there*, the warning voice screamed. *There's something not right about this guy.*

The man — Clint — stepped back and beckoned Conrad to follow.

Was he being irrational?

Oh what the hell. Matt would never have told him to drop by if Clint was a psycho. What did he think he was going to do to him anyway? An overactive imagination, that was his problem. Too many late-night movies on the Horror Channel. He was seeing psychotics where there were none.

He followed Clint inside.

The lights were out in the main gym hall. He could see the skeletal silhouettes of the equipment — dumbbells, running machines, cross-trainers. It looked like a fairly decent, well-equipped place, if you were into that kind of thing.

"What's up with the plumbing?" he asked brightly, keeping it light, to pretend that everything was normal.

"Sprung a leak," Clint said flatly. A man of few words.

Conrad made a mental note to self — if he drew this prize, donate it right back.

"Where did you say Matt was?" Clint asked. They had reached a small office in the corner of the main hall. There was a desk, computer, filing cabinet. Not much else.

"I'm not sure. Working, I think. He just called to say he couldn't make it. He works really long hours."

"It's Friday night."

"That won't make a difference. If he has work to do, he'll stay till he finishes."

Clint turned to face him, heavy butt perched on the edge of the desk. He focused on Conrad, eyes narrowed, looking hard. As though studying him properly for the first time. "Do you work out?"

"Me? Oh, God no." He laughed. It sounded nervous, even to his own ears. *Keep it together. Don't let the fucker intimidate you.* "I don't have time. My job keeps me busy. I'm always dashing about, here and there. So much to do. Especially with events like the one this weekend. I could really do with getting on now. If you have that prize I'll get right out of your hair."

Clint's mouth narrowed. He folded strong arms across his chest. "So what are you to Matt?"

Conrad's flesh prickled all over again. "We're friends. We've known each other for years."

"What does that mean? You holding a candle for him, or something? Got a schoolboy crush?"

"No. Nothing like that. We're just good friends. That's all. Now I really do have to get going."

"That's the thing, you see. You're going nowhere." Clint uncrossed his arms and moved his hands toward his groin. He stroked the hard bulge. "Like sucking cock, Conrad? 'Cause you're going to suck mine. You're going to suck it real good too, if you know what's good for you."

"There's been some kind of mistake," Conrad said, just about managing to keep his cool. "I don't know what your problem is but you can shove your prize. I'm going."

"Stay where you are," Clint snarled. He stood straight, one hand still stroking the bulge in his pants. "You see, I've got a problem. I was looking forward to Matt coming round here this evening. Been looking forward to it all day. Finally getting a chance to stick it to him. And *you* turn up in his place. You. I mean, shit, look at you. You're barely a man at all."

Conrad edged toward the door. "You've got the wrong idea. About both of us."

"Maybe. But I'm going to stick it to you anyway."

"Mister, that's *not* going to happen."

"What makes you so sure of that?" Clint said coolly.

The time for talking was over. Conrad turned and made a swift dash for the exit.

Clint was the bigger man but he was also faster.

Conrad was barely out of the office door when a huge arm wrapped around his neck, hauling him back against Clint's bulk. He struggled, gripping Clint's arm in both hands, trying to release his grip. Hopeless. He wriggled, trying to use his slighter size to his advantage, but there was no slack to maneuver.

"I like it when boys put up a struggle," Clint muttered, grinding his obscene bulge against Conrad's ass. The arm around his neck tightened its grip.

A sudden thought came into his mind. *Is Clint the Durham Strangler?*

It seemed far-fetched and yet he had his arm around his throat. He was choking him.

Conrad panicked.

His survival instinct kicked in. He fought, twisting, kicking Clint's shins, reaching behind, trying to find his eyes with his fingers. Seeking something to hold on to, somewhere soft, where he could cause some damage.

Clint put a hand on the back of his head. Pushed hard, forcing Conrad's throat against his solid forearm. He was choking, couldn't breathe, his vision began to dim.

With a harsh laugh, Clint released his hold. Conrad dropped to the floor. There was a sharp pain as his kneecap impacted with the tiles—it jarred all through his body. He gasped for breath. Reacting on instinct, he fought through the pain. He knew the danger he was in. There was no time to assess the situation, he had to get out. Now. He pulled toward the door.

"I don't think so." Clint chuckled, standing down hard on

the back of Conrad's injured knee.

The pain was excruciating. A wave of blackness rushed over him. He came close to passing out but the instinct to survive was strong. Keeping him conscious.

Clint reached down, put both hands around his waist and lifted him as though he weighed next to nothing. He carried him to the desk and threw him face down on top of it.

"No," Conrad screamed, as the larger man tore at his trousers, pulling them down with his underpants to bare his behind.

He heard the voice behind him say, "I'm going to enjoy this a lot more than you, my friend."

Then the real agony began.

* * * *

Clint walked slowly around the floor of the darkened gym. His thoughts came more easily in the dark and he did need to think. Today, everything had got away from him. The careful control that had served him well all these years had deserted him. From the moment Matt said he would come around tonight, he'd been thinking with his dick, not his brain. Stupid. Stupid. Stupid. Thinking like that could get a man in trouble. Worse, it could get him caught.

He had no intention of that happening.

This was Matt's fault. Making him lose his cool. If he hadn't asked for that stupid raffle prize, none of this would have happened. Letting him think he was coming over. Getting him hot and bothered. Sending this faggot round in his place. It was intolerable. Making him deviate from the plan and lose sight of the long game.

The long game was over. No chance of seeing it through to conclusion now.

Today's misdemeanors required a quick, clean resolution. Matt had made a fool of him.

For that, he would be punished — in the most severe way.

Clint moved back toward the office. The faggot was on

the floor. He was unconscious but still breathing. Just. With his trousers in tatters around his ankles, his body was a bloody wreck. When Clint was done with his ass, he'd stuck it to him with his boots, kicking him around the floor until his body stopped resisting. He'd lost it entirely. Allowing anger to possess him. So much frustration had built in him across the day. It wasn't enough to fuck this piece of shit. Not after all that. He had to fuck him up too. Boy, had he fucked him over, working up a sweat as he booted him all over the office. Giving him all he deserved.

Now what?

Clint prodded the body with the tip of his toe. He didn't move. He shoved him again, harder.

"Wake up, bitch," he snapped.

When there was still no reply, he knelt beside him and grabbed a fistful of hair. The hair was wet with blood, and as he lifted his face from the floor, Clint realized the damage his boot had done to the boy's features. His own mother would find it difficult to recognize the faggot now. Still, he wasn't dead yet, the bitch would talk.

"Wake up," he growled, smacking the side of his face with his palm.

Conrad whimpered.

"Where is Matt?" he barked, shaking Conrad's head. "Answer me. Where is he? You'll talk if you know what's good for you. I don't want to hear none of that shit about him working late. Where is he really?"

Conrad's eyes were swollen shut but from the change in his breathing, Clint knew he was awake. Clint repeated his question. When Conrad tried to speak, blood and saliva bubbled between his bust lips. Clint smacked his face again.

"I can't hear you. Where is he? Tell me."

Again, the answer was incomprehensible.

Shit. This was no good.

Clint let go, allowing Conrad's face to drop heavily against the tiles. He stood and left the office, returning a few moments later with a bucket of ice cold water. He tipped the whole lot slowly over Conrad's head. The little fucker was making plenty of noise now that he thought he was drowning. Screaming and spluttering, he tried to wriggle away from the downpour. Clint put a foot in the middle of his back, ensuring he went nowhere.

Conrad spat blood and water across the floor, gasping for breath. Clint was certain that his nose was broken. He leaned down and grabbed him by the hair again.

"Now listen," he hissed. "I reckon if I stick my cock down your throat right now, with that bust nose of yours, you won't be able to draw breath. Is that how you want this to end? Eh?" He shook his head like a terrier with a rat for effect. "Now, I'll ask again and this is the last time I'm going to ask nicely. Where is Matt?"

Conrad made a strange mewling sound as he tried to speak. Clint realized that his jaw was as broken as his nose. *Shit.* He really had lost his temper. Still, the little fucker could speak. He smacked his face again.

"Daaarrr..." Conrad spluttered, blood dribbling down his chin.

"What was that? Say it again."

"Daaaa..." He coughed, spitting more blood. "Daa. Daaale."

"Dale? Did you say Dale? Is that where he is? With the fucking American?"

"Yeeeeth. Yeeths."

Clint let go and sat back as a veil of cold fury descended over him. Matt was with the American. Damn it. He should have known. He banged a fist against the floor. For fuck's sake, why? What was so special about that bastard? From the day he'd arrived, the Yank had been nothing but an annoyance. One look and Matt had been smitten. First day at boot camp and he set his eyes on someone else. It was intolerable. Enough was enough.

Clint's plans for Matt were in jeopardy. No more games. There was no time. Suppose the fucker talked Matt into going to America with him. Where would Clint be then?

Denied the ultimate prize. That couldn't be allowed. He always got what he wanted. He always had and that wouldn't stop now.

He rose slowly to his feet. Calm descended on every part of him. He put his anger in a tight compartment. There would be time to indulge it later. But for now, a clear head, void of emotion, was essential. After tonight, everything would change. In all likelihood his crimes would be exposed. He might have to leave in a hurry. Not just the city, but the country. He was prepared for that. There was a fake passport and plenty of money in the safe. It might not come to that. Not if he was careful.

Only one thing was certain. Matt Blyth and Dale Zachary had to die. Slowly. Painfully. Tonight.

# Chapter Twenty

Dale was waiting at the open door when Matt pulled up in front of the house, high in the hills. The grin he'd been sporting all the way here widened farther. The sight of Dale was everything he'd been waiting for. It had only been a night, but it felt as if he'd been gone for weeks. It was so good to see him again. And damn it, if he didn't look great. Standing there, in a loosely fastened checked shirt, jeans, bare feet... He was the best-looking man Matt had ever seen.

Matt was out of the car and in his arms in seconds. "God, I've missed you," he said, squeezing him tight and pressing his mouth to his lips. He slid a hand beneath the shirt to caress his bare skin, pushing his fingers through the hair on his chest.

Dale held him just as tight, letting his hands fall to Matt's ass and squeezing. "You look good in a suit," he drawled. "I knew you would. You're the sexiest lawyer I ever saw."

Matt suddenly realized they were standing in an open doorway. He stepped back from Dale and scanned the courtyard behind and the distant tree line for any sign of photographers. "Where are the press?"

Dale pulled him back into his arms. "Nothing yet. Keeley Rank knows where I live, but I don't think any of the others have caught on. But the phone's been ringing nonstop since I got back. Apparently the studio is under siege again, but none of them have found their way up here. I'm past caring. I've made things right with the people who matter. Everything else is bullshit."

"I like this new attitude," Matt said, sliding a hand to

Dale's butt, helping himself.

"There's a whole lot about me you're going to like."

They went inside and closed the door.

He knew the house was just a rental but it was impressive nonetheless. The hall was large and airy with plenty of light coming from the upstairs windows. There were several rooms leading off from the hall. He saw through into a large living room, which had a stunning view of the sweeping valley below. "Wow, this is some place."

Dale grinned. "Yeah, I like it. I've never been keen on the town and city life. I much prefer living in the middle of nowhere. Come on, I want to show you something."

He took Matt's hand and led him into a large kitchen. It was modern but totally in keeping with the traditional style of the house. Delicious aromas wafted from the cooker — chicken, garlic, tarragon.

"You had time to cook too? I'm very impressed. Smells better than any restaurant I know."

Dale grinned. "Sorry to disappoint. That would be Mrs. Butterman, the lady who comes in to look after the place. She's a great cook. I called her to say I'd be back today and arrived home to find the slow cooker working its magic. She's a terrific lady and really spoils me. If it wasn't for our boot camp, and Clint whipping my ass into shape, I'd be twice the size I am now."

"I need a Mrs. Butterman in my kitchen. Think she could fit me in?"

"I'm not giving her up. You'll have to share." Dale picked up his tablet computer from the counter and gave it to Matt. "Take a look at this. I didn't want to send it till you got here."

The tablet was open on Dale's Facebook page. He had typed a statement into the status update field. *The murders that have taken place in Durham are a tragedy, even more so that the victims' stories are at risk of being lost amid speculation surrounding a television show and my personal life. In order to devalue any further gossip I would like to confirm right now that I am gay. In our modern, tolerant world, the sexuality of a relatively unknown actor should not be such a newsworthy event and I only hope this statement will rob my "outing" of any sensation. Our thoughts and sympathies should be with the young men who have lost their lives and the families who grieve them. For their sake, I apologize for the scurrilous headlines they might have to read this weekend and I hope that attention quickly moves onto what is really important — finding their killer and bringing him to justice.*

Matt handed back the tablet. "Is that how you're going to do this? Facebook, rather than a statement from your agent?"

Dale looked back the screen. "No. I've hidden enough. I'm not going to hide behind a third party now. This has to come from me. Anything else would just be...wrong. Do you understand?"

Matt put an arm around his shoulder, pressed a soft kiss against the side of his face. "Of course I do. Send it."

Dale's finger hovered over the send icon, no more than a second, before he tapped the screen. The message disappeared before the screen refreshed and there it was — made public for the world to see.

"Done," Dale grinned, shutting off the computer. "Let's celebrate."

He opened a cupboard and lifted out two champagne flutes. From the fridge, he produced a bottle and set about opening it.

"Where's your phone? It's going to start ringing any minute now."

Dale, midway through unwrapping the foil on the champagne bottle, stopped and pulled his phone from his back pocket. He turned it off. "You're right. No calls tonight. This is just about you and me."

"How do you feel? Now that it's gone."

Dale filled the glasses. "Wonderful, I guess. A little frightened, sure, but it's a relief."

"You have nothing to worry about. Nobody is going to

care. We have a saying here, you might not have heard it —
'Today's news is tomorrow's fish and chip paper.'"

Dale's brow furrowed. "I think I get what you're saying
but I have no idea what fish-and-chip paper is."

"Okay, then next weekend, when this really is old news,
I'll take you to the coast and you can find out for yourself.
Deal?"

"Can't wait."

He handed Matt a glass and they clinked.

"Cheers."

"And congratulations," Matt said. "To a new beginning?"

"I'll definitely drink to that."

They both drank. The champagne was cold and delicious.
Matt moved closer to Dale. He put his hand on the back of
his head and drew his mouth close. They kissed long and
deeply. Lips lingering, tongues thrusting. Matt held him
and kissed him and breathed in the heavenly smell of him.

"Want to see more of the house?" Dale murmured against
his lips. "Take a look upstairs?"

"Lead the way."

* * * *

Jamie, who hadn't eaten a thing since the coffee and
scones forced upon him by Barney Kilofer-James, stopped
at a takeaway restaurant on Craddock Street, bought a
steak pie and a portion of chips and ate them in the car
outside. He was starving and too impatient to wait until
he got home to eat. Something had been bugging him all
day. Something he couldn't quite grasp. He didn't know
what it was but...*something*. He hoped that, in satisfying his
hunger, he would give his brain a chance to function better.

The food was mediocre at best. The chips were greasy
and the pie was little more than salty gravy in a pastry case,
but they filled his empty belly. He turned on the radio.
There was a classical music concert on the BBC. Not his
usual thing but the big orchestral sounds were strangely

conducive to thought. Instead of heading for home, he turned the car back in the direction of the station. There was no point going anywhere else, not until he got a handle on what it was troubling him.

*What the hell is it?*

It had started mid-afternoon. Right after his visit to Barney. Something the old queen had said triggered the bug. But what? Jamie ran their conversation through his mind, trying to get a handle on that spark.

*Come on, boy, what the hell is it?*

The old man and his husband were screwing Aaron Oxford. No big deal there. Plenty of men and women met for casual sex. It wasn't something they were keen to share with family and friends but it happened. Aaron had visited the old boys a couple of times at their home. Again, no big deal. It was hardly enough for attachments to form. Besides the old guys just weren't that type. However much they liked Aaron, Jamie had a feeling he was lucky to get that second invite to their bedroom. He'd met men like them before. Once they'd had what they wanted, conquests were quickly discarded. Jamie rarely bothered with gay bars but when he did, he found the snatches of overheard conversation quite depressing.

*'Had him. And him. And I had him when he was worth having.'*

Barney Kilofer-James struck him as *exactly* that type.

So no, the old queens weren't out there killing young men through fits of jealousy. They were too busy searching for their next conquest.

The tech team had already run a search on Aaron's phone, computer and social accounts. He'd contacted a handful of people via a dating app looking for sex. So far none of those contacts had revealed anything suspicious. There was no evidence that he'd even looked at the profiles of any of the other victims. Dating sites always came under suspicion when there was a case of this kind, but Jamie had a feeling they weren't going to catch their killer on Grindr.

Barney had said he and his old man picked up Aaron and

brought him to their house. They had met him once in town and once outside a gym.

A gym.

Of course. That was it. The bloody gym.

That was what had been bugging him. The previous victim, Olly Raymond, also had a gym membership card among his possessions. It was slight, very slight. Two good-looking gay guys, going to the gym. It was hardly out of the ordinary, and the chances of them both frequenting the same place were almost zero.

But good detective work was all about making connections. If only to rule them out.

Still driving, Jamie brought up Barney Kilofer-James's number. The old boy answered straight away.

"It's Detective Dench. Sorry to bother you again, especially at this hour, I just have one more question for you."

"Detective," Barney purred. "How nice to hear from you again. I was just telling Tony what a delightful young man you were. What can we do for you? Maybe Tony's memory is better than mine."

"You told me you once picked up Aaron from outside his gym. Can you remember the name of that gym?"

"Oh God, now you're asking. Can't think of the name. It was on Dunston Street, just along from the butcher's and the hardware shop. Just a second." There was the sound of conversation in the background before Barney came back on the line. "Dexter's. Tony says the place is called Dexter's. I don't know anything about it. It doesn't look like much from the outside. We prefer Bannatine's. The facilities are so much broader."

"You've been a big help." Jamie hung up before the old man could invite him to join them at their gym. No doubt the sauna and pool were their favorite facilities.

After pulling up to the station, he hurried straight to his desk. The incident room was empty. Even on a major case like this, the overtime budget did not stretch to Friday nights. Jamie didn't give a damn about overtime. He was onto something. He logged into his computer and brought up the evidence log of items taken from Olly Raymond's apartment.

He scrolled through the list, looking for one thing in particular.

There it was.

One gym membership card.

The gym was Dexter's on Dunston Street.

Jamie logged straight back out of the computer and raced for the door.

Shit. How did they miss that?

*　*　*　*

Keeley stared at the words she had written. This story was going nowhere. It was useless. Worse than useless. She had nothing.

"Fuck!"

Tomorrow morning every tabloid paper was going to run with a variation on the Dale Zachary story. Those hacks hadn't even cottoned onto the closet fairy until today, and now they were stealing the story, *her* story, right out from under her. She'd been here all week, routing around the set of that crappy TV show, and she had no more than the other papers to show for it.

What should have been an exclusive scoop was a scoop of dog shit. She'd had to make up eighty percent of what she'd written. Not that *that* was a problem, she'd put out stories before that were ninety-nine percent made up, but still, she had a little pride in what she did. It should have turned out better than this.

Most of the people she'd talked to on the show had no idea their leading man was a cock sucker. Idiots. Like those two greedy bimbos she took to lunch today. What a total waste of time they were. They gave almost nothing, and what little she did glean from them would have to be credited to 'sources close to the actor'. She'd could hardly admit her sources where two stupid tarts from the makeup trailer.

She might be a gossip columnist but she had some standards. She'd be laughed out of the industry.

Maybe the problem was Dale. Other than the fact he'd been keeping his sexuality under wraps, and getting his dick sucked by one of the deceased, there was nothing to write about him. There was no scandal there. No drugs, no rent boys, no naked selfies to fans. The bastard was cleaner than Snow White, and that was no good to a writer like her.

Keeley saved the dismal file and shut the lid on her laptop, signaling to the hotel waiter that she was ready for another glass of wine.

*Think, woman, think.*

She needed to save this story and make it her own by morning. Her Sunday feature was already shaping up to be old news, but there had to be *something* she could do to rescue it, together with her reputation.

The Sunday Edition was looking to get rid of her. It hadn't been said in so many words, but she knew it was coming. The current editor was less than enthusiastic about the stories she turned in and the bastard was already testing new writers. That feature on George Clooney last month should have been hers, but he had given it to some twenty-five-year-old airhead straight out of college. And he pulled the piece she did on Katherine Jenkins entirely. "We are not in the business of character assassination," he had said, dropping her profile in favor of some shit about a flower show.

When did the rules change? Journalism had always been about character assassination. That's what people like her were there for. To tear down those people who got too high and mighty about themselves.

Like Dale Zachary.

There was a great story to be written there, if she could only find the angle.

There had to be one.

The waiter brought her drink with a fixed smile. He knew better than to make pleasant conversation with her. She'd made that very clear a few nights back.

So the TV show was a blank. The crew either knew nothing or were not prepared to talk.

There was an ex-wife and a kid somewhere. The other journos were already tracking them down. They were of no use to her. That was not where her story lay. It was here in Durham. She just had to find it.

Keeley drank her wine. The answer was really quite simple. She would have to use her own initiative. It hadn't let her down before. When every other tactic failed there was one thing she did better than anyone else—good old-fashioned snooping.

She would get to the bottom of Dale Zachary's story if it killed her. She drained her wine glass.

Keeley picked up her laptop and left the bar. The story was out there. It was time to bring it home.

* * * *

One night away had made their passion insatiable. Matt and Dale were all over the bed, kissing, groping, moving in and out of each other. Neither one could get enough. They had both climaxed already but remained hard and eager. Matt rolled under Dale and wrapped his legs around Dale's waist, drawing him deep inside, locking him tight.

"Fuck me," he growled, thrusting his ass against Dale's hips.

"I thought I did already," Dale said, teasing him with the just the head of his cock.

"No," Matt pleaded. "I want more." He thrust his fingers into Dale's hair and pulled his face above his, their noses touching. "More."

Dale thrust into him with long, deep strokes, giving him exactly what he wanted. What they both wanted. This was pure heaven.

Soon they were both coming again, holding each other tight as paroxysms of pleasure racked their bodies.

Finally spent, they relaxed, lying side by side on the rumpled bed, gasping for breath.

"I need to see you in that suit more often," Dale said, stroking Matt's thigh. "Man, what have you done to me?"

Matt laughed. "If that's all it takes. Putting on a suit is preferable to spending any more nights apart."

"I won't argue with that." Dale sat up, propping pillows behind their back, and handed Matt his glass of champagne.

It had lost its chill while they'd been making love but it was still delicious.

"Champagne in bed," Matt said. "This is a rare treat."

"Let's see if we can change that, eh? Let's have champagne in bed all the time."

He laughed. "Maybe not *all* the time."

"At least once a week?"

"Sounds good to me."

Everything was good for Matt in that moment. Though it was his first time in Dale's bed, first time in his house, it was all so comfortable. There was no awkwardness. Lying next to Dale, drinking champagne, he knew he belonged there.

It was a large bedroom, decorated in a neutral tones, in keeping with its rental status. But there were personal touches here and there. Dale had tried to make the place his own. There were photographs of him with a young kid, around twelve years old. That had to be Jack. Just from the photos, Matt could see so much of Dale in the boy. They shared the same dark blond hair and clear blue eyes. There was a pile of scripts on one of the dressers, the pages covered in handwritten notes and yellow Post-its.

"Where do you live when you're not filming?" he asked.

"Nowhere."

"What?"

"It's true. This is it. I live in hotels and rented apartments. I don't have a place of my own yet. I was waiting to see how things panned out for me in the UK before setting down roots. If I couldn't find work, then I couldn't afford to stay. I rented with another actor in South London for a while, but that's gone now. He needed a more permanent tenant and had to replace me when I came up here."

"What will happen when the show wraps?" Matt asked.

"I haven't thought that far ahead. My agent is negotiating a couple of offers, but nothing has been signed. Those offers could disappear when the papers come out tomorrow. If I'm lucky, I might get back into European horror films. I heard they're casting for *An Axe in the Dark 4*. Maybe they'll want me to play my twin brother. If not…"

"The series could be a success," Matt said.

Dale shrugged. "Could be. In spite of everything. I can't see it happening, though. There's just too much that's gone wrong for anything good to come out of this mess. There's no focus. I've worked on my fair share of stinkers and this gig is starting to smell. It's a shame, because it began so well. It had the potential to be great. Everything starts with good intentions, I guess."

"Don't be so down on it." Matt reached for the champagne bottle and refreshed their glasses. "Keep working hard and hope for the best. That's what I always do."

* * * *

Clint Dexter was back in control. His breathing, heart rate, blood pressure and emotions had all returned to normal levels. He'd fucked up in the biggest way. Losing it with the faggot at the gym—he couldn't go back from that. But now that he was thinking practically, he understood that it would all have ended today anyway. If Matt had come to the gym as he was supposed to, and Clint had been able to do the things he wanted, it was unlikely he'd have gotten away with it. Matt was too well-known. The police would soon come sniffing around. There was no way he'd have been able to continue like before. Things were always going to change today.

Even so, he'd fucked it up spectacularly.

He had to work fast if he was going to get away.

The gym wouldn't open until morning. No one would find Conrad before then. That gave him around twelve hours to make his escape. He'd taken cash from the safe in the office and picked up the emergency stash he kept at home. It was enough to get going.

Except he was going nowhere without the thing he wanted most.

Without Matt this would all have been for nothing.

Matt wasn't at home. He didn't expect him to be but it was worth checking anyway.

He knew exactly where to find him. With the bastard American.

It was all so fitting—he would kill two birds with one stone.

He had followed the American home from the studio one night and knew where he lived. The remote house in the hills was perfect for what he had in mind.

Clint Dexter always got what he wanted. Matt Blyth would be no exception.

# Chapter Twenty-One

*Funny what the eye sees without ever really taking notice.*

Jamie must have passed the gym on Dunston Street countless times but never paid attention until now. It stood on the main road, sandwiched between a kitchen design company and a bridal wear shop. He hadn't paid them any attention either. Why should he? He had no need for the services of any of them. He would never get married, his flat was rented and the gym was for losers. Well, maybe not losers, just people with too much time on their hands. He didn't need to work out when he had such an active job. He never gained weight. Older colleagues warned him it would be different when he was older. He would worry about that when the time came.

Right now, he was trying to find out what connection, if any, two of the murder victims had to this place. Did they know of each other? If so, that changed the thrust of the whole investigation. DCI Redgraves was working on the assumption that the victims were unconnected. If Jamie could prove otherwise – he could forget about going back to regular duty when the case was closed.

Darkness had cut in when he pulled up outside and approached the door.

It was locked and the shutters were down over the windows.

Weren't these places supposed to stay open late for the hardcore roid-heads?

He peered through the gaps into the metal shutters. Most of the lights were off inside. The skeletal silhouettes of equipment were lit by dull, emergency lighting. As he stepped back he saw the handwritten sign on the front. There was a fault with the plumbing and the note directed the plumber to use the back door. That was more like it. If the manager or any of the assistants were still around he could ask them to check their membership records. He didn't have a warrant and hoped it wouldn't come to that. This was a murder investigation after all. Any reluctance to help would be treated with the suspicion it deserved.

He walked to the end of the street and around the corner. The alley was dark but not so much that he couldn't see. He counted the doorways until he found the gate leading to the back yard of the gym. It didn't look promising. There were no plumbers' vans in the alley. Maybe he was too late. He tried the door anyway, on the chance the plumber hadn't arrived yet. It was Friday night after all, no one would come out in a hurry, not with overtime and emergency fees to be claimed.

But the door was locked.

*Damn it.* Jamie knocked, hard. There was no reply. He knocked again, even harder, banging the door with his fist.

"Police," he shouted. "Anyone in there?"

No answer.

This was so frustrating. Police work was all about patience, but he was loath to get so near to a puzzle and leave without a resolution. The sign said the gym would reopen in the morning, maybe he should wait till then. He could swing by here on his way to work and perhaps have a lead to follow by the time he reported to Redgraves. But he wouldn't be able to settle tonight, not when he could be on to something.

He leaned up to look through the window at the back. It was small, not really showing much of anything. There were bars across the frame. Beyond, he could see into a small office. There was a desk, a computer, magazines and folders spread across the surface. And...blood. What? Jamie grabbed the bars and pulled upward for a better view.

It looked like blood. Smeared across the desk and the

chair behind it.

He hitched higher, angling to see more of the floor. Stained papers littered the office and there, just visible, right beneath the window itself, what looked like a foot. A man's foot in a bloodstained sneaker.

Jamie's heart began to pump faster. Blood and adrenaline coursed through his body. He dropped down into the yard, digging his phone from his jacket. He called it straight in, giving his name and rank, requesting immediate back-up and medical assistance. But he couldn't wait. God knows what had happened on the other side of that door. The poor bastard might not have the time it would take for the ambulance to get here.

It might be too late already.

There was only one way to find out.

He had to get through that door.

Whoever had left had done so in a hurry, neglecting to turn the deadbolt. The door was secured by a single Yale lock. Putting his shoulder and all of his weight into it, he rammed the door. Once, twice, it gave on the third run. Jamie spilled into the tiny back kitchen. There was blood all the way to the door.

So much blood.

He proceeded with caution. From the pattern of blood on the floor he was certain whoever had done this had already left. It must have been too dark in the yard for him to notice the stains on the concrete. Regardless, his training came to the fore. A dead hero was no good to anyone. He advanced steadily, checking every corner, tuned in to danger.

He had a good idea of the layout from what he'd seen through the window. He turned the corner, into the office, expecting something awful.

What he found was worse.

The figure on the floor did not move. And the blood — there was so much of it. Its bitter scent assaulted his nostrils. He could even taste it, a horrible tang that caught in the back of his throat. It was impossible to know where it was all coming from. The man on the floor was covered in it. The poor guy's exposed buttocks gave some indication of the damage he'd been dealt.

The man lay face down, one arm flung above his head, the other at his side. Jamie reached for that nearest to him, grabbing the wrist, searching for a pulse. He felt nothing and pressed even deeper into the wrist. It was there. Thank God. It was weak and thready, but he could feel it.

Jamie grabbed his phone and called back in. "Tell the ambulance to hurry," he said. "We've got an unconscious male and a lot of blood."

What he'd learned in compulsory first aid training kicked in and he checked the man over from head to toe, searching for the most obvious injuries and a way to stop the bleeding. There were no puncture wounds. Most of the blood seemed to come from the man's head and his backside, which meant the damage was internal. He needed that ambulance right now.

"Hello," he said, loud and clear. "Can you hear me?" He put his mouth close to the man's ear and asked the question again. No response. But he was definitely breathing. Jamie tilted the man's head, very gently, to open up his airway. If he was unconscious, his biggest risk was choking.

As he moved the man and looked at his face, Jamie froze. Despite the damage, he recognized him.

*Oh, God, it's Conrad O'Brien.*

\* \* \* \*

"Hungry?"

"Absolutely starving," Matt replied. "I can't survive on sex and champagne. As tempting as it sounds."

Dale stroked his naked hip. "You've got to keep your strength up. The night is young."

The champagne was finished. They had consumed the rest of the bottle as they'd basked in the tranquil afterglow of their lovemaking. Outside, the evening had turned to darkness. Dale rolled off the bed and drew the curtains against the night. He padded naked into his dressing room and came back wearing a casual pair of shorts and a gray T-shirt, which looked as if it had been made especially to complement his muscular body. He handed Matt a pair of short lounge pants and matching T-shirt.

"Seeing as I forced you to come straight from work, why don't you put these on?"

"There I was, thinking you were going to keep me naked all weekend."

Dale gave his bare ass a playful tap. "If that's what you want, my love, don't get dressed on my account."

Matt slipped into the soft blue pants. "What would Mrs. Butterman say if she found out you were entertaining naked men with her casserole?"

"I expect she'd be jealous. 'Cause you're tastier than anything she could rustle up in the kitchen."

Matt laughed. "Did you learn that corny line in one of your movies?"

"Hey, that's bona fide B-movie gold. Come on, let's eat."

They went to the kitchen, where the scent of Mrs. Butterman's cooking was even more delicious than before. Matt's stomach rumbled loudly. He was hungrier than he'd thought.

"Can you hold out ten more minutes?" Dale asked, setting a pan of water on top of the stove. "I want to cook some rice to go with this. There are some rolls in the bread bin if you need something to tide you over."

"I can wait, just about." Matt gazed out of the kitchen window. The darkness beyond was absolute. Out here, it was so different to living in town, where the nights were never completely black. "No sign of the hungry press yet."

"Let's hope it stays like that." Dale tipped rice into the pan. "Maybe I overestimated their interest in me. Maybe an old actor coming out of the closet is no big deal after all."

"It's pretty remote out this way," Matt said. "They might not know where to find you."

"They always find you, believe me. Someone on the crew will give up my address if the price is right."

"Has anyone ever told you, you might be paranoid?"

"They don't have to. Believe me, I know that already."

"Maybe it's because of all those horror films you starred in. You see bogey men on every corner."

The pan of rice came to the boil. Dale poured two glasses of white wine and guided Matt to the kitchen table.

This was so unlikely. Sitting down to dinner with a man at home. When Matt was with Jamie, they had hardly ever eaten a meal at the same time. One or the other of them was always working late. Dinner, if you could call a diet of ready meals and takeout pizza dinner, was usually eaten on a tray in front of the television. Eating like this, with Dale, was so much nicer, more grown up. It seemed right.

"Cheers." They clinked glasses.

Dale sipped the wine then put down the glass. His fingers moved slowly around the stem as he gazed thoughtfully into the straw-colored contents.

"The long drive back here today, it really gave me a chance to think. Nothing to do but follow the road for miles and miles. I haven't had an opportunity like that in ages. When I didn't have to think about work, or a script, or Jack. When I could think about myself and what I was doing. Not only me, that sounds so egotistical, but about what was going on here. These murders. The wasted lives. Aaron and those other boys."

Matt nodded. "It does put a lot of trivial problems in perspective."

"Exactly. It made me realize that I've been doing everything all wrong. Moving around, living for the job, jumping from one shitty movie to the next. Never settling down. I don't even have a place to call home. I'm tired of that. I want more from life."

Matt reached across the table and put his hand gently on the back of Dale's. "Only you can make those changes."

"I know. And I'm going to. I want to reprioritize my life.

What I'm saying, badly, is that one of those priorities is you. I know it's only been a couple of weeks but I love you, Matt. And I don't want to throw that away by leaving town for the next job."

Matt's heart beat faster. In a quiet way, he'd also been worrying about their future and whether they even had one. He didn't want to spoil what they had right now by thinking too far ahead, but he was aware that when production on the series ended there would be nothing to keep Dale here. When his work took him all over the world, how could they ever sustain a relationship? However much they loved each other, realistically, he knew it had slim chance of working.

"For one thing," Dale said, "I've decided to take an extension on the house. I can take the lease until the end of the year. It will give me a base — a home — till I can find somewhere else. And, when the show is over, I want to take you away. How about it? Do you have any vacation time due? We could go someplace for a couple of weeks, somewhere quiet with plenty of sun. Just the two of us."

An unexpected mist came over Matt's vision. Tears of joy pricked the back of his eyelids. He blinked them away, smiling.

"It sounds like heaven."

They leaned across the table, their lips uniting, cementing their dreams for the future.

\* \* \* \*

Clint parked a little under a mile from the house, pulling onto a side track that couldn't be seen from the main road. He made his way cross-country to the exclusive development at the top of the hill. In its day, this would have been a working farm, providing livelihood and shelter to hardworking countrymen. Now, it was a privileged hideaway for pampered rich folk and their spoiled brats.

It gave him an honest degree of pleasure to know that after tonight, these overpriced barn conversions would lose a good chunk of their value, and the remote hill top location would no longer be such a desirable place to live. It would become a shrine for morbid tourists.

These peaceful hills would run red when he was done.

Three of the five houses on the site were lit up, including Dale's. But none of the neighbors were close enough to cause him any problems. He was a master of stealth.

When tonight was over and the investigation began, Dale Zachary's neighbors would shake their heads in puzzlement and declare they heard and saw nothing when the Durham Strangler struck. It gave him a thrill to envisage it. They would never sleep soundly in their beds again.

Not up here.

Yes, in just a few hours there would be a lot of negative equity in these former sheds. All those people with expensive mortgages on properties which soon wouldn't be worth shit. The expectation would have given him a hard-on, if he wasn't already rock-hard.

In perfect darkness, Clint crept closer to the house.

Matt's Nissan was parked outside. Of course it was. He'd have been surprised if it wasn't there.

His day had gone to hell so far, but tonight was playing out exactly how he wanted it.

He approached the house from the side, keeping clear of the sensor that would trip the front security lights. Not that anyone would pay attention out here. The lights were always being set off by badgers and foxes. No one would investigate, because no one expected any real intrusion. Not to their safe, exclusive world.

He followed the side of the house, around the garage.

There were lights in the kitchen window. Clint moved closer.

And there they were. Such a cozy sight. Matt Blyth and Dale Zachary, having dinner at the kitchen table. Look at them in their matching outfits. The perfect fucking couple.

*How cute.*

How pathetic.

There was wine on the table and they looked at eat other as they ate. Laughing, smiling, obviously in love.

He couldn't stand it. He wanted to destroy it.

He'd wasted enough time.

Silently, stealthily, he moved closer to the house.

* * * *

Whatever shit the world chucked at him tomorrow, Dale would remember how happy he felt right now.

It was perfect. The food. The wine. The man he loved. It took his breath almost every time he looked at Matt. Having him here tonight, in the only place he had to call home, well, it was everything he wanted. Life couldn't get better.

This was what he'd been searching for. All those years of covert affairs and one-night stands, so much wasted time. Except it wasn't wasted, because without everything in life happening as it had done, he wouldn't have taken the job in Durham and wouldn't be here now, sitting across from this handsome, clever, warm-hearted man.

Did he believe in soul mates? Not until now. Not until he found his.

"What are you smiling at?" Matt asked. "It can't be the empty glass."

Dale's grin was a mile across. "If I told you, you'd only say I was quoting lines from one my awful movies again."

Matt rolled his eyes. "Another rom-com moment?"

"There's nothing wrong with romantic comedies," he said, feigning offense.

"You would know. Seeing how you're the undisputed king of them."

"Don't forget the direct-to-DVD horror. I'm no slouch when it comes to that territory either."

Now it was Matt's turn to fake offense. "As if I would forget those. But you know what? I'm not in the mood for horror tonight. We've had more than enough of *that*. Let's stick with romance, shall we? Cheesy or otherwise."

"Got no complaints about that." Dale experience a rush of euphoria. He was the happiest man alive. "I want to celebrate."

"Celebrate what?" Matt asked.

"*Everything*. You. Me. Us. Coming out. I've never been happier than I am right now. If that's not worth another bottle of champagne, I don't know what is."

Matt raised both hands in mock surrender. "You twisted my arm."

Dale slapped the tabletop. "Let's do it." He shoved back his chair and hurried round the table, kissing Matt fully on the lips. "There's a fridge in the garage. I'll grab us another bottle. Stay right where you are, sexy."

Matt tapped his butt. "Not going anywhere."

"I love you." The words came easily now.

There was an interior door at the back of the kitchen, leading directly to the garage. He didn't use it for anything other than storage. It was too much hassle to bring the car in and out every time he wanted to use it, so he left it parked outside.

Scrambling in the dark, he located the light switch and turned it on. He was already pretty loaded, but what the hell. There was nothing in this second fridge besides booze. Now that he had Matt, he'd have a lot of reasons to drink champagne and celebrate.

He sang *Can't Get You Out Of My Head* as he crossed the floor.

The figure behind him was so fast and silent, Dale knew nothing until an arm wrapped around his throat and squeezed tight.

\* \* \* \*

Dale had told him to wait, but Matt's bladder had other ideas. A bottle of champagne, wine and now more champagne on the way — he had to make space for that.

He rose from the table. A little unsteady. The booze was

already affecting him, but in a good way—a great way—enriching the mood. He felt wonderful. He could get used to nights like this.

After locating the downstairs bathroom, he released a long stream. That was better.

This was some place Dale had found. His own little house was a shed in comparison. The downstairs toilet was double the size of his main bathroom at home. It was all finished to the highest standard. Kind of impersonal, like a five-star hotel, but impressive nonetheless. He couldn't imagine ever feeling at home in a place like this, not without massive changes, but he was grateful that Dale had decided to stay on.

He doubted Dale would want to move into his place either. But if things worked out, maybe, just maybe, when the lease on this place expired, they could look for a house together.

He was getting *way* ahead of himself.

Still, it was nice to dream.

He finished off and washed his hands. There was Molton Brown hand soap on the vanity unit, his favorite. So, they shared the same taste in bathroom products. That was a good start.

He smiled at his reflection in the mirror. His face was glowing from the collective effect of sex, alcohol and happiness. He looked goofy and yet he couldn't wipe away the smile. Not when he felt this good.

Swaying slightly, he headed back to the kitchen.

Dale still hadn't returned with the wine.

"Hey," he called, "what's keeping you? Are you brewing the stuff yourself?"

There was no reply.

He approached the connecting door. There was really no need for extra champagne. Dale didn't have to go to trouble on his account. He didn't need expensive alcohol to celebrate what they had going. He felt pretty fabulous as it was.

He didn't see the step down into the garage and tripped slightly as he went over.

"Whoa." He laughed. "I'm drunker than I thought. Maybe we should save the booze for tomorrow."

The sight that greeted him stopped him cold. The sobering effect was immediate.

To hit upon Clint Dexter was a shock in itself. What was he doing in the garage? It took another moment for his brain to register exactly what was happening.

Clint's bulging arm was wrapped around Dale's throat. Dale clutched it, trying to loosen the grip. His face was red, teeth bared and eyes bulging. Dale caught sight of Matt and managed to gasp one desperate word.

"*Run.*"

There was no possibility of him running. "What the hell is going on? Clint, let him go." He stepped forward.

"Stay where you are," Clint said coldly. Tightening his grip on Dale's throat, he raised his other hand, giving Matt a good look at what it held — the dangerous curve of a knife.

"Clint?"

"Just so you don't get any ideas, this is how serious I am."

With the speed of an attacking snake, Clint flicked the lethal blade against Dale's face.

A wound opened in his cheek. Strangely bloodless for a moment, before the red fluid oozed from the cut.

Matt's own blood turned cold. He didn't know why this was happening. Only one thing was certain, they were in trouble. Big trouble.

# Chapter Twenty-Two

He had experienced fear before. He'd looked into another's eyes and seen anger, fury, even hatred, but none of that prepared Matt for what he saw in Clint's eyes. Nothing.

They were empty. Devoid of any soul.

Blood poured from the wound on Dale's face. A crimson stain that covered his chin.

"Dale, are you all right?"

Clint tightened his hold around Dale's neck and moved the knife back toward his face. "Unless you want to say goodbye to these pretty looks, keep your mouth shut until I tell you," he threatened. "This is a paper cut compared to what I'll do."

Dale looked directly into Matt's eyes, flashing a warning to do what Clint said. He didn't have to speak. A look said everything.

Matt tried to assess the situation and make rapid sense of what was happening. There was no sense. Clint had his lover by the throat and a knife to his face. He'd already shown what he was capable of. The cut on Dale's cheek was evidence of that. What the hell was this all about? He was crazed, that much was obvious, but what had brought it on? What did it have to do with them?

There was only one thing he could do. Go along with him. For now.

"We'll do what you want," he said, raising his open hands. "Just don't hurt him."

Cold eyes regarded him for twenty seconds, thirty — it seemed like hours. What was going on behind those eyes? Impossible to know. There was no emotion. Looking into

those blank holes, a question suddenly came into his head —
was Clint the Durham Strangler?

He couldn't be. That was impossible. This was not the
strangler's MO. And yet, he had his arm around Dale's
throat, and the emptiness of those eyes spoke of nothing
but madness.

The Durham Strangler?

Matt was more afraid than ever. He had to get that sick
bastard away from the man he loved.

Clint inclined his head toward the door. "Back through to
the kitchen."

Matt did what he was told, keeping his hands raised
where Clint could see them. *Don't do anything to startle the
fucker.*

He stepped into the kitchen. Clint followed, arm still
around Dale's throat, knife at his face, a slow shuffling two-
step.

"Don't try anything stupid," he said. "Or I'll take one of
his eyes out."

Matt raised his hands higher. "I'm not doing anything,
Clint. You know I wouldn't." With supreme effort, he kept
his voice level and calm. He'd dealt with enough angry
dickheads to know the slightest thing could unbalance
them. Something as small as a perceived change in tone.
He couldn't afford to do anything that might provoke him.

"Far enough," he said as Matt drew level with the table.
He loosened his hold on Dale's throat.

Dale sucked in a huge lungful of air. Clint shoved him
toward the table.

"Sit," he barked.

Dale's eyes met Matt's again. *Keep it together*, they were
saying. Matt could properly see the cut on Dale's face — a
two-inch wound from the cheekbone down into his beard.
At least it looked clean. The amount of blood made it look
worse than it was. If they got out of this soon, it should
stitch together without much trouble. It was a big 'if'.

Clint took something from his jacket pocket and threw it

on the table toward Matt. Cable ties.

"Bind him to the chair," Clint said, waving the knife. "Wrists and ankles. And make it tight. Try anything brave and I'll take that eye. This is the only warning you'll get."

Clint and the knife were too close to Dale. Matt couldn't risk it. Tying him up might be suicide for both of them, but in that moment, he had no other option. He took the cable ties and set about Dale's first wrist.

"Tight," Clint barked. "I'm watching. If there's as much as a millimeter slack, I'm gonna do some cutting."

Hands shaking, Matt struggled with the fiddly ties, trying to thread them the wrong way before figuring out how they worked. At last he had fixed his lover to the chair by hand and foot.

Had he also signed his death warrant?

Clint gestured with the knife for him to step away before moving in to check the fastenings. Satisfied, he straightened up, finally lowering his weapon.

"Clint," Matt said, trying to inject a tone of calm reason to his voice. "Why are you doing this? We haven't done anything against you. Whatever you think is wrong, this is not the answer. Talk to me, please."

"*Fucking*, weren't you?"

"What?"

"You were fucking. You said you would come to the gym tonight but instead you came here to fuck him."

A fresh wave of horror hit him. The cool manner he'd tried hard to uphold crumpled. "Where's Conrad? What have you done to him?"

Clint's face betrayed no emotion. "What I wanted to do to you. I *fucked* him. Only I didn't go so easy as I might have done with you. He was useless. Couldn't even make me come."

Matt felt the world shrivel around him. His best friend — what hell had he sent him into? *No. No. No.*

"You bastard," Dale roared, spitting blood across the table.

Clint struck a blunt fist against the side of Dale's head. "You'll get your turn, Yankee, but not until I'm ready. Like I gave it to your friend from work, little Aaron. He was nice. A real sugar butt. He put up a struggle too. I like it when they do that." He laughed. It was a humorless sound.

"Aaron?"

There it was. Matt's worst fear confirmed and a nightmare descent to a deeper level of hell. Clint Dexter *was* the Durham Strangler.

They were dead men.

"Clint," he said, grasping for any desperate line of hope. "You said you wanted me tonight. Let Dale go and you can have me. I'll do anything you want."

"No," Dale cried.

"That's not how this works," Clint said. "You're not in your courtroom now, big man. *I* call the shots. No bargaining. No negotiation. This goes my way."

The calm tone of his voice was terrifying. There was a sickly white pallor to his skin. His face glistened with sweat. Everything about him was at odds. He was clearly out of his mind.

"I will kill you," Dale said, straining hopelessly at his restraints.

"That sounds like something you would say in one of your movies." Clint laughed. "Only much less convincing. The only thing you're going to do tonight is die. Maybe you'll get a fuck, maybe not. It depends how generous I feel once I'm finished with your boyfriend."

"Don't touch him. Don't you dare."

"Or what?" Clint said calmly. "You're tied to a chair, big man. And even if you weren't, I could break your neck before you laid a finger on me. I'm the real killer, Yankee. You only play at it."

Matt fought to think rationally. Dale was tied up. He wasn't. For whatever reason, Clint had decided not to restrain him too. If they were to have any hope of survival, he had to make sure it stayed that way. He could arm up later, right now he had to focus on staying free.

"You," Clint said, pointing the knife at him. "Strip."

It made little difference now. He was only wearing shorts and a T-shirt. Better to be naked than chained. He took everything off and stood in front of Clint, defiantly meeting his icy gaze.

"You could have been so much better, without the distraction of this," Clint shoved Dale's shoulder. "Missing sessions. Eating garbage. Drinking fucking champagne. You could have been perfect. *I* could have made you perfect."

"He is perfect, you asshole."

Clint delivered a back hander to Dale's face. "I wasn't talking to you."

"You're a psycho!" Dale spat.

Clint hit him again, harder. Dale's head jerked sideways, spraying blood across Matt's chest.

"Stop it," Matt begged. "Please."

Clint looked straight at him, mouth curling cruelly at the corners. "Seeing how I like you so much, I'm going to afford you a favor. Something I didn't do for all those other men. Aaron and…Conrad, was it? I'm going to let you know what happens next. I was going to kill you both, but on the way over here, I had a change of plan. Sweet, huh? Once we're done here, Matt and I are going to take a journey. North. To Scotland. One of the islands, some place we can lie low till all this Durham Strangler shit dies down. Not much for two men to do up there to pass the time, except fuck. We'll be doing a lot of that."

"You crazy bastard," Dale snarled.

Clint smacked him around the head and continued. "Once the heat is off, we'll take a fishing boat out of the country." He smiled. "Now, I'm saying *we*, that's supposing I haven't grown tired of you by then. I guess it's up to you to make sure I don't."

"You won't get one second of pleasure out of me," Matt said defiantly. He would sacrifice himself to prevent Clint from taking out his twisted desires, but Dale's survival depended on him pulling through. He couldn't give up now.

"That's where you're wrong," Clint said. "I like a man who fights back. Now I'm going to see how much fight you've got in you. Let's go upstairs."

*Was he kidding?* "Upstairs?"

"That's right. As much as I'd enjoy Dale watching me fuck you right here on this table, I figure what he can't see will torture him a whole lot more. I reckon he'll go out of his mind, imaging what we're doing on his bed. Besides, I've wanted you a long time, Matt. I want the first time to be special. Just the two of us." He laughed again. "Romantic, like the two of you before I arrived."

"You're out of your mind."

Clint stroked the obscene bulge in his pants. "If you'd rather your boyfriend *did* watch this first time, I could go for that too."

The pain in Dale's eyes was too much to bear. With tears burning his eyes, Matt turned toward the hall.

"It's this way."

Dale's howl of rage and frustration tore through the house.

"That's a nice arse," Clint said, walking up the stairs behind him. "I knew it would be. I've got an eye for these things."

Naked, Matt felt exposed enough already without Clint's lecherous eyes on his behind. But modesty was the least of his problems. He was seconds away from going into the bedroom with a serial sex killer. What the fuck could he do now?

"You can walk as slowly as you like," Clint quipped. "We've got all night. Besides, those nice slow steps you're taking give me an opportunity to admire your ass and think about all the ways I can destroy it. I have a lot of experience in that area." A low chuckle. "And I've been thinking about you and your body for longer than most."

Every word caused his flesh to crawl, but Matt didn't

show it. He had too much experience, fronting things out in court, to betray his fear to a madman like Clint. Except he was frightened. Terrified.

They reached the turn in the stairs. Ten more steps to the top. Time was running out.

*Think, Matt. Come on man, think.*

What could he use as a defense up here? He hadn't set foot in the house until tonight. It wasn't enough time to get to know the place.

There was an en suite bathroom off from the bedroom. If he was quick enough he could lock himself in there. But then what? There was no phone. No way of raising the alarm. He would be safe, for now at least, but leave Dale to the mercy of Clint and his knife. That was not an option. Clint could do what he wanted to him if it would spare Dale.

Clint had already told them he wasn't going to kill Matt tonight. Whatever happened, he still had hope of saving Dale. Hope was all he needed.

They entered the bedroom.

"Nice," Clint said, regarding the rumpled sheets.

Less than an hour before they had been in ecstasy upon that bed. Their own little heaven. Now it was a living hell.

"Is that why you stood me up?" Clint asked. "So you could be with him, in there?"

"Clint," Matt said, turning to face him, open arms, his expression wide. "I didn't know you wanted me in that way. How could I? You never gave any indication that you...liked me, until tonight."

It was a long shot trying to reason with a psycho, as if it were nothing more serious than a co-worker with an inappropriate crush.

Clint's knuckles whitened around the handle of the knife. Matt took a careful step backward, closer to the bedside cabinet.

"Don't try stalling me with that crap," Clint said. "I'm the Durham Strangler, remember. Not one of your no-hope clients. I don't want to buy you dinner and roses. You're *my* fucking dinner."

In two long steps, Clint covered the room and was upon him. Adrenaline took over.

Clint's arms came around his torso.

Snake-fast, Matt's arm went behind his back, his hand gripped the neck of the empty champagne bottle. Whipping back around, he smacked the bottle over the crown of Clint's head. He heard a sickening *thunk* and the force caused the bottle to shatter.

Fragments of glass rained over both of them. Matt backed into the cabinet.

Clint staggered. Stunned. His face was blank for a second, until he shook the pieces of glass from his head. His eyes came back into hateful focus.

"Boy, you're gonna regret that in every way."

He came at Matt with the force of a crazed bull.

* * * *

Dale attempted to move. The plastic cable ties cut deep and had drawn blood from all four limbs, but there was no give in any of them. Clint had chosen well.

That bastard. Dale's rage threatened to consume him but he had to keep a lid on it. Blind fury would not get him out of this.

He *had* to get upstairs. God knows what that sick fuck was doing. He'd heard the broken glass moments before, then a heavy thud. *Matt. Poor Matt, what is he doing to you?*

He'd never felt so useless. Incompetent. Unable to protect the man he loved. This was the worst feeling in the world.

Try again. Try harder.

Deep breath. Willing his entire body to relax, go soft. Devoid of tension, he tried the wrist straps again. Easing back, using minimal force, he tried to wriggle free. Nothing. It was useless.

*Fuck. Fuck. Fuck.*

That evil bastard had killed Aaron and all those other men, now he was upstairs with Matt and there was nothing he could do to stop it.

Dale let loose a primal scream of anger. Tears and blood ran down his face.

"*Be quiet,*" the voice was a whisper, close to his ear.

He snapped his head around.

Keeley Rank held a finger to her lips. "Be quiet, for God's sake." She tugged at the restraints on his wrist. "Scissors?"

He didn't know where she had come from, or why she was there, but in that moment she was a gift from heaven.

"Top drawer, left of the sink," he whispered.

There was another heavy thud from above. The ceiling shook and the contents of the cupboards rattled. Keeley froze, looking upward.

"Get me loose," Dale urged. "Hurry."

Carefully, Keeley opened the drawer and located the scissors. She crept back to Dale and snipped the plastic ties. The relief was instant. Dale flexed his fingers to restore the circulation.

"Let's get out," Keeley urged, helping him to his feet.

"He's got Matt upstairs."

"I've already called the police," she said, taking his elbow and urging him toward the door. "Let them handle this."

Dale stood firm. "No. He's insane. The second he hears the sirens he'll go berserk, like a cornered rat. Matt will be dead."

"You don't know that. C'mon, let's get out. The cops can handle him. They're the experts."

He shrugged her away and started opening drawers. What could he use for a weapon? *Shit!* If he was in the States, he'd have a gun on the property and could blow that fucker's brains out.

Knives were the only option. And the element of surprise. Clint thought he was still trussed to the chair. If he could get up there undetected, he'd have surprise on his side. It was better than the alternative—nothing.

Dale grabbed a carving knife and a large chopping knife, the biggest two in the block. He'd never had to wield one of these for real but all those horror movies had taught him a thing or two about handling them.

"Dale, don't do this," Keeley urged.

"He'll kill Matt if I don't."

"He'll kill you too," she said. "Would Matt want that?"

"I don't mind dying to save him. Go outside," he said. "Wait for the cops. When they arrive, tell them exactly what's gone down. Tell them to turn right at the top of the stairs. It's the bedroom at the front. Tell them not to wait, to come straight up."

"Fuck," she said, heading for the back door.

When his mind was set, that was it for Dale. There was no going back. Fear would not put him off.

A loud cry from upstairs. Matt.

Dale took the stairs on the balls of his feet, the light tread of a cat. He was alert for the sound of sirens outside. Nothing yet. The moment Clint heard them coming, it would be over.

Matt let out another cry.

Killing was too good for this bastard, but right now Dale would do what he had to. Matt had suffered enough.

This ended now.

With his back to the wall, he crept along the landing.

Clint's confidence and lust had done him the biggest favor. So hungry to get to Matt, he'd left the bedroom door open.

They were on the floor beside the bed. Dale edged into the doorway for a better view.

Clint had Matt pinned down. He was on top, pants around his ankles, hairy ass thrusting.

"Let me in, cunt."

Matt cried in pain.

Finally blinded by rage, Dale surrendered to his violent impulses.

He crossed the room, both knives raised. He brought his

right hand down with sudden force. The blade slid over Clint's shoulder blade before slipping into a space between his rib. Dale came in fast with the second knife, jabbing into the soft tissue of Clint's waist. The blade went in to the hilt.

Clint reared with a scream, clutching his back. He fell to the side of Matt, writhing in agony. He stared at Dale, a look of question and disbelief on his face, until Dale's knee impacted, full force, with his nose.

Matt pushed up onto his hands and knees. Dale was there, putting arms around him. He hauled the sheets off the bed to cover him.

As he led him from the room, Dale heard the police sirens distantly on the hill.

The nightmare was over.

# Epilogue

*Twelve months later*

"The award for leading actress in a television series goes to...Roxanne Maxwell for *Blood Falls on Stone*."

The announcement met with a rapturous cheer from the audience at the Theater Royal Drury Lane. For those watching the live broadcast at home, the moment was just as sweet. *Blood Falls on Stone* had won in every category it had been nominated for so far—Best Drama, Best Supporting Actor for Adrian Nelson and now Best Actress for Roxanne Maxwell. The crime show that had been so reviled by the press just a year earlier, had risen to the top of the heap at the British Academy Television Awards. It was an unrivaled reversal of fortune.

"She looks beautiful," Conrad O'Brien said, raising a glass in honor of the woman on his TV screen.

"She certainly deserves it," Danny Frost said, clinking glasses with his lover, carefully watching Conrad for any signs of forced bravado. When *Blood Falls on Stone* had finally made its tortured way to television in January that year, Danny wasn't sure Conrad should even watch it. The show was much too close to the ordeal Conrad had suffered for him to benefit from seeing it.

"Your best friend's boyfriend is basically playing the guy who attacked you," Danny said at the time.

"Rubbish," Conrad told him. "Dale is not playing Clint Dexter. He was a victim of the man himself. What Clint did to me has nothing to do with this show. He was killing before this program was even thought of."

"Even so—"

"Even nothing. If Matt can watch the man he loves play a killer after everything they went through, so can I. I want to see this. I need to."

Conrad had been right. As dark and disturbing as the series was, especially the central performance from Dale Zachary, it was nothing compared to the horror he'd lived through.

After Jamie had discovered him on the floor of Dexter's gym, Conrad had spent three days in a coma. Months of physical and psychological recuperation had followed. He'd never told Danny exactly what had happened to him and Danny hadn't ask. He didn't need to know. He had been there to pick up the pieces and that was what mattered most.

Roxanne Maxwell paid tributes to the victims of Clint Dexter in her acceptance speech. Conrad's eyes prickled with tears as he listened.

Danny moved closer on the sofa and put an arm around his shoulders. "Okay?"

Conrad sniffed and wiped his nose on the back of his hand. He nodded. "I'm alive. Those other men weren't so lucky."

Danny nodded and placed a soft kiss on the side of his head. Things weren't perfect. They might never be again. But they were getting better.

For now, that was as good as anything.

\* \* \* \*

Jamie Dench watched Roxanne collect her award on the TV in the staff room of Durham Police Station. Ordinarily he never watched award shows like this but tonight was different. He didn't know why, other than he was looking for some kind of resolution.

Everyone was keen to point out that the murders committed by Dexter had nothing to do with *Blood Falls on*

*Stone*. Except they did. It was bullshit to claim otherwise. Dexter had murdered one of the crew and planned to kill the leading man. How could anyone say there was no connection? It was willful ignorance.

Jamie watched the crime drama when it came out, and despite his reservations, he had enjoyed it. The show deserved all the praise it was getting now. And he didn't hate Dale Zachary. Not anymore. How could he? After everything Dale had been through. And saving Matt's life.

No, the only one Jamie had to hate was Clint. What he had found in that gym would haunt him forever. The things that bastard had done to Conrad. No wonder the poor guy blanked out so much of it.

It could easily have been Matt. God knew what Dexter would have done to him if Dale hadn't come through.

Jamie carried the burden of guilt too.

If he had gotten to the gym an hour earlier, he could have prevented everything that had happened that damned night. Conrad, Matt—Jamie had to live with that. He could have stopped all of it if he'd only been quicker.

Nevertheless, his career was flourishing. He'd been promoted to Detective Sergeant and given a permanent position in MIT. It was what he'd always wanted. In the aftermath of that night, he became a bigger workaholic than before, putting in more hours and working harder than any other member of the team

He had to. For the sake of future victims of crime. For his own sanity. He was always trying to make up for the hours he had lost tracing Dexter's gym.

He had a long career ahead of him.

Maybe that would be time enough.

* * * *

In the space of a year, Keeley Rank had gone from journalist to a full-blown celebrity herself. Backstage at the television awards, she drank champagne and quietly toasted her own success. The landslide victory of *Blood Falls on Stone* would only boost sales of her book, *Track-down – Hunt for the Durham Strangler*, which was already a bestseller. With the publication of the paperback version set for next week, once again Keeley found herself in the right place at the right time.

While everyone involved in the show went out of their way to distance it from the crimes of Clint Dexter, Keeley was keen to play up the comparisons. Some badly researched interviewers even made out that the show was based on her book. A tiny fact she neglected to correct. Why should she?

The greater the buzz she could generate about the book the better. She was the hero of the story, after all.

In reality, she'd been spying through Dale's windows in the hope of adding some spice to the outing story she planned to write on him. It was pure chance that Clint decided to target Dale and Matt at the same time. Her lucky star was shining bright. Right place, right time again.

*Track-down* told a slightly enhanced version of those events. Ingenuity and courage had led her to Dale's house that night. So what. It was a little artistic license. Dale and his boyfriend would be dead if it wasn't for her. Not that you would know it—those ungrateful bastards. They wouldn't even give her a quote for the front of the book.

"Hey, Keeley, great result tonight. Can we get a picture?"

"Sure," she replied, posing happily for the eager photographers. Since becoming a celebrity, she'd undergone a dramatic transformation. Twenty pounds lighter with a sleek new hairstyle and expensive wardrobe, she looked better than most of these TV bitches.

"Keeley, is it true you're doing *Celebrity Big Brother*?" asked one of the hacks.

"Oh, I'm hardly a celebrity," she said coyly. "I'm just a writer."

Her agent was negotiating hard to get her the Big Brother gig but the producers had yet to come up with a satisfactory fee to secure the deal. She wasn't one of the desperate has-beens or two-bit bimbos who usually populated the show. If they wanted Keeley Rank, they would have to pay. Big.

She was the woman who caught the Durham Strangler, for fuck's sake. That had to be worth something.

She was already working on a follow-up book about Clint Dexter. Her first was knocked out in a hurry — understandably so. Every true crime hack and misery merchant rushed out their chronicles in the wake of the murders. But it was her title, with its unique selling point — the woman who caught the killer — that had risen to the top of that steaming pile.

The publishers were still processing the enormous demand they had for pre-orders when they commissioned a second, more in-depth book. This was to dig deeper into Dexter's history — a real mud-raking scandal piece on the notorious killer. The sort of thing she excelled at.

What a pity the fucker had to get himself killed.

Lousy bastard.

Clint survived the attack by Dale in the bedroom. Both of the knives he drove into him missed vital organs by millimeters. When he had been well enough to be discharged from hospital and face police questioning he had refused to cooperate. He made 'no comment' replies to every question put to him and when they took him before the court he had entered a 'not guilty' plea on all counts.

Keeley had been delighted.

The evidence against him had been overwhelming and he would go to prison for life but a 'not guilty' plea meant the case would go to trial. A guilty verdict was certain but the trial would keep the story alive for weeks, months. Witnesses, survivors, relatives — all would be called upon to give evidence against him. She would even take the stand herself to give an account of that bloody night.

Key witness in a brutal murder trial.

You couldn't buy that kind of publicity.

It would also make a great prologue to her second book.

She was certain Clint had an ulterior motive for taking the

case to court. He was never going to get away with it. He wasn't insane enough to think he would. No, Clint had a different aim — one she couldn't wait to write about. He was obsessed with Matt Blyth. The only way he could ever see him again was when he gave evidence across a courtroom.

That was the real reason he had held out.

Only it wasn't to be. Remanded in Durham Prison, Clint Dexter was *The Man* — the Durham Stranger — he could do whatever the hell he wanted. But there were bigger men than Clint in prison. Men who didn't appreciate his bullish ways.

Clint had been found dead in his cell a month before the trial was listed to start. He had multiple stab wounds to his neck and chest. No one among the staff and prisoners saw a thing.

So a piece of shit died in prison. The world still turned and Keeley still had her book deal.

"Any chance you could hang around?" one of the photographers asked. "We'd love to get one of you together with Dale and Matt."

Keeley moved on, pretending she hadn't heard.

She had saved their lives but the guys had been pretty vocal in damning her book.

It was a reunion none of them was in a hurry to see. Especially not tonight.

* * * *

Roxanne Maxwell left the stage with her Best Actress award and received the most rapturous applause of the night so far. When she dedicated her award to the victims of Dexter, her voice cracked and the tears that poured from her beautiful eyes were genuine. A palpable wave of emotion ran through the crowd. Many tearful eyes were discreetly wiped amid the applause.

In the third row back, Dale and Matt were on their feet. They cheered and clapped louder than anyone. There were no tears for either of them. They had cried enough this last year. It was behind them. Tonight was a celebration.

"Your turn next," Matt said, patting his lover's knee as they sat back down.

"We'll see," Dale said modestly. He took nothing for granted. It had been a clean sweep so far, with the show winning every award it was nominated for. Best Actor was all that remained to be announced. He was the bookmakers' favorite. The industry favorite. He would love to win. But if he didn't, it would be no big deal. He already had everything he wanted — health, family and the love of his life.

In the last year he had journeyed to heaven and hell and all the way back. The physical injuries Matt and he received were the quickest to heal. Cuts and bruises. A scar down his cheek.

The psychological damage had taken a greater toll. Dealing with the knowledge that Clint had been stalking Matt for months. That he had been killing other men while keeping Matt's death in reserve, as if it were some kind of grand prize. All those lives destroyed or damaged. Poor Aaron and Conrad. Conner Welsh and Olly Raymond.

Until that night at the house, Dale's biggest fear was that he would be outed in the press. That small concern had been put in perspective.

They got through the aftermath together — Dale and Matt. Sleepless nights, waking nightmares and agonies. They understood what they'd been through better than any of the doctors or counselors they were sent to see. The doctors weren't there in the middle of the night.

Slowly things got better. The nights, while not untroubled, become less disturbing.

Matt had gone back to work first. "I need things to return to normal. To deal with other people and their problems, not just my own."

The prospect of Clint's trial had hung over them like a black cloud. The crazy fuck had pled not guilty. They would have to relive every awful detail of that experience again, only this time in a courtroom, standing across from the man who'd put them through it.

Matt had been right.

They needed a distraction. They needed to go back to work.

Only *Blood Falls on Stone* was hardly a distraction. Having almost fallen victim to a serial killer, did he really want to continue playing one?

"Daryl Stone is a character," Matt had told him over a soul-searching conversation at the dinner table. "He's *not* Clint Dexter. And you're an actor — a bloody good one. You need to finish what you started."

He was right again.

After an enforced hiatus, production on *Blood Falls on Stone* picked up three months later. The scar on Dale's face was obvious. They had offered to hide it with makeup but he had refused. It was part of him. He'd had to accept it. The change to his appearance had made it necessary to re-shoot some of his earlier scenes, but in every way it was a smoother, less troubled production than the original block. There were no tempers, no diva behavior, no protests. The only visitors to the front gates were well-wishers and autograph hunters.

Aaron Oxford's presence was missed the most, but the producers promised that when the show eventually aired it would do so with a dedication to his memory.

The cloud of Clint's trial disappeared midway through the shoot when the bastard was found dead in his cell. Dale had felt nothing but relief.

That night in bed, he had held Matt even tighter than usual.

"Being a lawyer, I know I should stand up for justice and the right of every man to have a fair trial," Matt said, head lying softly on Dale's chest, "but not him. We know exactly what he did. Prison was too good for him, with its gyms and libraries, not to mention all those vulnerable young men it would give him access to. He would flourish. I'm glad he's dead."

"I am too," Dale had felt no guilt in saying it.

*Blood Falls on Stone* defied all expectations when it had screened. The overnight viewing figures came in at over nine million. It had been the highest rated show each week for all six episodes. Critics fell over themselves to praise the acting, the writing and the production.

A second series was commissioned before the first run had finished.

It was a smash.

Everything was fine again.

Next weekend would be Matt's birthday, his thirtieth. He didn't want a party so they were flying to Malaga, in Spain, to celebrate in the sun. Dale would make sure it was special and spoil him every moment they were away.

The award for leading actor in a drama was next. An expectant hush fell over the audience as the nominations were announced. A show reel of all four actors began to play.

Dale reached for Matt's hand and drew closer to him as the footage played. With his mouth close to his ear, he asked the question he'd been building to all year. "Will you marry me?"

Matt turned. His eyes were moist in the flickering light of the screen, but his smile was wide. "Yes."

"The winner is...Dale Zachary."

The crowd took to their feet to applaud Dale's victory, unaware that he had already won the greatest prize imaginable—the heart of the man he loved.

# More books from Pride Publishing

*A reporter and the thief he's investigating both fall for a golden dancer, forging a ménage of love and lies that could send one to prison and one to the morgue.*

*Getting calls from the dead in the middle of the night isn't*
*Oliver's idea of fun…*

*Andrew had no intention of ever going back home. But circumstances force him to face his painful past and the friend who betrayed him.*

*Leading a double life can be challenging, as Reaper well knows.*

# About the Author

**Thom Collins**

Thom Collins is delighted to make his debut as a Pride Publishing author. His love of page turning thrillers began at an early age when his mother caught him reading the latest Jackie Collins book and promptly confiscated it, sparking a life-long love of raunchy novels. He's been writing for as long as he can remember and recently celebrated his 21st year in print. He has adopted a number of pseudonyms in that time but is probably best known as Thom Wolf, author of gay erotic fiction. His stories featured in dozens of popular gay magazines throughout the 1990s leading to the publication his first novel Words Made Flesh in 2000. In addition to his novels, he has written several novellas and short stories for both print and digital publication.

Closer by Morning is the book he has been building to all that time and marks his debut as a mainstream romantic author. He loves creating strong sexy characters in a world of glamour, excitement and danger. He's currently working on the first novel in a trilogy of romantic thrillers.

Thom is married and lives in Durham, North East England. He loves all kinds of genre fiction, especially bonkbusters, thrillers and horror. He is also a cookery book addict with far too many titles cluttering his shelves. When not writing he can be found in the kitchen trying out new recipes. He's a keen traveller with a fear of flying that gets worse with age, but since taking his first cruise in 2013 he realised that sailing is the way to go.

Thom Collins loves to hear from readers. You can find contact information, website details and an author profile page at https://www.pride-publishing.com/